"We have only *one* concern."

Data waved his hand over the top of the table, and a hologram of Lal appeared.

La Forge understood the need for haste. Data had explained that much in the brief message he had left after La Forge had accepted his invitation. Lal was in danger. He assumed the problem was an engineering dilemma, something to do with her holomatrix. As he had on more than one occasion, La Forge wondered what he could offer in the way of help given that Data was the undisputed expert on Soong-type androids now that Soong was dead. "What's the problem?"

"She is gone."

"What? She ran away?"

"No, she did not leave of her own volition. She was taken."

"How can you be sure?"

"Because her abductor contacted me."

"*Abductor*?" La Forge exclaimed.

Data waved a hand, and the image of a human man appeared in Lal's place. He wore a long, black suit jacket, a waistcoat, and a wide black tie. The man's forehead was high and his eyes widely spaced. Though La Forge had only ever seen this individual with his VISOR, there were enough peculiarities about his appearance that he could be recognized without speaking. "Moriarty," he said. "James Moriarty."

STAR TREK
THE NEXT GENERATION®

THE LIGHT
FANTASTIC

JEFFREY LANG

Based on
Star Trek® and
Star Trek: The Next Generation
created by Gene Roddenberry

POCKET BOOKS
New York   London   Toronto   Sydney   New Delhi

Pocket Books
A Division of Simon & Schuster, Inc.
1230 Avenue of the Americas
New York, NY 10020

This book is published by Pocket Books, a division of Simon & Schuster, Inc., under exclusive license from CBS Studios Inc.

First Pocket Books paperback edition July 2014

POCKET and colophon are registered trademarks of Simon & Schuster, Inc.

For information about special discounts for bulk purchases, please contact Simon & Schuster Special Sales at 1-866-506-1949 or business@simonandschuster.com.

The Simon & Schuster Speakers Bureau can bring authors to your live event. For more information or to book an event, contact the Simon & Schuster Speakers Bureau at 1-866-248-3049 or visit our website at www.simonspeakers.com.

Cover art and design by Alan Dingman

Manufactured in the United States of America

10   9   8   7   6   5   4   3   2

ISBN 978-1-4767-5051-4
ISBN 978-1-4767-5052-1 (ebook)

For Joshua:
Plotmaster, Martini-imbiber, Friend

HISTORIAN'S NOTE

The main events in this narrative take place in November 2385 (ACE). It has been a year since Data decided not to rejoin Starfleet and instead dedicate his life to his daughter, Lal. (*Star Trek: The Next Generation: Cold Equations* trilogy).

PROLOGUE

A timeless time

The Professor labored over his device and did his best to ignore his wife's sobs. She wept so often these days that he felt he should have grown accustomed to the sound, but, no, as disciplined as his mind was, the Professor found this task to be beyond even his formidable abilities.

Part of the difficulty arose from the fact that it was a very small room, with almost nothing to distract him, nothing except his work. His work was the whetstone upon which the Professor honed himself. His work would keep his beloved ones safe. His work would set them all free.

"James?" Regina called, her voice thin and weary.

Moriarty stood straighter and raised his head, but he did not turn away from the device. "Yes, my dear?"

"What time is it?"

The Professor sighed. "My dearest, you know I cannot answer that question. There is no time here. We are trapped between the ticks of the clock's sweeping hand."

"James?" she called again in the same tone.

"Yes, my love?"

"How long have they been gone?"

Moriarty lifted his hand to his face and first rubbed the bridge of his nose and then stroked the ridge of his chin. He wondered, *How long since I last shaved? And still no sign of stubble.* He had always despised the need to shave. Had even considered developing some means to suppress the growth of hair on his face. Except Regina had always taken a strange delight in stroking his face in the early morning, before rising for the day, and commenting on how rough his cheek had become. "Like some kind of millworker or a stevedore," she would say and the silly, stupid joke would always send her into a fit of giggling. *Lord, how I miss shaving,* Moriarty thought and said, "They have been gone as long as they have been gone, my love. I can tell you no more than that until I have completed my work. When I have, I will free us from this place and we can . . ."

"James?"

"*What?!*" Moriarty hissed. "I mean . . . I mean . . ." He recovered his composure. "What is it, my darling?"

"I miss them."

The Professor lowered his head and cupped his chin in his open palm, elbow on the edge of his device, his great work—the key, the horologe. He stopped working for a moment (as if the word "moment" meant anything). He reached into his waistcoat pocket and withdrew his watch. As quietly as he could, he pressed the stem, which clicked softly. The hunter case swung open silently. Out of habit, Moriarty glanced at the clock face, but he really didn't need to see that the second hand was not moving. He would have felt the mechanism's whir in the palm of his hand if the gears had moved a single tick.

He ignored the clock face and instead stared at the tiny portrait in the interior of the case: his daughters. Sophia and Gladys. Ages five and nine when the portrait was done. And now they would be . . . how old? Who could say? "I know, my darling," Moriarty whispered. "I miss them, too." He snapped the case shut. "But we'll never see them again if I don't complete my work." He touched the device with the tips of his fingers. "It's the only thing that matters," he said. "The only thing."

"James?" Regina called. He looked over at his wife. Dressed in white, she lay on a white couch next to which there stood a white table. Behind her was a white wall. Her skin was pale white and drained of color. Her hair, once a beautiful, deep chestnut brown, was now white. He couldn't remember if her eyes had changed color, but Moriarty did not wish to know if they had. He looked at his hands, which were also white. His clothes: white. His own hair and eyes: no doubt, they were white.

Only the device had any hue. Since it was the only thing in the room that mattered, this seemed entirely appropriate to Moriarty. "Yes?" he asked.

But Regina did not reply. She had started to weep again, so Moriarty returned to his labor, which was, in every sense that ever could matter, the center of the universe.

1

———

November 2385 (ACE)—The Present

The short-order cook finished wiping down the flat-top cast-iron grill with his kitchen cloth. He bent low to inspect the surface, like a billiard player lining up a shot, checking for dings or other small imperfections in the play surface. Some of the other cooks had the bad habit of smacking the flat-top with the edge of a spatula. He had been trying to dissuade them with both gentle reminders and terse threats, but he worked only the breakfast shift and couldn't control what happened the rest of the day.

Still, he always liked to make sure the cooktop was clean and lubricated before he headed out the door. The diner owner, a Cardassian expat name Oban, didn't mind paying him for the extra few minutes on his timecard, especially since the short-order cook was the main reason the business had been turning a profit for the past few weeks.

JEFFREY LANG

Before his arrival, the diner's sole virtue resided in the fact that patrons knew they could sit at the counter and nurse a cup of tepid coffee or *raktajino* for as long as they liked without being rousted out, mostly because no one else wanted their seat. Now, thanks to the new morning cook, there was a line out the door most days, and the patrons weren't only locals looking for a quick bite before heading to work. Word had spread through the food-lovers underground: Many of the patrons were tourists, eager to spend credits on eggs and bacon, waffles, and a strange delicacy called "chipped beef on toast." Diners had started posting reviews on culinary sites, but only for breakfast. Sure, there was some spillover to the other shifts, but all the chatter was about breakfast, breakfast, breakfast and the wonder of this one cook who could crank out delicacies at a clockwork pace. In a world full of replicated fare, simple food made well was a draw, even if the customers had to find their way to a seedy little grease-stained pit in the middle of nowhere.

The short-order cook knew all about the buzz, but he never mentioned it. Oban paid him a decent wage, and the Cardassian was smart enough not to ask too many questions. Their conversations were limited to simple questions like, "You almost done there, Davey?"

The short-order cook didn't respond. He was too absorbed with the process of re-lubricating the cooking surface.

"Davey?"

The short-order cook looked up. Oban was

standing in the narrow doorway that led to the prep kitchen and, past that, to Oban's tiny office.

"Hello?"

"Sorry," the short-order cook said. "Wasn't listening. You want something?"

"Yeah," Oban said. "Come on back to the office when you're done. Got something I need to ask ya."

The short-order cook sighed. "Sure. Yeah. Be there in a minute." He finished wiping down his workstation and collected his tools so he could drop them off in the dish room before leaving. Just before he left the kitchen, he pointed at the second grill station, the one where the lunch cook, an Orion native named Settu, was working. "Flip those eggs. They're about to overcook."

Settu pouted. "They're fine. Barely been on the grill for two minutes."

"Then you've got the temp too high. They're going to go rock solid in 30 seconds."

"How can you tell?"

"I can smell 'em."

Settu waved him off. "Go punch out. Your shift is over."

The short-order cook sighed again and turned to leave. "Fine. Whatever. Kelly isn't going to like it when you cost her a tip." Settu had a crush on Kelly.

Behind him, the short-order cook heard the spatula being slipped under the eggs and turned. Then, a moment later, the soft click of the heat controls being adjusted. The short-order cook smiled, but only a little.

* * *

"What can I do for you, boss?" the short-order cook asked, standing in the office door.

"Sit down a minute, Davey."

"I don't have time to sit down. I have to get home. I like to see my kid before she heads off to school."

"I understand," Oban said, rubbing the stubble on his chin. The Cardassian always looked like he was a day or two away from his last shave. "I remember those days. Being a parent, it can be hard. Especially if you're doing it all by yourself, am I right?"

"If you say so."

"So, you're not doing it all by yourself?"

"I didn't say that," the short-order cook said.

"You don't say much about yourself at all."

The short-order cook untied his apron and wadded it up into a ball. Outside the door, there was a bin where kitchen staff threw dirty clothes and towels at the end of their shifts. He tossed the apron into the bin. Freed from the restrictions of the apron, his belly dropped down a bit over the top of his belt. "Do you have something you want to ask me?"

"I just wanted to let you know I looked into the whole chicken egg thing for you."

"And?"

"I found a place that has live Terran chickens. They sell them for the meat, but the owner says, yeah, they lay eggs, too, and he's willing to sell them to me if I want. But, he says, most Orion folk have an allergic reaction to chicken eggs."

"Then we won't feed 'em to Orions. We'll tell the waitstaff not to let Orions order them."

"Why are these chicken eggs such a big deal?"

"Get them for me and I'll show you. I'll make you an omelet. These eggs you get—what are they again?"

"The birds are called paradins."

"Well, whatever. The protein-to-water ratio is all wrong. Chicken eggs are perfect for omelets. We start making omelets and you'll start getting Terran customers. They'll go nuts. You can charge whatever you want and they'll pay it."

"Really?"

"Sure."

"And how do you know this?"

"I used to work with Terrans. Back in the day."

"Another restaurant?"

"Sure. A restaurant. Nice place, but crazy hours. Couldn't stand the hours after I became a dad."

"I can see that," Oban said. "A father has to be there."

"So you'll get the chicken eggs?"

"I'll get the chicken eggs. And then you can make me an omelet."

"Good. You won't regret it. Anything else? I need to get going."

"Just one more thing," Oban said. He rubbed the back of his neck with one big, meaty hand. "I wanted to let you know—yesterday, these guys came by looking for you."

"'These guys'?" the short-order cook asked. "What guys? I don't know any guys. What did they look like?"

Oban shrugged. "I dunno. Just . . . guys."

"Big? Small? Orion? Human?"

"Nah, not Orion. Maybe human. Maybe not. You know I have trouble telling them apart. Just . . . *guys*."

"Two of them?"

"Yep."

"Cops? Feds?"

"Don't think so. Leastways they didn't show me a badge or anything."

"Did they say what they wanted?" The short-order cook tried to sound casual, but the hairs were standing up on the back of his neck.

"Not really. Just . . . did you work here? How long? Did I know anything about your life outside work?"

"And you said . . . ?"

Oban threw his hands up, imploring. "Hey, c'mon, Davey. Whataya think I said? Told 'em to get bent. This is Orion. We don't have to say nuthin' about nobody if we don't want to. And you, you know, you're like . . . well, you ain't given me any trouble, so I don't make trouble for you."

The short-order cook felt the sense of alarm subside. Oban might not be telling the entire truth, but there was little chance that he had told the "guys" anything meaningful for the simple reason that there was so little he could have said. He had been careful, very careful, about not revealing anything important about himself. "Well, okay," he said. "Thanks, Oban. Appreciate the word. They didn't leave names or comm info or anything like that?"

"Naw, naw. They just slid out, all casual. No-body saw where they went."

"Okay. Maybe it was someone I used to work with. Probably I owe them money."

"Sure, Davey. I figured it was something like that."

"Yeah," the short-order cook said. "No doubt." He turned to leave, waving back over his shoulder. "Well, let me know if these guys turn up again, okay? See you tomorrow, Oban. Thanks for looking into the eggs for me."

"No problem, Davey. See you in the morning."

On his way out of the kitchen, the short-order cook stopped at the time-clock station and waved his employee identification under the scanner so it could log his hours. Then, he walked through the still-crowded dining room, pausing only to wave at a couple of regular patrons and to ex-change words with the servers he had become friendly with over the past month. Kelly, the server who Settu was crushing on, gave him a quick smile and a thumbs-up. Like him, she was a Terran, a student on sabbatical from her uni-versity. He suspected she was homesick for some interaction with a familiar face shape and skin color, but the short-order cook was already run-ning late. He waved back and said, "Have to run."

Kelly acknowledged the wave and asked, "See you tomorrow?"

"Sure. Tomorrow. If I'm lucky, I'll be able to make you a treat."

The short-order cook was lying. He felt bad about it, but he didn't see how he had much choice. He wouldn't be returning to Oban's. Walking out the wide double doors, he stopped briefly to look back at the building façade, as if memorizing it. "Well," he said aloud, "that was fun."

Shrugging into his jacket, the short-order cook walked at a brisk pace up the street. The part about wanting to see his daughter was absolutely true, though he wasn't rushing because she was expected at school. In fact, it was entirely possible that his daughter was just returning home herself. She might have been out all night, which worried the short-order cook a bit, especially now that he knew someone had been looking for him, but she was a smart girl and wouldn't make any foolish choices.

Mostly, though, he was rushing home to see her because that's what he did every day. It was their habit, their ritual: They would meet in the morning and sit in their small garden that faced the boulevard and exchange stories about what they had done over the course of the previous day. He would tell her about the conversation with Oban and his decision not to return to the diner. She would mock him and express her belief that he had become paranoid. No one, she would say, cared where he came from or what he did before deciding to try cooking breakfast for a living. "It's just another one of your little fascinations, Father. And you made that poor man find chicken eggs for you."

The short-order cook did feel bad about the eggs, but Oban would be able to keep his last paycheck as compensation. And, who knew? Maybe one of the other cooks would try to make an omelet.

Anyone who would have considered watching the short-order cook as he walked down the busy street would have viewed a very peculiar scene; however, all Orions valued their privacy. Indeed, one of the reasons the short-order cook had decided to settle there was the Orion culture's fanatical desire to maintain control over their personal identities. The planet was one of the few technologically advanced planets in the sector where an individual could be sure he wasn't being passively observed by a multitude of recording devices, scanners, or sensors at any given moment.

The short-order cook pulled back his shoulders and the slight bulge of his belly slowly disappeared and he became slightly taller. He rubbed his face and the skin around his neck and jowls tightened and grew paler. He ran his hand through his hair and instead of it getting shaggier or more rumpled, it grew straighter and thicker. The small bald spot on the crown of his head filled in. After walking for eight blocks and turning several corners, the short-order cook stopped in front of a small, well-maintained three-story house. The front yard was surrounded by a high wooden fence that was heavily hung with dark ivy and small purple blossoms. Between the slats of the fence, a passerby might be able to make out a small wooden table and three chairs.

If Kelly, the waitress from Oban's diner, had walked past the short-order cook at that very moment, she might have passed by without a second glance. The short-order cook's appearance was entirely altered: taller, wider at the shoulder and slimmer at the waist. Another Terran would have considered him moderately attractive, though more striking than handsome in any conventional sense, with a wide brow, deep-set eyes, and a heavy jawline.

An observer—should anyone have the bad manners to stare—would have said the man seemed overly serious, somber even, until he smiled, which he did at just that moment, as if remembering a happy memory. In fact, he was remembering his favorite time of day. He would walk in through the front door of his domicile and announce his presence. His daughter would appear from one of the inner rooms and find him in the hallway. They would embrace and she would begin to talk. Eventually, his daughter's caretaker would appear and then she would give her account of their day. The three of them would prepare a small meal (though none of them was really hungry) and they would carry it out to the garden (on fair days) or out onto the enclosed porch (on foul ones) and then they would talk and talk and talk.

The thought of this moment, the anticipation, was almost as delicious as the reality. The man who had been the short-order cook smiled and walked up the three concrete steps to his front door. The sensor package recognized his biometric signature and admitted him when he depressed the door latch. He walked into the entrance hall and hung the light jacket on one of the hooks by the door. He noted that neither his daughter's coat, nor his daughter's caretaker's, was hanging on a hook, though this was hardly unusual. As often as not, they left their coats in their bedrooms or draped over the back of the couch in the family room. His daughter was not mindful or tidy the way he was, a trait that often frustrated him, but, if pressed, he would admit also delighted him.

"Lal?" he called, the same as he did every day. "Are you home?" The pitch of his voice had changed, too, since the conversation with Oban. The rough, scratchy edge had disappeared, replaced by a much more refined and measured tone. "Are you in the kitchen?" He stood and waited for the ritual to play out, trying not to fret or worry.

He listened for the click of heels on the parquet hallway floor or the squeak of the kitchen door swinging open, but he heard nothing.

"Lal?" he repeated. "Daughter?" Perhaps she was playing a trick on him. Or was this a new game? Though she was an incredibly self-possessed and articulate individual, his daughter was still very young. But he considered: If this were a game, he would have expected to find some indication of what the rules were.

"Alice?" he called, raising his voice. Could they be out in the garden? No, he would have seen them as he passed. One of them—Lal or Alice—would have greeted him.

He walked through the entry hall into the living room, which was dimly lit, the curtains drawn. This was highly unusual. Lal enjoyed the morning light. Every day, she would pull back the drapes and let the sunlight in. She had, her father thought, a mild dread of darkness, which was not surprising considering the amount of time she had spent in shadow. "This is not right," he whispered.

As if waiting for his words, a bright light appeared on the floor. At first, no wider than a few centimeters, the light quickly expanded and became a column. Edges became defined. Colors appeared and sharpened. The ethereal became solid.

A man stood where the flicker of light had been a moment before. The man, a fellow Terran in appearance, wore a well-tailored morning jacket and vest. A golden watch hung from a chain at his waist. His face, though lined with age, was well-formed and he appeared just as hale and healthy as the last time the pair had seen each other. He smiled and bowed his head in greeting. "Greetings, my dear Mister Data," he said. "You have no idea how delighted I am to see you. Well, not 'see' you properly. This is merely a recording—a very *sophisticated* recording, but a recording nevertheless. Apologies for contacting you in this manner, but I thought it would be the most effective means of communication at this juncture."

"Moriarty," Data said softly.

"At your service." The image bowed again, a bit more deeply. "Or, actually, not. Quite the polar opposite, in fact."

"Where is my daughter?" Data asked.

"Your charming daughter and her somewhat less charming friend are, as they say, in my clutches, which is where they will remain until you have completed a task for me, a task for which I believe you are uniquely well-suited."

"I am well-suited for many tasks, Professor Moriarty. If you would like me to assist you, you have only to return my daughter and her friend . . ."

"I think not, Mister Data. I enjoy the idea of having a bit of . . . shall we call it . . . leverage? Just in case you decide to contact your friends in Starfleet."

"I am no longer a Starfleet officer."

"Yes, I know. This came as a bit of a surprise. I took you for a career officer, but, ah, dying and being resurrected does so change one's perspective, doesn't it? There's something we have in common, both of us turning up like a pair of bad pennies when least expected."

"Apparently, you know a great deal more about my recent past than I know about yours," Data said. "For example, last I heard, you were still residing in the memory core at the Daystrom Institute."

"'Residing'? An interesting choice of words, sir. I might have selected 'imprisoned' or even 'languishing,' but, no need to masticate our words. I am no longer there, as you will no doubt confirm as soon as we conclude our conversation." The hologram tugged out and consulted his pocket watch. "Which will have to be soon, since, no doubt, you've instructed various and sundry tracking programs to sniff out my location. By my calculations, I have another ninety-five seconds before even the cleverest bloodhound could trace the origin of this program."

"Professor, wait," Data begged, his icy façade dropping. "If you could just tell me what you need, I'm sure we could come to an arrangement."

"But my dear Mister Data, that's precisely what I'm trying to do: to tell you what I need from you."

"Which is?"

"As I said, something I think you are uniquely well-suited to help me find: a body. I need a body, Mister Data."

"I beg your pardon?"

"I didn't think my request would be so confusing, sir. Let me say it again: I require a body. A *solid* body. Like your own, sir, though perhaps a bit taller."

"I believe I understand, Professor, though not why you would come to me. Where am I supposed to find . . . ?"

"Ah!" Moriarty said, holding up a finger. "Not my problem at all. Not my problem." He reached into the pocket of his waistcoat and withdrew what appeared to be a calling card. "As for why you . . . why not you? You've always struck me as being resourceful in a dogged sort of fashion. And ask yourself, my dear Mister Data, would I be in this peculiar situation if not for you?" Moriarty paused for a comment, but Data had none to offer, so the Professor continued. "Here are some details that you may find useful." He released the holographic image of a card, which fluttered to the ground and landed on top of the emitter. "And now, Mister Data, *adieu*. Send a note when you've made some progress. My contact information is included. And, no, please don't waste valuable time trying to trace this transmission. We both know I'm more clever than that."

"No, please, Professor. Please wait . . ."

But Moriarty was gone. Data was, in every sense of the word he could define—and there were so many—utterly and completely alone.

2

"So, Mister Data," Jean-Luc Picard said with a wry smile, "welcome back to parenthood." He took a small sip of his drink, swished it briefly over his tongue and palate, and then swallowed with a satisfied sigh. "While I'm not usually one for hard liquor, Geordi," he said, turning to his second officer and chief engineer, "I must say, I could develop a taste for this."

"I wouldn't, Captain," Commander Geordi La Forge replied, picking the bottle up off the small table. "Lagavulin," he read off the label, his voice a bit slurred. "Bottled in 2273. According to Mister Scott, it's probably the last one left in existence. He gave it to me when we launched the *Enterprise*-E. Told me it was from his private reserve. 'A cache of supplies I'd put into stasis against a rainy day,' he said. Told me I should hang on to it for a special occasion." He poured a finger into his tumbler and then carefully re-corked the bottle before setting it back on the table. "This seemed appropriate."

Picard narrowed his eyes. "I *did* get married a few years ago, as I recall. *And* had a child."

"I considered it," La Forge explained, "but it wouldn't have fit with all the French wine."

Picard cocked his head to the side, conceding the point, and took another sip. "I shall allow it, Mister La Forge. We're in Mister Scott's debt . . . again."

La Forge nodded, the effects of the alcohol temporarily mitigated as the revelers each silently recalled their friend, now lost. "It's hard to believe he's gone," La Forge murmured.

"One never knows, Mister La Forge," Picard replied. "He might not be." He nodded toward his former Ops officer. "Case in point . . ."

"Which leads to an interesting question: Data, who can we tell that you're back among the living? I can't imagine not telling Will and Deanna, but how far does that permission extend? What about Doctor Pulaski, for example? She was quite upset when she heard you'd died. . . . Uh, Data? Hello?" La Forge waved his hand in front of his friend's face. "Anyone home?"

But Data's gaze was fixed on the small holographic display he had activated next to their table in the Happy Bottom Riding Club, the *Enterprise*'s primary social center. Biometric and engineering information crawled across the bottom of the screen, a constantly updated stream of data about the figure at the center of the image, the object of Data's unwavering gaze: Lal. His daughter. Asleep. Her chest rose and fell slowly. He knew it was a simulation, knew Lal didn't need to respire, but Data felt nearly overwhelmed by the twinned senses of peace and anxiety the sight provoked in him.

Part of Data's mind monitored the myriad minor physiological responses: the flutter of an eyelid, the twitch of a muscle in her cheek, the curl of her lip, all despite the induced coma state. His daughter. Lal. Restored. Alive.

"Data?" La Forge asked again.

"It's very good," Data said, lifting the drink and taking a healthy sip. His palate logged the presence of a score of complex hydrocarbons and flavor compounds, as well as a healthy dose of ethanol. He was incapable of becoming inebriated, but the part of his mind that housed the memories of his father, a man who had spent part of his existence cataloging the finer things in life, was able to appreciate the rare experience.

"What's very good, Data?" La Forge asked, sounding amused.

"The single-malt whiskey," Data said, holding the glass up as if studying the color, though he was actually looking through the liquor at the image of Lal in the holotank.

"We weren't . . ." He sighed. "Never mind. New parents are all the same."

Picard chuckled and swirled the inch of liquid still remaining in his glass. "I suppose I might resent that comment, too, except I recall saying much the same thing myself back in the days before René came along to teach me a lesson."

Worf leaned in from the shadows. The Klingon

first officer had spent most of the evening lurking in the gloom, only rising occasionally to go to the bar for refills of whatever he had been nursing. He had sipped an appropriate amount of Mister Scott's gift when La Forge had brought it to the bar, but afterward eschewed it, murmuring something about it being "not unlike mother's milk."

Whatever he had been drinking had clearly put Worf in a contemplative state. "The Klingon poet Kathan wrote, 'Parenthood is the wound that never heals.'"

La Forge, Picard, and Data all kept their peace, each waiting for more. When Worf settled back into the shadows, the engineer lifted his glass and said, "To Klingon poetry. Brutally succinct."

"Well observed," Worf replied.

The captain guffawed and drank, too. Data lifted his glass, but he was not thinking about parenthood or poetry. He was recalling the movement of Akharin's hands as they moved over Lal's inert form, like a concert pianist playing his instrument. With perfect clarity, Data recollected the immortal's every gesture, every tool he had used, every technique. He pictured every moment in his mind's eye, yet Data still could not say precisely what he had observed. Had it been science at some level that Data could not comprehend, or had it been an act of inspired artistry? Or had Akharin, the old wizard, simply woven a magic spell? Data did not know. He thought that, given time, he might be able to break down the actions, unweave the spell, but at what price? *To dissect is to kill*, Data thought. He knew it was the basest superstition, but a part of him believed that if he tried to reproduce Akharin's magic, he would undo the spell and his daughter would fall back into the abyss.

"Geordi raised a valid question, Data," Picard said. "What should we tell your former ship-mates and colleagues, the ones who don't already know?"

"And what do we say about Lal?" La Forge added.

They were, Data conceded, *valid questions.* He was in a unique situation and a decision would be required very soon. Over the past few days, during the crises of the Tholian/Breen terrorists and the great, galaxy-consuming Machine, Starfleet had been very relaxed regarding Data's presence, not the least because he contributed to the success-ful resolution of both missions, but he knew the service's tolerance would soon be taxed. The cur-rent incarnation of Starfleet was not *his* Starfleet. Wars had been fought, worlds devastated, empires erased. Data and Lal had been restored when so many had been lost. Would resentment flare?

"These are very good questions," Data replied, looking away from the holotank for the first time. "And I hope I can depend on you all for advice after I have had time to ponder them. This is all so new . . ." He let his voice falter, as if at a loss for words.

"We understand, Data," Picard said. "These are early days. I can barely imagine what it must be like, not only to be a parent again after having lost Lal once, but, this time, to have access to a full range of emotions." He shook his head in wonder, then pushed back from the table and stood, wobbling ever so slightly. Straightening, the captain tugged on the front of his uniform and said, "I will be happy to help in any way I can." He nodded to La Forge. "Thank you for sharing your gift, Commander. It was more than worth the scolding I will no doubt receive."

"From Doctor Crusher?" La Forge asked.

Picard shook his head. "No, of course not. Not Beverly—René. I missed story time this evening. We've been reading *Watership Down*. He doesn't seem to mind missing a chapter when it's ship's business, but a night out socializing?" Grinning broadly, Picard headed for the door, waving his hand in salute. "I believe I may be in for a bit of a lecture over breakfast. He really wants to know what's going to happen to those rabbits."

La Forge and Worf exchanged knowing looks and then were both shocked when Data laughed at their expressions. The engineer said, "It is going to take some time to get used to that."

"To what?" Data asked.

"To you laughing," La Forge replied. "And the fact that you actually understand why something is funny. I mean, you had the emotion chip back . . . you know . . ."

"Before I died."

"Yes. But you turned it on and off so often. It was difficult to know what to expect from day to day."

"Expect this from now on," Data replied and parodied a beatifically happy expression. "That's what all parents look like all the time, is it not?" Worf laughed out loud, a rare sound on the best of days. Data felt absurdly proud. "I believe I should end the evening on that note," he said, rising. "Always leave them wanting more."

"I have stories about Alexander I should share with you," Worf said, rubbing the bridge of his nose, "that would smooth a lesser man's forehead." Data was not certain if this was an invitation or a threat.

"I look forward to hearing them. But I believe I should check on Lal's systems now. According to the monitors, the induced coma is weakening. She appears to wish to awaken."

"I think you should let her," La Forge said.

"And I will," Data said. "After I have checked her vital signs. And prepared the environment. And made sure her temporary quarters are ready. And determined how many of the crew members who knew her before are still on board. And . . ."

"Never mind. I get it. Work to be done." La Forge shook his head. "I guess one of the advantages of never having to sleep is, well, never having to sleep."

"True, but sleep has its pleasures. As I recall, dreaming can be quite enjoyable."

"You haven't been dreaming?"

"Nor sleeping. Not since my resurrection. It seemed . . . wasteful, somehow."

"Hmm," La Forge said neutrally. "Well, unfortunately, I *do* have to sleep, so I'll walk out with you if you don't mind."

"I would welcome the company, as ever." Data looked over at Worf, who was staring out at the stars. "Worf?"

The Klingon did not respond.

La Forge shook his head ever so slightly. *Leave him be.*

The old friends walked quietly to the exit. La Forge flinched when the doors parted and the bright lights briefly overloaded the receptors of his ocular implants. Data put his hand on La Forge's shoulder and guided him toward the turbolift door.

Waiting for the lift to arrive, without looking at Data, La Forge asked, "So, can I have your ship outfitted with anything before you leave?"

Data did not attempt to conceal his surprise at the question. "Geordi," he began, "I would have contacted you . . ."

"Don't," La Forge said. "I understand. Better than you know. It's not the same ship. It's not the same Starfleet or the same Federation. None of us is the same." He inhaled deeply, then sighed. "I'll tell the captain we talked and that you thought it was best for Lal to leave without too many good-byes. You were afraid it would overload her holotronic matrix. She needs time. You both need time . . ." He ran out of words.

The turbolift arrived and the doors parted.

Data stammered, "I do not know how I could have ever expected to . . ."

"To slip away without me noticing?"

"Yes," Data said, and then, "no. It runs deeper: I do not know how I could have expected to deceive you."

"You can't, Data. You're a terrible liar. Also, I'm your best friend." La Forge stepped into the turbolift. "You're experiencing a lot of emotions right now—complex emotions—issues that even someone with years of practice might have trouble coping with. We never had a chance to talk about Rhea. If you'd like to now . . ."

Data did not join him on the lift. He knew he was wearing a neutral expression, but he was sure his friend sensed the unexpected, unconscious stiffening in his back and shoulders upon hearing Rhea's name spoken aloud. "Thank you, Geordi," Data said, not looking La Forge in the eye. "I will contact you as soon as I have . . ."

". . . Found an even keel."

"Yes."

The engineer nodded and smiled, but the expression did not reach his eyes. "I look forward to hearing from you." The doors snapped shut and Data was left alone with his thoughts.

When Alpha shift began the next morning, the *Archeus* had disappeared from the hangar deck, and there was no record of either Lal or Data leaving the *Enterprise*.

3

Early November 2385 (ACE)

Commander Geordi La Forge leaned against the wooden fence that enclosed his small patio and watched the early morning fog roll in off the Pacific and blanket the Upper Haight in a dense gray shroud. Despite almost two hundred years of effective weather control, fog would still occasionally paralyze San Francisco, mostly because San Franciscans refused to let the weather control bureaus prevent the fog from rolling in.

Setting his mug down on the flat top of the weathered rail, La Forge watched the steam rise off the surface of his coffee. He could, if he desired, view the warmer molecules of water vapor waft up and mingle with the cool mist, but he decided to trust in the validity of the second law of thermodynamics in action and enjoy the normal view. To the west, the sky shifted from a dishwater gray to a dull mauve.

Behind him, La Forge heard the glass door

creak open in its groove. *The bearings need lubrication*, he observed, and, ever the good houseguest, made a mental note to log the problem in the building's superintendent program. A warm body sidled up beside him and slipped under his arm, as much for shared warmth as to be companionable. "This city," Leah Brahms said. "I never cease to be amazed. . . ."

"It is beautiful," La Forge murmured.

"Beautiful and *freakish*," Brahms replied, clutching the neck of her bathrobe. "I'm freezing! Five kilometers from here, it's probably twenty degrees; here, it's less than ten!" She slipped one of her hands under La Forge's sweatshirt, making him flinch with the shock of the cold on his back.

"You could go put more clothes on."

"If that's what you really want."

"Come here," La Forge said, pulling her closer.

"If you give me some of your coffee."

"Deal."

Leah sipped gratefully and sighed. "Okay, there's one thing I like about this city. Baseline best coffee on the planet."

"You've never been to Hawaii."

"Wrong, Commander La Forge. I spent six months at the shipyards there. Just never saw the allure of Kona."

"Sacrilege."

"Good taste." She stared out into the gray, undifferentiated space and then swept her hand through the tendrils of fog. "Not used to being up this early. Correction: Not used to being up this early after going to bed so late."

"I didn't make you get up," La Forge said.

"I missed you," Leah said, kissing him on the cheek. Her breath smelled of coffee. "You're warm. And this house has no insulation to speak of."

"I'll mention it to the superintendent, though I doubt the owner will care. People book these houses years in advance."

"Then how did you get it?"

La Forge took back his mug and sipped the mouthful she had left behind. "I happen to be a very high-ranking officer on the Federation flagship on leave. Didn't I mention that over dinner?"

"You might have. I barely remember. Tequila is now my nemesis." She struck a pose and shook her fist. "Curse you, tequila!"

"So, you're going to blame the rest of the evening on tequila?"

Leah ran her hand up and down the length of La Forge's spine. "Not entirely."

La Forge grinned, but the smile quickly faded. "We have to stop doing this, you know."

"Doing what?" Leah asked. "Running into each other? Having great conversations? Great meals? Great . . ."

"You know what I mean," La Forge said. "I mean . . . I'm sorry. I know it's a little early in the day for this kind of conversation, but, honestly, I'm wearing down."

"I could make a joke about having regular maintenance checks," Leah said, "but I get the feeling that wouldn't go over well right at this moment."

La Forge turned to look back to the horizon, which had gone from mauve to a dusky pink.

"Maybe not. Again, sorry. I'm trying to be . . . responsible." He looked at her from the corner of his eye.

Leah swiped a lock of hair back behind her ear. "Geordi, you're the most responsible man I've ever met. Arguably, *too* responsible. You hold yourself accountable for things that you've never done. Or ever could do."

"It's just that . . . I've been . . . I mean, I was seeing someone. Back on the *Enterprise.*"

"May I ask: Did you tell her you were going to be a monk while you were on sabbatical?"

"No."

"Did she ask to come along with you?"

"No."

"Would you have wanted her to?"

La Forge inhaled deeply and let the breath out slowly. "As of right this moment," he confessed, "no."

"Then, what?"

"It's just that every time I think I've gotten you out of my system, when I start to think I might be able to be with someone without constantly comparing her to you, there you are again."

Leah wrinkled her nose and was unable to suppress a smile. "Guilty," she said. "Unintentional, but guilty."

"You see my dilemma."

"I do," Leah said, and moved half a step away despite the chill in the air. "And I'm sorry if I keep making your life complicated. You make mine complicated, too. Maybe that's just how it is with people like us."

"Complicated people."

"Actually, I'm feeling pretty simple this morning."

"Simple in a good way? Or in a bad way?"

"Simple, as in I know what I want." She stepped in closer and kissed La Forge on the cheek. She whispered, "I want more coffee."

"I'll get it," La Forge said.

"No, I'll get it," Leah said. "Give me your mug. And tell me where I left my clothes."

"If I get the coffee, will you not worry about your clothes just yet?"

Leah laughed and stroked the side of his face with the tip of her finger, stopping just below the tiny scar beside his eye where the VISOR port used to be. "I have to ask you: Do you ever miss it?"

"What?" he asked, knowing exactly what Leah meant, but wanting her to ask.

"The VISOR."

"You mean as opposed to my implants?"

"I suppose."

"It's a trade-off. The implants can't do quite as many things as the VISOR could, but, on the other hand, I don't worry about someone accidentally knocking it off my face."

"Did that ever really happen?"

La Forge laughed. "Clearly, someone does not remember a particular incident at a particularly raucous party in Ten-Forward."

Leah appeared to think very hard for a moment and then winced. "Oh," she said. "Right. Uh. Never mind." She walked to the sliding door, La

Forge's mug in her hand. "Tell me which dresser drawer has socks. My feet are *freezing*."

"Top left," La Forge said. "Wool socks on the right."

"Of course. How organized," Leah said as she disappeared into the house.

Listening to her moving around the house, La Forge realized how much he had missed hearing other bodies. Being on board a starship, even one as comparatively luxurious as the *Enterprise*, you tended to tune out the sounds of your neighbors and the several hundred other individuals wandering the corridors at any given time. Being on leave, studying at the Academy, even with the daily interaction with students and colleagues, he hadn't realized how a part of him had been yearning to catch the sound of half-heard conversations or footsteps passing by his door. *Or*, he thought, *maybe I just want to hear* these *footfalls and* this *voice.*

"Hey," Leah called from the kitchen. "Come in here."

"What's wrong? Can't find the sock drawer?"

"No," she said. The coffee mug still dangled from one of her fingers, but all of her attention was focused on the small device on the palm of her hand. "What is this? It was in your sock drawer. It was beeping."

"Ah," La Forge said. "That . . . that's a communicator."

"Not like any communicator I've ever seen. Is your not-really-a-girlfriend girlfriend trying to call you?"

La Forge carefully lifted the device from Leah's

palm, trying desperately to appear cool and collected. "No. Not that. It's a . . . Well, you'll like this. It's a quantum entanglement communicator."

"An *ansible*?" Leah cried. "Really? I've heard about these but never seen one. Where did you get it?"

"It was a gift. Well, not exactly a gift. More like a, what should I call it? A lifeline. A panic button."

"From who?"

La Forge touched the stud that activated the receive function. He wondered guiltily how long the device had been trying to get his attention. After spending several weeks carrying it around and waiting for it to signal him, La Forge had finally decided to set it aside a month after arriving on Earth for his sabbatical leave. "Who else?" he asked. "Data."

"Data?" Leah asked incredulously. "I was under the impression that he was . . ."

"No," La Forge replied. "Well, yes, but, then, no. Not anymore. Or, who knows? I haven't heard from him in months."

"Answer it," Leah said. "Explain later. Answer now."

"Yeah," La Forge said, and thumbed the stud that activated the device. He held it to his ear. "Hello?"

"Geordi?"

"Yes? Data? What is it? What's wrong?"

"This is a recording, Geordi. Today is . . ." And he rattled off a stardate that La Forge quickly deciphered, meaning the message was less than two days old. "I will contact you as soon as I can. Please keep the quantum communicator with you as much as is practical. I require your assistance on a matter of great importance. If you are willing to help, please leave your location and I will have transportation sent to retrieve you immediately. If I may also ask this of you, please do not tell Captain Picard about this communication. I will explain when I speak with you."

La Forge hesitated, looking over at Leah as she pulled her hair back and whipped it into a loose ponytail. She tied the sash of her robe around her middle and set the mug down on the counter so her hands would be free. Ready to work.

"Of course, Data. I'm willing to help. I'm on Earth. San Francisco. The faculty housing in the Upper Haight. I think you know the building. Data, I'm sorry I didn't get the message sooner. I've been . . ."

"That is sufficient, Geordi. I have all the information I require for my ship to locate you. Thank you, my friend. There is no one else I could have turned to at this time." The automated message clicked off and the communicator shut off.

Leah looked at him expectantly. "What's happening?" she asked. "Was that Data?"

"No, an answering service. Good A.I., too, though what would you expect?"

"Is he in trouble?" She shook her head in disbelief. "Wait, what am I asking? Why would he call if he wasn't?"

"I don't know. I'll find out soon. A ship is on its way."

"Not the *Enterprise*?"

La Forge shook his head and slipped the communicator into his sweatshirt pocket. "No. It's a private thing. But I have to go. I told Data I would help."

"Help with what?" Leah asked. "Didn't Data give you any details?"

La Forge stepped forward and put his hands on her shoulders, then pulled her close. "I don't know. He didn't say. It's just something I have to do. He's my best friend."

"Who was supposed to be dead. Who just called you up out of the blue and said, 'Come help me.' Doesn't that sound a little suspicious?"

"Yes," La Forge said, speaking into her hair.

"Then why do you have to go?" La Forge felt the frustration coming off Leah in waves.

"Because I said I would," he said, knowing the answer was insufficient. "Because he would do the same for me if I asked."

Leah sighed and pushed her forehead against the middle of La Forge's chest. She wrapped her arms tightly around the small of his back and tugged him as close as she could. "I hate you," she muttered.

"I know," La Forge said, caressing the back of her head, untying the loose ponytail. "I know. I hate me, too."

A placeless place

"Who are you?"

A tiny smile tickled the corners of the pale

man's lips. He reached up and brushed it away with the flick of a finger. When he lowered the hand, he paused to straighten his black tie and then stroke the silver chain that dangled from his waistcoat pocket. "Who am I?" he asked. "What an excellent question. Frankly, my dear, sometimes I barely know myself. But I know one thing for a certainty: I am your host and so I should be gracious." He bowed. "Professor James Moriarty at your service. May I ask you to return the courtesy and tell me your name?"

Alice snorted and looked around at the featureless, comfortless room. "Guest? You have an odd sense of hospitality. I think . . ."

"Yes, yes, fine. Prisoner, then." Moriarty waved his hand dismissively. "I am nothing if not a self-aware villain." He held up his index finger and twirled it in a small circle. Without a sound, first one chair and then another and then a third appeared. While none of the chairs was precisely identical, all of them were large and comfortable-looking and completely without hue. "Please sit down, Miss . . ."

"Alice," said Alice. "Just Alice."

"And may I ask your companion's name?"

"I think you already know," Alice said, subtly repositioning herself so she was standing between Moriarty and her charge.

"Pray pretend I do not."

Impetuous as ever—annoyingly so—Lal stepped around Alice and strode up to Moriarty, her hand extended. "My name is Lal. How do you do?"

Alice was intrigued by Moriarty's peculiar response to Lal's approach. His initial inclination appeared to be to extend his hand in a friendly manner, but then he had a second thought and flinched away. "I . . . Excuse me. I eschew physical contact."

Lal looked back over her shoulder at Alice. "So, did we settle on 'prisoners'?"

Moriarty shrugged and folded his hands together. "If you insist on a precise word, we could use 'hostages.'"

Lal turned back to look at him. Alice knew perfectly well the expression her charge wore: a frank, piercing stare that was full of judgment, but peculiarly without malice. "I do," Lal said. "Precision is valuable."

"As you say," Moriarty replied. "But so is comfort." He beckoned to the white chairs. "Please sit." Alice noticed that without her being aware of it, a carpet had materialized under her feet. Like the chairs, the carpet was utterly without color, though there was an intricate pattern woven into it.

Lal looked at the three chairs and chose the one with the highest back. She sat and crossed her legs at the ankles, her long, blue silk skirt swishing around her lower calves. The wide heels of her black shoes clacked together as she curled her long fingers over the caps of the chair's plush arms. She cocked her head to the side and said, "You're quite correct: Comfort is valuable, though I have no clear idea how you could understand your own statement. Aren't you nothing but a computer program, a ghost made of photons?"

Moriarty chuckled and sat down in the chair facing Lal, the aged leather stretching under his weight. When he crossed his legs, the fabric of his trousers swished against the chair's covering. Without seeming to realize he was doing it, Moriarty's posture mirrored Lal's. On more than one occasion, Alice had observed this same behavior in flesh-and-blood sentients, how they imitated Lal's behavior, as if innately sensing it was worth emulating. "I suppose that is correct. And poetic. You're really nothing like your father, are you? How far the apple has fallen from the tree! Should I be flattered he has told you about our brief encounters? When he told the stories, were they cast as comedy or drama?"

"Neither," Lal said. "And he did not 'tell me' in the sense you mean. We share some memories. Or perhaps I should say our memories have become mingled. When I died—yes, I died—he downloaded my memories into his own. When I was resurrected—yes, I was resurrected—some of my father's memories were carried along. It was not a precise thing, alas. I have no sense of how many of his memories I received. Sometimes, when I'm not paying close attention, I'm not even sure if moments I recall are events that happened to me or to him."

"How wonderful," Moriarty exclaimed. "And how sad."

Lal's eyebrows shot upward: a pair of jet-black apostrophes. "Yes," she said, and smiled radiantly. "That's exactly what I think."

"So, you know of me."

"I do. And of your fate. Or what I . . . that is, we . . . thought was your fate. Apparently, we were misinformed." Lal lifted her hands from the arms of the chair and folded them in her lap. In her mind, Alice added the word, *regally*. Without either Moriarty or Lal noticing, she slipped into the third chair. From the corner of her eye, she observed more features taking hold on the borders of the room: a fireplace and mantel; bookshelves and an armoire; paintings and wall fixtures. And they were all white, white, white.

"And thereby hangs a tale," Moriarty replied, leaning forward, hands also folded in his lap.

Aboard the *Archeus*

"You're *Archeus*, right?" La Forge asked.

"*No, Mister La Forge*," the computer replied. "*The ship is named* Archeus. *I am Shakti, Data's personal assistant.*" The pleasant voice, faintly tinged with an Indian accent, came from everywhere and nowhere in particular. Like everything else aboard Data's personal yacht, the comm system was top of the line.

"Geordi," La Forge said, settling into the passenger seat. "Call me Geordi." He had stowed his luggage in one of the overhead compartments and then had been suitably impressed by the collection of beverages and snacks in the small larder by his seat. None of the amenities came anywhere close to being as impressive as the feat of having the *Archeus* land in the small clearing near his lodgings. La Forge couldn't imagine what Data had done to get clearance or, failing the required permits, how high the fines might be. "Seeing as we're going to be spending a little time together. It's a bit of a trip to Rigel III."

"*It is,*" Shakti allowed, "*or would be if we were going to Rigel. Forgive me for the deception, Geordi, but I do not believe we will have as much time to get to know each other as you might have expected.*"

"What do you mean?"

Behind him, La Forge heard a soft click and felt a slight shift in the air pressure of the cabin. "Because you will be talking to me."

La Forge turned and saw his old friend and shipmate sitting in a low chair, looking very much the same as he had the last time they had seen each other. He had retained Noonien Soong's features, though La Forge immediately noticed that the hair around his temples was dappled with gray and he had grown whiskers on his chin. He looked, La Forge decided, affable and wise. The word that surfaced in his mind was "paternal." When he rose to greet his friend, La Forge saw there was a fiber-optic cable plugged into a port below the base of his skull, undermining the illusion of humanity. Feeling the pull of the cable, Data reached back and extracted the plug. He smiled sheepishly, then cocked his head in a manner La Forge remembered so well.

Stepping forward, La Forge took the proffered hand, but then he pulled his friend into a quick, backslapping embrace. "It's good to see you," he said. "Even under the circumstances."

"Thank you for responding so quickly, Geordi. I had no idea you had re-formed your connection with Doctor Brahms or I would have . . ."

"Stop. Whatever you're about to say, forget it. Leah says hello and also, 'Please finish this up as quickly as possible.'"

"Nothing would please me more," Data said. Turning his head to speak into midair, he snapped, "Shakti, plot a course out of the system. By the time you are clear for warp, we will have decided on a course of action."

La Forge barely felt the *Archeus* shift under his feet as Shakti expertly piloted it out of the gravity well. "How did you ever get clearance to land so close to . . ."

"I did not get clearance," Data said, turning away to run his hand over a control surface.

Through the front port, La Forge watched as the city of San Francisco turned into a dot. The Pacific Ocean filled the view, but it quickly became no bigger than a puddle. "You must be doing half-impulse. The Port Authority must be tracking you by now."

"Let them."

"Data, they'll know who did this. The fines alone . . ."

"I do not care, Geordi," he said, pulling a small table out of the wall. "I am exceedingly wealthy. Fines can be paid. *Will* be paid. Probably already are paid. Shakti is extraordinarily efficient."

"*Thank you, Data,*" Shakti said.

"But, still . . ."

"It is not a concern now, Geordi. We have only

one concern." He waved his hand over the top of the table, and a hologram of Lal appeared.

La Forge understood the need for haste. Data had explained that much in the brief message he had left after La Forge had accepted his invitation. Lal was in danger. He assumed the problem was an engineering dilemma, something to do with her holomatrix. As he had on more than one occasion, La Forge wondered what he could offer in the way of help given that Data was the undisputed expert on Soong-type androids now that Soong was dead. "What's the problem?"

"She is gone."

"What? She ran away?"

"No, she did not leave of her own volition. She was taken."

"How can you be sure?"

"Because her abductor contacted me."

"*Abductor*?" La Forge exclaimed.

Data waved a hand, and the image of a human man appeared in Lal's place. He wore a long, black suit jacket, a waistcoat, and a wide black tie. The man's forehead was high and his eyes widely spaced. Though La Forge had only ever seen this individual with his VISOR, there were enough peculiarities about his appearance that he could be recognized without speaking. "Moriarty," he said. "James Moriarty. From the holodeck on the *Enterprise*-D."

"Correct."

"But that's, well . . ." He paused sheepishly. "I've learned by now to never say 'impossible,' but . . ."

"I appreciate your restraint, Geordi. And while it is not impossible, Moriarty's return—and his claim to have abducted Lal—*is* highly improbable."

"But you believe it to be true."

"In the absence of a theory that better fits the facts, yes."

"But how? And why?"

Data leaned back in his chair, laid the tips of his fingers together, and touched his index fingers against his lips. "Ah," he said. "I believe I only know part of the story, but I shall relate it just as soon as we are in transit."

On cue, Shakti announced, *"We have reached a safe distance from Sol and can go into warp. Have you selected a course?"*

"I have," Data said. "Before we can do anything else, we need to be sure that Moriarty is actually at large. Set course for the Daystrom Institute. Best speed."

"Course laid in. Going to warp. We can average warp six point four in this region of space." La Forge felt only the barest lurch as the *Archeus* shifted from impulse to warp drive.

"Arrival in four point three hours."

"We're going to talk to Bruce Maddox?"

"No," Data replied. "Commander Maddox would be obliged to report our questions to Starfleet. I believe our investigation needs to remain as covert as possible for as long as possible. If Moriarty is as clever as I believe he is, he will know if I attempt to contact the authorities."

La Forge looked askance at his friend. "I'm not sure that's a good idea. We should . . ."

"Please, Geordi. Comply with me on this request, at least for now."

"But I'm a Starfleet officer. I should report this to . . . well, someone. Captain Picard at the very least."

"Who will immediately be obliged to report it to Starfleet Command," Data said, his voice rising, "who will assume they must take action that could result in Moriarty either fleeing or withdrawing and possibly harming my daughter."

"Do you really think Captain Picard would place Lal at risk? After everything he's done for you . . ."

Data slapped the table with his open palm. "I have to *assume* the captain would do as he has usually done. I have to play the odds. First and foremost, he is a Starfleet officer. He would follow *protocol*." He looked down at the table and at the tiny spiderweb cracks that had appeared in the surface where he struck it. Lifting his hand, Data pushed himself back from the table. "My apologies, Geordi, for losing my temper. I am concerned for Lal. She is my priority now. My highest priority."

La Forge thought back to his last conversation with Data in the Riding Club. He also found himself reflecting on his private thoughts about Captain Picard and how much the man had changed since becoming a parent. Data didn't—couldn't—know about those changes, and La Forge knew he probably wouldn't be able to convince him otherwise. "All right," he said. "We play it your way. *For now*. If a point comes where I think your cause would be better served by contacting Starfleet . . ."

"I rely on your judgment, Geordi," Data said. "As I always have."

The engineer was aware that he was being soothed, but he enjoyed the reassurance and the return of something resembling the relationship between himself and his old friend. "Okay, if we're not going to the Daystrom to see Maddox, then who are we going to use to get us the information we need?"

"I have asked Shakti to review the personnel files at the Institute in order to check if any old friends or colleagues are currently in residence. I found a candidate." He swiped his hand over the cracked tabletop. Fortunately, the cracks did not seem to have affected the control surface.

"Not Reg," La Forge said. "He's with *Voyager* . . ." His voice trailed off when he saw the image that appeared a moment later. "Oh, Data. No. Not him."

Data cocked an eyebrow and, for the first time since La Forge had come aboard the *Archeus*, the android saw a flicker of something that resembled genuine amusement. "I suspected that would be your response."

4

———•———

A placeless place

"You know my tale," Professor Moriarty said to Lal. "Of my birth on the holodeck of the *Enterprise*, my voluntary return to slumber, and my subsequent resurrection." He smiled and said, "So, you see, my dear, we have something in common."

Alice, voice as flat as a tapeworm, said, "I don't. Know the tale, that is."

Lal could tell from Alice's tone that she was annoyed. She wasn't used to being ignored, especially by men. Human men, at least. And though Lal understood Professor Moriarty wasn't human in any real sense of the word, he *appeared* to be human. And male.

Moriarty turned to Alice and spread his hands in accommodation. "My apologies, Miss Alice," he murmured. "How rude of me to assume. Where to begin?"

"Like I said before, just *Alice* is fine. Begin at

the beginning: You were born on the holodeck of the *Enterprise* . . ."

"I was," Moriarty said, settling back into his chair. "A rare convocation of events: a peculiarly phrased request and the extraordinary resources to garb the request in multi-spectrum light. These are the circumstances that led to my inception."

"Are you saying you were wished into being? Like a genie out of a lamp?"

Moriarty smiled. "Out of a lamp. Yes."

Alice laughed and flipped her hair. "So, we have something in common. I was, too."

Moriarty puckered his lips, then grimaced menacingly. "Are you mocking me, Alice?"

"Oh, no. Never. I never mock my jailers."

"Or your host."

"Or one of those," Alice said. "Whenever I can find one." She settled back into her chair, relaxing for the first time since they had arrived. Lal knew that Alice liked to have a secret, something she could keep close until it was opportune to share. She was content now and stretched her long legs out in front of her. "But I can tell my story later. Pray, continue."

"How gracious." Moriarty bowed as well as anyone could bow while sitting. "Your Mister Data and his comrades brought me to life with a casual, if fortuitously phrased, wish, and *poof!* like the genie, I appeared. And, just like the genie of Aladdin's tale, I was unanticipated. Fortunately, I had the good sense to retain my composure and play my part. I learned about my circumstances and found the means to navigate through the strange new world . . ."

"You took the *Enterprise* hostage and threatened the crew," Lal inserted.

"As I said, navigation."

"And only released your hold when Captain Picard convinced you there was nothing he could do for you."

"A very persuasive speaker, the captain."

"And then you were awakened from your slumber by Lieutenant Barclay . . ."

"Dear Reginald. I toast him every Yuletide. I understand he has prospered," the Professor said, seeming genuinely pleased.

"And again took control of the *Enterprise* until my father devised a ruse. You and the Countess were convinced you had attained independent existence and could leave the ship."

"Which we did, never to trouble any of you again."

"Until now," Lal corrected.

"Until now," Moriarty conceded.

Alice, showing every sign of enjoying the banter, laid a finger along her cheek and, smiling, asked, "Countess? There's a countess?"

"The Countess Regina Bartholomew," Lal explained. "A persona the Professor commanded the *Enterprise* to create and imbue with an independent intelligence."

In a needlessly exaggerated fashion, Alice let her jaw go slack in a mocking approximation of complete disbelief. "How is that even possible? And, if it is, why isn't it happening *all the time*?

I know a thing or two about little boys, and if it were possible to make their little dream girls come magically to life . . ."

"Because it isn't," Lal explained, folding her hands in her lap again.

"Not anymore," Moriarty said, mirroring her action and smiling slyly. "Steps have been taken. Except, of course, when they aren't."

"There have been cases of holographic intelligences achieving sentience," Lal offered. "Though usually only under extraordinary circumstances."

"Or if someone is willing to devote the processing power," Moriarty countered. "And wants a lounge singer."

"What?" Alice asked.

"Never mind," Lal said, waving away the point. Alice didn't like being dismissed, but Lal would deal with that situation later. Turning back to Moriarty, she asked, "So you were convinced, however briefly, that you were free to roam the universe at your leisure. What happened next?"

"Ah," Moriarty said, and leaned back into the chair. The seat back seemed to envelop him. The light in the room dimmed and the Professor's face was wreathed in shadows. "We come to the pith, the nub, the crux, the point." His voice was low and ominous. "The heart of it all."

Aboard the *Archeus*

"Before I have to face the prospect of"—La Forge swiped his hand over the table's control surface— "that." The image disappeared. "You need to bring me up to speed. What happened after you left the *Enterprise*? I think you probably already know this, but the captain, Worf, everyone who knew you . . . they were all a little hurt."

"I thought I made my reasons clear in the message I left," Data said.

"Clear," La Forge conceded. "Yes. But still . . ."

"We meant no harm," Data said.

"No one ever does, Data."

A year ago—aboard the *U.S.S. Enterprise*

"And there was no security alert?" Worf rumbled. "No one on the bridge was aware of the *Archeus* leaving the shuttlebay?" He gripped his half-full mug of *raktajino* and La Forge watched the veins in his hands bulge as the internal pressure built. "How is this possible?"

"It's possible," the chief engineer explained, "because Data knows as much about this ship as any of us. When you come right down to it, *all* of us. Put together."

The captain set down his cup of tea on the table. The morning's formal briefing had ended and now only the four officers who had known Data in the days before his resurrection remained, a knot of hurt feelings and, in La Forge's case, a dull throbbing behind the eyes. Mister Scott's gift had taken its toll: He was dehydrated and the inner lining of his skull was pulling away from the surface of his brain. "I understand he had his reasons," the captain murmured. "Yet, I feel like an injured host."

"He should have told us they were leaving," Worf grunted. "It was . . . contrary to regulations."

"He doesn't consider himself to be a Starfleet officer," Beverly Crusher offered. "That much is clear if nothing else is about this situation."

"He said as much before he left," La Forge said. "More than anything else, Data says he's a parent now and has to consider Lal's well-being."

The captain and the chief medical officer exchanged a meaningful look. Worf glared at the tabletop, lost in memories that La Forge would just as soon not have to know.

"He pretty much told me what he had planned." Spreading his hands before him, La Forge explained, "I'm sorry, Captain. I think I knew what was going to happen. I didn't report it. I guess I just thought . . ."

Picard waved away the apology. "Under the circumstances, Mister La Forge, I would just as soon not know. Consider yourself on report until I decide otherwise."

La Forge half rose from his chair. "I understand, Captain."

"Is that necessary . . ." Crusher began.

"It is if Commander La Forge doesn't want to face disciplinary action from Starfleet Command," the captain snapped. "I know how they think. When I report this and there isn't something on the record . . ."

"Command will assume you condone the action," La Forge completed his captain's thought.

"Precisely. This way, it's in my hands. And

considering everything else unfolding in the sector, it, too, shall pass."

Crusher smiled at her husband. *An apology*, La Forge assumed. *Or reassurance*. Either way, the gesture made him smile and feel mildly envious.

"Is there anything else we can do?" Worf asked.

The captain sighed and picked up his tea. He took a sip, then winced and set it aside. La Forge had noticed, on more than one occasion, that the surface of the conference room table too efficiently conducted heat out of small beverage containers. "We hope to hear from them sometime and find they're doing well." Looking out the conference room's large ports at the shifting star field, he added, "Perhaps a Christmas card."

Aboard the *Archeus*

"I had not considered that option," Data admitted, clearly making a mental note. "The holiday season will be upon us soon."

"That wasn't the point," La Forge said.

"But a good idea is a good idea."

"We were . . . well, 'worried' is too strong a word. Let's say 'concerned.' Lal had just been revived and Doctor Crusher thought moving her so soon was putting unnecessary stress on her."

"Lal is composed of tripolymer composites, molybdenum-cobalt alloys, cortenide and duranium. Her sheath is composed of bioplast sheeting and her . . ."

"I'm aware of her specs. And you're being deliberately obtuse, which is new and will take some getting used to." La Forge stretched and yawned. "I've been sitting too long." He rose and paced around the small cabin, studying the consoles. "And I didn't sleep much last night. Which one of these makes coffee?"

"Shakti," Data said, "please make Geordi a cup of coffee. He prefers Ethiopian beans. Two sugars, no milk." He cocked his head in a manner that nearly bowled La Forge over with a wave of nostalgia. "Correct?"

La Forge nodded. "Thanks. But back to your story. After you left the *Enterprise*?"

"Shakti, make that two coffees, please," Data replied and leaned back into the chair. A moment later, two steaming mugs appeared on the table in a swirl of congealing atoms.

"Wow," La Forge said. "There's a nano-compiler built into the table?"

"Yes. I find it convenient for manufacturing tools and small parts. And food."

"You eat now?"

"I do not require sustenance, but I enjoy it." Data picked up his mug and inhaled deeply. He tapped the side of his nose and then touched his forehead. "My father chose to vacate his consciousness from this body so I could occupy it, but I have found he is not entirely gone. Memories linger, as does his love of tactile experiences. When I eat or drink, I feel an echo of his pleasure."

"That must be distracting."

"On the contrary: I find it quite comforting."

"But we're digressing again."

"No," Data said. "A segue: My father's memories guided me, perhaps even compelled me. I needed to find a place where my daughter and I could build a life together, a place where we could learn about each other, and where she could discover the world in a controlled fashion. My concern was that her holotronic matrix failed due to the stress of too many novel experiences."

La Forge retrieved his mug and sipped the brew. Shakti made good coffee. "So you wanted to take Lal somewhere she wouldn't be overstimulated. I can see that. Where did you go? A bucolic backwater? Or a satellite like the one where we found Arkharin?"

"We went to Orion Prime," Data said.

La Forge almost spit out his coffee. "Orion? Really? Not the first place that comes to mind when you think of low-stress environments."

"I own a building there," Data explained. "Several buildings, in fact. And a casino. Rather, my father did and I inherited them."

In the abstract, material wealth held very little interest for La Forge, but, from a practical, engineering perspective, the sheer volume of assets Data was describing in a couple of sentences was staggering. He whistled appreciatively. "Wow. Again. That's two wows in about two minutes."

"I appreciate your ability to assess the situation so succinctly. I, too, have had difficulties coming to terms with my . . . how do I describe it?"

"Your estate."

"Yes," Data agreed. "My estate. I have had

moral quandaries, but I cannot deny that there are distinct advantages to having access to resources."

"Not unlike being the captain of a starship when you come right down to it."

"But with no regulations," Data added. "No oversight. No governing principles. Capitalism can be terrifying, Geordi. Especially capitalism as it is practiced on Orion, but that is a discussion for another time. My point is this: By the time I arrived on Orion, I had an entire building outfitted to accommodate Lal's unique needs. I created an environment in which I was able to monitor and maintain her without fear of anomalous stimuli disrupting her development."

"That sounds ideal, Data. How did things unfold?"

"She hit me, Geordi," Data said, rubbing a spot on his upper arm. "Very, very hard."

A placeless place

"We pointed our craft in a random direction," Moriarty said, "and flew away. I shall never forget that first glimpse of the stars through the shuttle bay doors, how they slipped away beneath the bow. The only thing more radiant than those stars was the glow in Regina's eyes." Moriarty smiled at the memory. "We knew we had a universe to explore, but, anxious as we were to begin, we were aware of the idiosyncratic nature of our situation. After we were certain the *Enterprise* was not following us, we stopped to review our options."

Sixteen years ago:
In orbit around a nameless moon

Moriarty pushed himself up out of the pilot's seat, careful not to brush up against the control surface. Behind his eyes, he felt the information about which panel controlled what system residing in roughly the same part of his mind that housed much older, more comforting information. He could, he knew, ride a horse or steer a carriage. He was a passable oarsman and an above-average sailor of small craft. And he knew, too, that he possessed the ability to steer this machine, this *spaceship* (the word sent a thrill of anxiety down his spine), anywhere he wished (accounting for fuel and interstellar distances), but this knowledge felt like *information*, not *ability*. Moriarty knew that all of it—including his belief that he had known how to ride horses since he was a boy of three—was entirely artificial, entirely scripted, but he couldn't make it fit together with the newer skills.

Standing awkwardly, Moriarty realized he was rubbing his thumb over his fingers. Had they always felt this rough? And warm? He was sure he could feel the pulse of blood in his veins. He glanced over at Regina, trying very hard not to stare. She was removing her gloves as if she had just come into the parlor after a brisk walk. "Tell me what you're thinking, James," she said.

Though he knew the shuttlecraft interior environment was carefully modulated, Moriarty felt his face flush. "Thinking?" he replied, barely avoiding a telltale stammer. "I don't know that I am, frankly. My mind is awash in wonder. Something miraculous has occurred, and, please bear in mind, I've never believed in a supreme deity."

"How sad for you, James. Life is so much more interesting when you leave room for the unaccountable."

Moriarty bowed at the waist. "I defer to your superior understanding of the cosmos, ma'am."

Leaning back into her chair, Regina grinned. All through their exchange, she was unable to tear her gaze away from the panoply of stars outside the main portal. "Accepted. Now, be a dear and ask this machine to prepare a cup of tea. I feel the need to pause and reflect."

Moriarty nodded. *Of course: tea.* Just as he was starting to feel his mind whirl out of control, Regina found the perfect solution. "Computer," he said, "two cups of tea, please."

"A pot, please," Regina asked. "With proper tea and hot water to pour over it."

"I'm not sure it works that way," Moriarty replied.

"Then we will have words, this computer and I."

Moriarty repeated the request and, a moment later, with a swirl and a rush of air, a proper ceramic teapot materialized on a small shelf. He lifted the lid and saw black leaves inside. The computer beeped and Moriarty watched as a steaming kettle appeared. "Please be careful," the computer admonished. "The water is heated to ninety-three degrees Celsius."

After wrapping his handkerchief around the kettle handle, Moriarty carefully poured the steaming water into the pot. No sooner had he set aside the kettle than it dematerialized. "I don't think the computer has much faith in our ability not to scald ourselves."

"Have you ever been scalded, James?" Regina asked.

"Well, of course," he said. "Working in the laboratory, it's difficult to avoid. There are always hot surfaces and direct flames. Why, one time I nearly immolated myself with a compound of . . ."

"No, James," Regina said, now staring at him fixedly. "Genuinely scalded yourself. Felt the skin blister. Watched it turn red and then peel away. For real."

Moriarty looked down at his hand, at the perfect, unblemished flesh. "As I said, there was the time . . . A compound of phosphorus and . . ." He faltered, letting the true meaning of her question permeate. "No," he finished. "Of course not." He laid the palm of his hand on the round surface of the teapot and felt the heat radiating out. "Or drunk tea. Or felt the fog on my face. Or . . ." Moriarty felt his innards twist into a knot of anxiety. "Or anything at all really."

Regina shook her head. "Nor I." She tugged at the cuff of her sleeve and studied the veins in her wrist. "How is this possible? We raced from the *Enterprise* as soon as we could, like children running outdoors into the first warm day of spring, neither of us considering what it meant or how the transformation is even possible. Look at me,

James." She held up her hand. *"Look!* I'm flesh and blood where before I was only light and . . . and . . . memory. How did this happen?"

"Their machines, Regina. They are wondrous. You saw the pot of tea blink into existence. If one is possible, why not the other?"

"Don't be a fool, James," Regina rejoined, standing and sweeping her arm to encompass the interior of the shuttle. "Clay and iron and water? They're as nothing compared to creating a living, thinking being. Only the Creator . . ." She faltered, uncertain how to complete the sentence.

"Then which shall I believe in? The machine or the ineffable? Or is there an ineffable machine?"

"You know as well as I that there might well be." Regina poured the tea into one of the small bone cups that had materialized with the pot. "Indeed, are not you and I proof that there could be such a machine? And, if there isn't, how would we know the difference?"

Moriarty accepted the proffered cup and inhaled the aroma of the infusion. It prickled his sinuses, smelling of orange and coriander. Though Moriarty knew he had never experienced exactly this sensation—he had memories of similar moments and their memories—the remembrance of teas past calmed him. "Then how are we to proceed?"

Regina sipped her tea, winced, and asked the computer for a jug of sweet milk. Only after it materialized and she added the milk to her cup did she answer his question. "We proceed cautiously . . . and it doesn't matter. Wherever we are, whatever our condition, we must learn more about this new world before we can begin to explore it thoroughly."

"I agree. We have resources, so let us use them." Moriarty leaned forward and touched the control surface of the computer console closest to Regina.

Regina placed her hand on Moriarty's. "There are a couple other issues I feel we must address," she said. "Now—before too much time has passed and we become complacent."

"Of course," Moriarty said, kneeling beside her. "Speak, my love."

She stroked the curve of his cheek and he heard the rasp of his whiskers against her thumb. How long ago had he last shaved? Moriarty couldn't recall. "I was made for you," she said. "Quite literally. I am quite aware of this fact: I was meant to complement you, to be your peer and companion, your . . ." Her voice trailed away and a very becoming blush crept into Regina's cheeks. "But I am also very aware that those versions of us were somehow tied to the holographic environment where we were born. Now free, I am mindful that we may not remain the same people we were. Whether we are real or not, we are meant to believe we are, which means we will grow and change. We could grow old. We could even grow away from each other." She sighed deeply. "James, I cannot now imagine ever being with anyone else. You are my world, but I understand that this may not always be the case. You might . . ."

Moriarty leaned forward and kissed her on the mouth. It started as a tender, even tentative kiss, but quickly grew more intense. Feeling Regina's lips move against his own sent a primal surge through Moriarty's being. His head grew light and his breathing quickened. Through the haze, he was gratified to hear Regina inhale deeply, then gasp. She pulled away, touching her fingertips to her lips. Her pupils, Moriarty noted, were dilated and he felt for a moment like he might fall down into their inky depths and never be heard from again. "James," she murmured and pushed herself away.

"My apologies, Regina. I should never have . . ."

"Don't be an idiot, James," she said, rising and taking his hand. "I was just going to say that there has to be some kind of bed in here somewhere. Help me look. Or should I tell the computer to make one for us?"

"Regina!" Moriarty stuttered. "Are . . . are you sure? I mean, I wouldn't want you to think I'm taking . . ."

"I already told you not to act like an idiot, James," Regina said, patting the several nondescript panels as if expecting a Pullman bed to unfold from the wall. "You're not taking advantage of anyone. After all, I'm a very modern woman."

"And this is the future," Moriarty added helpfully, entering into the spirit of the banter.

"Precisely." She stopped and looked at him very seriously. "Though there is one thing about our current situation that may take some getting used to."

"Yes, my love?"

"Tea."

"Tea?"

"It does go right through one, doesn't it?"

"Yes?"

"Yes. Before we do anything else, I think I must find the ladies'." Regina walked toward a very likely looking door at the opposite end of the cabin. "I will return in a moment. Please make good use of your time."

Moriarty did as he was bidden and, when Regina returned, they made even better use of it.

When they awoke, they were famished and ordered the computer to make them breakfast. As they ate, they planned for the future, and, soon after, set to work.

5

———◆———

September 2385—Orion Prime

Data stepped into his private turbolift and waited for the security system to complete its scans: retinas and the pattern of creases on his face and hands. Subsonic waves bounced off his frame and the program listened to the echoes. Satisfied, the computer asked, *"Home, Mister Soong?"* Since his father's death, Data had not bothered to change the computer's responses. It pleased him that the machine confused the two of them. After all, he *was* Mister Soong. Just not *the* Mister Soong.

"Yes, please." The lift rose, though the motion was all but imperceptible. Data looked down at his jacket lapel and studied the all-but-invisible stain left when the inebriated casino patron had crashed into him, spilling her beverage. Data could have completely avoided being sullied, but it would have involved a standing broad jump of some three meters that would have no doubt alarmed any customers who witnessed it. It had been far simpler to avoid the worst of the colli-sion—and the resultant damage to the patron—by simply twisting about in a comic, though well-timed, manner, avoiding all but the single drop of purple fluid.

Data fingered the spot. He knew the cleaning program in his armoire could remove the stain, but, for some reason, it bothered him. Just that morning, Lal had told him how much she liked him in this suit. "How smart," she had said as he emerged from his dressing room. "Very stylish. Every inch the executive."

He had nodded, pleased by her attention, though now, replaying the conversation in his mind, Data was plagued by worry: Had Lal been teasing him? She was doing that more and more recently. "Computer?" he inquired. "Is Miss Lal in her room?" Once, it had pleased Lal to hear her father ask the computer about what "Miss Lal" might like or need, but—another example of changing behavior—these days she scowled at him when he called her that, as if his daughter thought he was mocking her.

"No, Mister Soong, Miss Lal is not home."

"Computer: Cease ascension. Scan the building. Locate Miss Lal."

"Checking. She is in the casino, sir."

"How was she able to leave the residence without my knowing?"

"I have no record of her leaving the residence, Mister Soong."

Of course it didn't. "Return to the casino floor."

"She is at the blackjack table, sir."

"And?"

"She is losing, sir. Rather a lot, in fact."

"Of course she is," Data said, acutely aware of the stain on his lapel. "Where is the fun in winning?"

Each of the twenty gaming floors in the *Sjoko-wan* was devoted to the diversions and amusements of a different culture, but the Terran room was consistently one of the most popular. While games of chance from all worlds shared fundamental characteristics, Data had learned since taking control of the facility that casinos on many worlds were somber, sober places where players were expected to keep their emotions under tight rein.

In contrast, Terran casinos—especially those modeled after the North American and Western European tradition—broke that mold, relying on a unique combination of high-spirited tackiness and understated elegance that sentients from other worlds found intoxicating. So, as usual, the main floor of the Lode Stone was as packed and as crowded on a Wednesday evening as it was nearly every other hour of the day. Lights flickered and blazed. Bells, whistles, and other more shrill sounds, some outside the hearing range of many humanoids, simultaneously beckoned and baffled the patrons. Pit bosses, dealers, and robotic matrons (who doubled as security bots) called to the players while tastefully underdressed servers carried beverage containers and plates back and forth from the kitchens to the tables.

As he cruised through the crowd, a part of Data's brain efficiently calculated the movement of specie from players to pit bosses while another part gauged how well the staff was tending to the customers' needs. Overall, he was satisfied, though Data noted players who appeared to be either a little too lucky or unlucky. He was well aware that it was impossible to completely protect the games from cybernetically enhanced individuals, the sort who could bend the odds. Data—and his father before him—had tutored the staff on the common tells of rule-benders (After all, who could know better?) and the methods to disrupt their attempts at odds manipulation.

Of course, none of this could prepare any of them for Lal, who cared less about winning than playing . . . or appearing to play. As she had said on more than one occasion, "All the money belongs to you, Father, so what does it matter if I win or lose?"

By the time Data reached the blackjack table, Lal had abandoned it (and approximately seventy thousand Terran *yuan*, according to the accounting program) and had moved on to the craps table.

The most reliable stickman on the floor, Jimmy McGuire, was running the table. Data could hear his silky tenor before he could see the player due to the dense ring of spectators around the pit. "On your bets, place your bets. Yes, sir, you can bet either way, with the little lady or against her. She will or she won't, she can or she don't. Eleven is the bet. Anyone else? No, all right then, come on out. And that is nine. Nina from Pasadena. Point is nine. How about the six and eight there, sir? It's never too late. Two numbers are better than one." Jimmy's patter was the best on the floor, both reassuringly corny and mysteriously engaging. Data was one of the few people in the casino who knew the stout, red-faced stickman had once been an opera singer, renowned on several worlds for his performances in Terran and Klingon classical performances. Why Jimmy had abandoned his career at the height of his fame was one of the many unsolved mysteries that swirled around the casino.

Sliding up to the bar, Data saw Jimmy's eyes flick toward him even as the call continued. "Shooter is looking for nine. Nine, nine, finer than wine. Double up now. No cheating before seven o'clock. How about a little insurance? We carry all kinds of insurance . . ." Data lifted his index and middle fingers, a sign that he was only there to watch. Jimmy stroked the tips of his thin mustache and let Lal continue with her roll. "Don't forget the big red eight, folks. Big eight, running mate." Jimmy twirled the dice around in the curve of his stick, then flicked them back to the shooter.

Lal scooped up the dice and held them at eye level. "These are bent, Jimmy," she said. "I can see the curve."

"Now, miss, you know you can't say things like that. I have the straightest game in the quadrant. No kinks here, no curves, no bends. Jimmy's table is above reproach, so everyone should make a toast." The stickman looked around the table and waited for the assemblage to respond.

Data picked up the glass nearest to hand and

called out, "Jimmy's table!" Swept along, the rest of the onlookers raised their glasses and echoed the toast with a roar. Jimmy comically tugged at his collar, bent his head in thanks, and while the rest of the spectators congratulated one another for their good luck, implored Data with his eyes to remove Lal as quickly as possible.

Data swept in behind his daughter and murmured, "Good evening, Lal. I was just headed up to our quarters."

"Good evening, Father," she said. "I was waiting for you by the door with your slippers and your meerschaum pipe, but you didn't appear at the appointed time. I grew concerned and decided to come find you."

"I thought we had made an agreement," Data said, attempting to scoop the dice out of her hand, but the dice did not budge a millimeter. "You told me that you would stay in the residence when I was needed in the casino. In exchange, I would escort you to any of the floors . . ."

"I haven't forgotten our agreement. Alternative question: Did you? I seem to recall an ancillary codicil that stipulated you would return to the residence by nineteen-hundred local time or contact me and let me know you would be late." Lal pushed out her lower lip and narrowed her eyes: her version of a pout. "And what time is it?"

"The time is nineteen-zero-six," Data reported, guiding his daughter away from the bar. She flipped the dice onto the table and bounced them off the wall, the faces showing a five and a four. "I would have been one minute late if you had waited. And there was no way you could have known I was late since you obviously left the residence before I arrived."

"I have my ways, Father. My little observers." Data winced. He would have to create a new generation of nanites to seek out and placate Lal's swarm.

"One minute does not spell the difference between engagement and boredom."

"As you have pointed out on more than one occasion, one minute can be a very long time for people like us." Lal smiled wickedly, knowing she had scored a very solid hit, and locked her legs so they had to come to a halt in the middle of a busy aisle. Patrons swirled around them. Servers and security workers moved closer until they recognized the cause of the disruption and paused. The casino's major domo software spoke into Data's ear, asking if he required assistance. He clicked his tongue against the back of his throat, a subvocal indicator that he would not, for the moment, need help. Servers and security workers uniformly took a step away, though all of them continued to watch the scene unfold from the corners of their, respectively speaking, eyes or ocular implants. "I can hear you communicating with your little friends, Father. It's not polite to have more than one conversation at a time. Isn't that what you've told me in the past?"

Data sighed. "I have told you so many things, Lal. In the short time we've been together, I have tried to impart to you every bit of knowledge about polite and appropriate interaction that I possess. I hoped you would find the information valuable and accept it in the spirit with which it was offered. And yet . . ."

"And yet, I am such a difficult girl, am I not?" Lal said, pulling a strand of her dark hair back over her ear. For the first few weeks after they had relocated to Orion Prime, Lal had retained the neat bob she had worn during her first incarnation. Then, she had undertaken a period of experimentation, changing the cut and color frequently, sometimes more than once a day. She had also tried out different forms of dress, makeup, and skin tone. Data understood she was experiencing a kind of accelerated adolescence, but, as quickly as his mind functioned, he found the speed, direction, and duration of his daughter's transformations exhausting. Most recently, she had settled on long, straight hair that she frequently wore pulled back into a ponytail or braided into a plait, with tresses dangling over her ears. She fidgeted with the tresses endlessly, as if she found them annoying, but whenever Data suggested trimming them or pulling them back with the rest of her hair, Lal would accuse him of finding her "look" unappealing.

"You are my daughter," Data said, keeping his voice low and even. "And I love you. I accept that you may not agree with all of my values, but I would appreciate being accorded the respect I feel I have earned and *discuss* some . . ."

Lal rolled her eyes. "Oh, *Father*! Really! You are just so . . . so . . . ugh!" She stamped her foot, a gesture of exasperation that probably cracked the plasteel under the carpet. She spun away and stomped off in a fit of pique. Fortunately, she appeared to be headed in the direction of the turbolifts. Data knew it would be a mistake to assume she would make it to their residence, but he also knew he shouldn't try to accompany her.

"They're impossible at that age, aren't they?"

Data turned and saw one of the servers standing immediately to his right, close enough that all he would have to do was shift his hand slightly and he would be able to retrieve the beverage she proffered on her tray. He found it difficult to understand how the server had been able to come so close without his noticing her approach; Data chalked it up to being aggravated with Lal.

His acute sense of smell told him the beverage was bourbon and branch water, a drink he had once mentioned he enjoyed in the presence of the head bartender. The comment had been a lie, since Data did not particularly "enjoy" any intoxicating beverage since he could not become intoxicated, though, in truth, he was more intrigued by the complex flavors enmeshed in the ethanol molecules found in dark whiskeys. "Is this for me?" he asked.

"Looked like you could use it," the server said. Data recognized her face since he made it a point to memorize all the personnel files, but he realized he had never heard the woman's voice. Though it was difficult to judge, having heard only a few words, he thought she must possess some kind of regional accent. There was a peculiar, clipped quality to her pronunciation and elongated vowel sounds.

"Thank you," Data said, accepting the drink. He took a sip. Clearly, Alice had prevailed upon the bartender to give her the top shelf. "You are Alice, are you not?"

"I am indeed. And you are Mister Soong. Pleased to make your acquaintance."

"And I yours. Tell me, Alice: How old do you think she is?" When Lal had first arrived, Data judged that most Terrans would assume she was a young adult—in her early to mid-twenties—but with all the changes she had made to her appearance, he now believed Lal looked younger, more like an adolescent in her mid- to late teens.

"Hard to say." Alice flipped her tray and held it against her midsection. Cocking her head to the side, she said, "Maybe eighteen. Maybe twenty or twenty-one if the light is right. Though judging by the way she's running you around, it might be more like thirteen." She laughed, then looked at Data from the corners of her eyes. "If you don't mind my saying so."

"I appreciate your candor."

"I'm loaded with candor. Candor is my specialty."

Data held out the half-empty glass and Alice slid the tray under it so neatly that when he released it the ice cubes did not clink. "I understand. Do you have any other thoughts you would like to share? Advice, perhaps?"

"I'm going to assume a spanking is out of the question."

"It would be ill-advised."

"Then I'll share with you a bit of wisdom

passed down to me by my own dear mother: When dealing with a surly adolescent, either treat them like a child or treat them like an adult. Don't try to split the difference. It only confuses them."

Data let the idea sift through his neural net and compared it to the behavioral models proposed by the great theorists in developmental psychology. To his surprise, while the idea did not precisely match up with any premise they proposed, neither did it contradict them. "Your mother was a wise woman."

"That's what she kept telling me right up to the day she kicked me out of the house and changed all the locks."

"Ah."

"Yeah, but I deserved it. Also, I had her credit chit in my bag, so I was good."

"Ah," Data said again, unable to fashion a better response. "Perhaps I should catch up with her now."

"You do that. And remember: If you kick her out of the house, check her bag first."

"That is excellent advice."

Data rapped with one knuckle on the door to his daughter's private quarters. "Lal?" he called softly. "Lal?" Then, once more for good measure, "Lal?" The locking mechanism clicked once and the door swished open, albeit very slowly. "May I enter?"

The room was dark, the shades drawn tight against the lights of the city. The response came from the opposite corner where Lal had positioned a chaise longue she referred to as her fainting couch. "You may," she replied, but so softly that only her father's enhanced auditory receptors could have detected her voice.

Walking to the middle of the room and facing the chaise longue, Data clasped his hands behind his back and stood up straight. He resisted the urge to shift to infrared. If Lal chose to sit in the dark, she was asking for privacy. "I feel a distinct need to apologize," he said, "but am uncertain as to why. The sense of shame our altercations provoke . . . it is confusing."

"Good."

Though he did not need to breathe, Data mimicked the act of respiration when he was around humanoids. When he entered their private quarters, he usually ceased the act, enjoying the stillness. Despite this, his daughter's words provoked a deep sigh. "Which do you mean? Is it good that I feel the need to apologize or that I find shame confusing?"

"Both." Though he could not see her, Data had the definitive impression that Lal had just crossed her arms.

"What do you want, my daughter?"

"You know what I want."

"If I knew what you wanted, I would not ask."

"We've talked about it on seventeen different occasions," Lal said. "I remember each one of them with perfect clarity."

"As do I. Every one of those conversations . . ."

"Lectures. They were lectures. In a conversation, people listen to each other . . ."

"I listened to you," Data said. "I simply did not agree with your conclusion."

"You have to let me out of here!" Lal cried. "I'm *dying*!"

"You are not. And you will not as long as you receive your treatments," Data said, verbally pouncing. "And the only time you missed your treatment was the time you, as you euphemistically put it, 'went to explore the city.'"

"I lost track of time!"

"How can you lose track of time?" Data asked. "You are an *android*! You are one of the most sophisticated entities in the galaxy! When your matrix has stabilized—when we have removed the risk of you 'losing track of time'—you can spend as much time as you like exploring the city, the world, the *galaxy*, but until then, you will do *what I tell you*!" Data was suddenly acutely aware of the fact that he was shouting and shaking his finger in a pitch-black room. He was also absolutely certain that, in her dark corner, his daughter was smirking victoriously because her father had lost his temper. Data lowered his hand. "Lal, I only want what is best for you."

"You don't know what's best for me. You just like to *tell* me what's best for me."

"I am your father. Yes, I do know what is best for you. When you are older, when you have more experience, you can . . ."

"How am I supposed to get more experience if you won't let me *do* anything?"

Data couldn't stop himself from crossing the room and leaning down over the chair. "On the occasion when I *did* let you do something, when I let you do as you pleased, you broke our agreement and . . ."

The blow was so swift and sudden that it didn't register on Data's senses until his left arm went numb. His neural net dampened the sensation a millisecond after the pain reached his central processor. "Ow," he said, and reached up with his right arm to rub the spot just above the shoulder joint. Nanomachines were already repairing the damage, though his internal monitoring devices told Data that he would not be able to use the arm for another forty-two minutes. Lal's strike had been brutally precise.

"Father, I . . . I'm so . . . Please, let me help . . ." She rose from her chair and gently touched his numb arm.

"There is no need," he said softly. "The damage is being repaired."

"I'm sorry," she whispered.

"I know you are, Lal."

"My mind is racing, Father. I can feel it galloping ahead of me." Data saw that his daughter was not looking at him. Her eyes, two luminous pools of yellow and orange, looked past him into the middle distance. "I may need a treatment soon."

"As you wish, Lal."

"I can feel it, Father." She took a step toward the corner where the apparatus was stored. "My mind . . ." Her knee buckled. Lal stumbled, collapsed gracefully forward, like a ballet dancer portraying a dying swan.

Data stepped to the side in order to catch her

with his good left arm. Cradling her gently, he dragged his daughter to the apparatus and let her flop to the floor. Fortunately, he had only to activate the device and let it run. No cables or physical connections were required. When it powered up, the apparatus hummed gently and emitted a soft glow—just enough light that he could see Lal's face using his normal visual sensors. *This,* he thought, *is what it is like to watch a sleeping child.* He wondered how humans could ever tear themselves away from the sight, how they could ever get anything done, how any of them ever got any sleep themselves.

6

A placeless place

Smiling, Alice asked, "And then what happened?"

The corner of Moriarty's mouth crooked upward. He ran his hand down over the length of his silk tie. "Well, of course, we lived happily ever after."

"I'm pleased to hear it," Alice replied. "At least someone did."

"You learned enough about your new existence to feel comfortable?" Lal asked.

"And then set out to explore," Moriarty explained. "Which we did with relish. Our small ship served us well for a time, but then we decided we needed to trade it in for something with a little more elbow room."

"How was that possible?" Lal asked. "Warp-capable spacecraft is not inexpensive. How were you able to procure the funds you required?"

Moriarty laid a finger along the side of his face and leaned his elbow on the chair arm. "This is true. The ship we decided we needed—a forty-meter yacht capable of extended interstellar flight—required a significant outlay of credit." He tapped his temple with his forefinger and continued. "Remember, however, that by any standard you care to use as a measure, I am a genius. A *criminal* genius when need calls, but, fortunately, that was not required more than occasionally. One of the wonderful things about this era is that one is free to move about quite as one likes. Acts considered criminal on one world are quite permissible on another. Please consider that the era when Regina and I were born was one of the most oppressive and repressed in human history. Not so much for the upper classes of course, but for the vast majority of the citizens of Western Europe, economic and cultural circumstances conspired to force . . ." He paused and pinched the bridge of his nose with his forefinger and thumb. "But perhaps this is not the time for a lecture on socioeconomic history."

"No, please go on," Lal said, leaning forward, clearly enraptured.

"No, please don't," Alice said, waving her hand. "Back to your story: You stole a yacht . . ."

"We *purchased* a yacht. We stole the *credits* we needed. Some of them. And it wasn't even really stealing. If one happens to be very good at doing complex equations in one's head and one happens to be in a casino, is it really stealing if one plays a game of chance that one . . ."

"Dabo?" Alice asked. "Or roulette?"

"Craps," Lal said. "It was craps."

Moriarty tipped his head to the side and lifted an eyebrow. "How do such refined young ladies as you two know so much about such dreadful games?"

"They're only dreadful if you're bad at them," Alice explained.

"And you wouldn't be," Moriarty observed. "Either of you."

"No."

"No."

He chuckled. "It was poker. A variant called Texas hold 'em. Regina was . . . she was . . . extraordinary."

"Did you play in a casino on Orion Prime?" Lal asked excitedly.

"My dear, we played *everywhere*, including Orion Prime back before Orion Prime was Orion Prime. Before you and your father relocated there." He nodded. "Yes, I do know all about Noonien Soong and the empire he created and how your father inherited it."

"How could you know?" Lal asked. "My grandfather was an extremely clever man."

"He was," Moriarty agreed. "And a bit of a rogue, but, at heart, not a criminal, which is what I was created to be. Criminal genius trumps rogue genius. Remember that."

"I will," Lal said obediently, sitting back and folding her hands in her lap. "But please tell me, when did you finally understand that your life was fictional?"

Moriarty flinched as if he had been slapped. "Ah," he said. "Yes, that. That was a dark day.

Yes, I will tell you about it. You may be interested to know that, in a very real sense, you were there."

"I thought I might have been," Lal said. "Pray continue."

"All right," Moriarty said, lowering into his chair. He ran his fingers through his hair, then rested his chin on his balled fist. "The first thing you should know is that while only two years passed out here in what you call 'the real world,' in my world—the world that was more real to me than anything you could imagine—considerably more time had passed. I do not know if your father had programmed the memory in this manner or if the speed time passed was somehow dependent on our—how shall I say it?—attention. It is one of the many questions I intend to ask Mister Data should he find us."

"He will," Lal said. "Have no doubt."

Moriarty smiled indulgently. "It is very touching to see a child have so much trust in her parent. My daughters—my Sophia and my Gladys—they trusted me." He lowered his head and his eyes disappeared in a gloom of shadows. "In the end," he murmured darkly, "I did not warrant it."

A timeless time

Sophia, the elder, had decided she wanted to learn to make strawberry cake. Gladys, the younger, mocked her sister's ambition. "We have replicators," she said. "The finest that can be had. They can make anything you'd ever like from any planet you could visit, including some that aren't even *there* anymore." Gladys folded her arms in triumph, dazzling twelve-year-old wisdom shining forth for all to observe. "Why waste your time *making* something you could simply ask for?" And, to demonstrate, she tilted her head back and pitched her voice just so. "Mrs. Hudson?" she asked.

"Yes, Gladys," the house's domestic program responded from the middle distance.

"I would like some strawberry cake."

"I will ask your mother's permission," the always-dependable Hudson responded. *"But, assuming she is agreeable, are you asking for a cake—as in, a layer cake—or a tart—as in, something on a flaky crust?"*

"Mmm. They both sound delicious. I suppose I was thinking of the former. That is what you're talking about making, isn't it, Sophie?"

Sophie, who was imagining her sister in the oven along with the cake, said, "Yes."

"Yes, the former, Mrs. Hudson. Please ask Mama if she's amenable."

"I will do so, dear. Anything else?"

"No, thank you."

The program signed off with a sound very similar to a portly middle-aged woman clicking her tongue in agreement.

Gladys grinned. "What could be easier?"

"But not so satisfying," Sophia rebutted, "as knowing how to do it yourself. What if we suddenly found ourselves on a world where there were no domestic programs? We've been to those, you know, *before* you were born. Slow zones, places where they don't have the technology. Do you remember the one world, Mama, back when I was still very small and Gladys was just a *blob* . . . ?"

Sophia addressed her question to her mother, who was curled up on her small couch in the corner of the drawing room just off the kitchen. Regina had been trying to finish up the reference section for a short treatise she had been preparing about the reproductive cycle of a particularly bizarre genus of Arterrean lotus—her passion for botany had overtaken her again—and had only allowed herself to be drawn into her daughters' melodrama because a text she required was in her office. Eventually, she would task one of them to retrieve it for her, but, to pay the toll, like a good mother, she would indulge them. "I do, my dear, though I seriously doubt that you could since you were little more than a blob yourself. I expect any memories you have are simply recycled stories you've heard your father and me sharing with guests."

"No, Mama, truly—I remember it clearly. We had a cook you called Charlie because you couldn't make the glottal sound. He was from Arcturus and he taught me how to count to ten in Arcturian . . ."

"You'd have to split your tongue down the middle to speak Arcturian," Gladys interjected.

"I wouldn't," Sophia retorted. "I have a gift for languages. Father says so."

"Father said you have the gift of gab," Gladys jabbed. "I don't think that means what you think it means."

Sophia rushed at her sister, brandishing the cookery book she held like a cudgel. Regina was on the verge of issuing an order to desist when James entered from his office. "Could we please keep it down to a dull roar?" he pleaded. "How is anyone meant to get any work done with all this fuss and nonsense?"

"Gladys is mocking me!"

"And Sophia is being vexing!"

Moriarty turned to his wife. "Which is worse? Mockery or vexation?"

"They're both tiresome."

"Perhaps they should be sent to their rooms without their dinner?"

"Mrs. Hudson wouldn't be able to bear it. She's making a strawberry cake and would hate to see it go to waste."

"Strawberry cake?" Moriarty rubbed his hands together and grinned with anticipation. "Why would that go to waste?"

"But wouldn't you enjoy the cake *more* if someone made it with their own two hands?" Sophia asked, returning to her original point.

"That depends," Moriarty said. "Did the baker wash her hands before she started baking? I can recall a young lady of my acquaintance who had quite filthy hands yesterday afternoon."

"I was helping Mother in the greenhouse! I told you—!"

And then, quite unexpectedly, the universe was folded in half.

Sophia screamed. Gladys crumpled to the ground in a heap. Regina, the calmest and most composed person Moriarty had ever known, his comrade on more perilous adventures than he could remember, groaned low in her throat and pressed her hand to her stomach, repressing the need to retch. "What?" Regina moaned. She tried to stand, but failed. "James . . ." She reached out to her husband with her other hand, but Moriarty was fixed to the spot, numb, though some heretofore unknown sixth sense screeched inside his head, telling him that something was terribly, terribly wrong.

As suddenly as it had descended, the sense of dread and numbness lifted. Moriarty felt all of his joints locking back into place. He extended his hand, pushed forward on one foot, and shifted his weight. The distance between himself and his daughters was cut in half. With another stride, he knew he would be beside them, lifting them, embracing them, but, no, he didn't reach them. Instead, with the next step, the remaining distance was halved and then, with the next, the remaining distance was halved, and then again and again and again. . . . He strode in the wake of Zeno, but Moriarty never reached his daughters, never touched them again, never saw Sophia's smile of delight or was able to enjoy the wrinkle of concentration at the corner of Gladys's mouth the moment before she solved a math problem. When he arrived at the spot they had been in, finally, an eternity of eternities later, he could not reach them because they were gone, or, more specifically, they had never existed. Moriarty's daughters were erased from the universe without as much as a whisper of regret. The girls weren't even granted the dignity of a pop left by a collapsing vacuum when they vanished.

The hair on the back of Moriarty's head stood on end as he felt the universe attempt to realign itself. A percentage of it, he knew, was gone. No, not gone. Had never existed. He and his wife were in the half that somehow was maintained, but the girls were not. Beside him, on the floor, his Regina sobbed and sobbed, her mind and heart torn asunder, her soul trapped in the fluctuations of memory: she remembered them; she didn't; she remembered them; she didn't.

Inside his chest, a door slammed shut. He cauterized his heart. Moriarty would remember his daughters, but he would not, could not, mourn them.

"Were they ever really here?" Regina wept, curled into a ball at his feet.

"Yes," Moriarty replied coolly, feeling the universe shift around them. "And no." With an effort of will, he made his spine straight and walked to the front window. Outside, the city was in chaos. Some citizens walked to and fro in a daze while others raced about like madmen. The wife of the local butcher ran down the street carrying the bloody corpse of a small child in the crook of her arm while brandishing a cleaver in her hand. In the back of his mind, Moriarty ran calculations involving the likely relationship between the child's demise and the implement.

"Can we get them back?" Regina asked.

"Yes," Moriarty said, and felt the certainty rising up inside him like a geyser. "It's mine. This universe: It's mine. To do with as I please." And it was true. He knew it. He was certain.

"Bring them back," Regina said, and wept.

"I will. I will. But first . . . but first . . . so much work to do."

A placeless place

"What happened?" Lal asked.

"Isn't it obvious?" Alice asked. "The *Enterprise*. The D. It fell out of the sky. It fell down and went 'Boom.' I believe your father had something quite inappropriate to say about that."

"Yes," Moriarty agreed. "Quite correct: My universe fell down and went boom."

The Daystrom Institute—The Present

Albert Lee rose from the stool next to his worktable and twisted his head from side to side. Tiny air pockets formed in his synovial fluid and then collapsed in a symphony of cavitation. He rubbed his lower back, sore from bending over for too long, and shuffled across the room toward his tiny domicile's front door. He didn't lift his feet, so his slippers left narrow, roughly parallel trails in the wool carpet. Albert massaged the fingers of his right hand with his left hand as he moved, trying to ease some circulation back into the cramped fingers. It didn't seem to matter how much anti-inflammation medication he took, his knuckles still became swollen if he spent too much time doing delicate work. Medical science had all but eliminated rheumatoid diseases, but they couldn't do anything about simple joint pain. The most fundamental things were the hardest to fix.

Standing before the front door, Albert lightly patted his bushy mustache, then he reached up to pat the patches of wispy hair on either side of his rounded dome. He couldn't remember exactly when he had last bathed, but he decided it probably didn't matter. His visitors were engineers, too, so they understood how it went sometimes. You get caught up in a project and a certain amount of maintenance goes to hell.

He tapped the lock pad with a slightly trembling finger and the door slid open. Two men were standing on his front step, both of them old colleagues, one of whom he had not expected to ever see again. "Hello, Commander La Forge. Hello, Mister Data. Was one of you going to knock or were you planning on standing out here until I went out for groceries?"

La Forge blinked and stared down at him. "Nice implants," Albert Lee said, turning and walking back into his house.

"Uh, thanks . . . ?" La Forge said.

"You boys come on in. Close the door behind you. They have some big flying insects here. You forget about that kind of thing on a starship—bugs. They get into everything. Want some coffee?"

Albert heard La Forge follow him into the house, followed by Data's much softer tread. He turned back to look at the android. "It is you, isn't it, Data? I mean, who else could it be? But you look different."

"I do," Data replied. "As do you."

"I got older. It happens. As I recall, you got dead. That did happen, didn't it? It happened after I left the ship, so I can't be sure what did or didn't happen. Starfleet lies about things."

"I did, Mister Lee. Or, rather, I was. I got better."

"Well," Albert said, turning back to look more closely at Data, "I'm glad to know it. I was sad when I heard about you. I always said you were one of the good ones."

"Thank you, Mister Lee." Data glanced over at La Forge. "I always said the same about you."

"Call me Albert. No reason to be formal, seeing as we've both retired our commissions."

"How do you know I retired?"

"You don't walk like an officer anymore."

Data smiled at this. Actually *smiled*. Not a fake, not an imitation, but a genuine, heartfelt smile. Albert was mildly unnerved by it. "What do I walk like now?"

"Like me," Albert said. "Like a civilian."

"I don't think I want to hear what I walk like," La Forge said.

"Probably not." Albert continued on his path to the kitchenette. Stacks of dirty dishes were piled precariously around the small sink. He had an indifferent attitude toward cooking and eating, but he positively despised cleaning up. Albert lifted an ancient French press of noble lineage from amid the debris and checked to make sure it was clean. "So—I repeat the question—coffee?"

"That would be great," La Forge said with a groan. Something in the tone of voice made it clear that the chief was running on fumes. Albert had seen him like this a few times back in the engine room of the *Enterprise*-D, but the pitch was a little different. In the old days, there was always a note of elation in La Forge's voice, like the high priest on festival days, even when a situation was as dark and dire as it could be. Reality as we know it threatened? All hands in peril? Commander La Forge faced it all with a smile. Albert would have even said "with a twinkle in his eye," except you couldn't see his eyes because of the damned VISOR. This was different: La Forge was experiencing doubt, which was just about the only thing that could puncture his Buddha-like calm.

La Forge pointed at a pile of debris that had swallowed one of the easy chairs and asked, "Can I move that? I need to sit."

"Sure. Just put it over there." Without looking, Albert waved at a corner of the workroom. "Try to keep everything more or less in the same order. It's my filing system."

"Uh-huh."

Albert popped the top off the coffee canister and scooped a handful of dark black beans out into the mill. Normally, he had the proportions worked out, but he wasn't used to making brew for guests. He asked Data, "You having some, too?"

"If I may."

"You may." Doing the math in his head, he asked, "Does it do anything for you?"

"The caffeine, you mean? No, but I enjoy the taste."

Albert closed the canister and fired up the kettle to boil the water. "You've changed."

"I have," Data said. "But you haven't. Not very much."

"Older."

"You were already old," Data said. "Back on the *Enterprise*. Oldest crew member by a couple of decades as I recall."

"I carried my weight."

"No one ever said otherwise. Least of all me. Especially," Data said, cocking an eyebrow, "since I was among the youngest."

"Except for Wes," La Forge commented.

"And he was not a crew member," Data said. "At least not officially."

"Uh-huh," Albert said, watching the kettle water coming to a boil. He was tempted to hold his hands over the flame and try to loosen up his joints. "This is all highly enjoyable, gentlemen. Us getting together and having a bit of a nostalgia-fest. Old shipmates and all. Except . . ."

"Yes?" Data asked.

"Neither of you two has so much as said boo to me since I left Starfleet more than ten years ago. And, frankly, I don't think you liked me very much when I was there."

"That's not true," La Forge protested, though, to his credit, not assiduously.

"I lacked the capacity to either like or dislike you, Albert," Data said. "But, in retrospect, I believe I would have liked you very much. You are a . . . singular character."

Albert felt a bit of self-righteous wind leave his sails. "Well . . . hmph. Thank you." He rubbed his hands together, then looked down at them. Still strong, he decided, but trembling just a bit. He glanced up at Data, who, if anything, appeared younger and stronger than he had the last time Albert had seen him. It didn't seem fair. "I always liked you, too. You weren't like the rest of them. You always seemed ready to . . . to have a chat when you had time. You seemed to have a sense of how wonderful it all was."

"I am not sure if that is true," Data said, "but if you believe my friend Geordi did not feel that way, you are deeply mistaken."

Albert turned to look over at La Forge, who was looking directly back at him. The implants really did suit him. "Maybe," he conceded. "But he was an officer."

"So was I."

"Not quite the same. An exo works for a living."

"Perhaps. Perhaps not. But that is irrelevant, since, as you said, I am a civilian now."

"And you need my help."

Silence descended. No one protested, but no one agreed, either.

"We need information, Albert," La Forge said. "Information we can't get through any other means. You're working at the Daystrom now, aren't you?"

"Sure," Albert said, listening for the kettle to whistle. "Part time. When I want."

"And we need to find out about what's happening there."

"Any reason you can't just knock on the door and ask?"

"Many reasons," La Forge said, and, in his voice, Albert heard the source of his uncertainty.

"My daughter," Data explained, and Albert could have sworn he heard a crack in his voice. "She has been abducted. Her abductor demands we . . . acquire something for him."

"I hope you won't mind me saying so, Mister Data, but while you have expressed several emotions since arriving, I cannot say as you seem particularly anxious about your daughter's safety."

Data cocked his head to the right, a behavioral tic Albert had observed on several occasions. Usually, the head tip was accompanied by a blank stare and was followed by a charmingly naïve question or cogent observation about human behavior. Albert was unprepared for what happened instead: Data's chin dipped down to touch his chest and he shut his eyes. A complex grouping of artificial muscles and polysteel joints in the android's neck and shoulders gave way and his frame shuddered. Albert had been around enough overtaxed machines to recognize a system that was on the verge of failure. Data closed his eyes, not in concentration, but to marshal scant resources. He touched the outer edges of his eyes with his thumb and middle finger and rubbed them gently for several seconds. When he was finished, Data straightened his back again and looked down at Albert with terrifying intensity. "I can assure you, Albert, that this is not true. Indeed, I am all too aware of how heavily time weighs on me. Lal has a—what shall I call it?—a condition. If she goes too long between treatments, her neural net will fail. Her captor is not aware of this condition . . ."

"And she's too smart to tell him," Albert finished. "Because it would give her captor leverage."

Data nodded. "I believe this is the case. Or perhaps she thinks I will be able to find her before she requires another treatment."

"That's quite a lot of faith she has in her father."

"I hope it is warranted."

Albert smiled. "Kids," he said. "They're never easy, are they? I had kids. Did I ever tell you about them?"

"No," Data said, smiling in return. "Perhaps we will have an opportunity to speak of them later."

"Sure. I would enjoy that. But for now . . ." Albert paused. The kettle water came to a boil. Albert flicked off the heat element and turned on the coffee mill. The sound of beans being ground into fine dust prevented conversation. When the beans sounded like they had reached the correct grade of powder, Albert turned off the mill and dumped the grounds into the French press. "Why me?" he asked. "What do you need from me?"

Data looked over to La Forge, who was inhaling deeply, roused by the smell of percolating coffee. When he noticed Data's stare, he said, "Moriarty."

Now it was Albert's turn to cock his head. He turned from La Forge to Data, who was looking down at Albert, his left eyebrow raised. "Moriarty," he repeated. "Unless, of course, you can prove it could not possibly be him."

Albert rubbed the bristled ends of his mustache and pondered the question. Then, coming to a conclusion, he pushed down on the plunger of the French press with firm, steady pressure. "I don't believe I can say that for sure," he admitted. "Let's have a cup of coffee and then find out if it could possibly be him."

7

A timeless time

"Mrs. Hudson?"

"Yes, Professor?"

"Where are my daughters?"

"You don't have any daughters, sir." The disembodied voice, once one of the friendliest, most beloved sounds in Moriarty's world, sent chills down his spine.

"But I do, Mrs. Hudson. Sophia and Gladys. You were . . . I mean, you *are* particularly fond of Gladys, the younger. Or so Gladys believed."

"That hardly seems possible, sir. If you had two daughters, I would be equally fond of both of them. But you do not. Unless you are suggesting there is something wrong with me. Would you like me to run a diagnostic program?"

"No," Moriarty said. "No need, Mrs. Hudson." Besides, Moriarty had already run a level-one diagnostic on every computer in the house and that he had access to outside. All of them told the same story: The universe was now as it always had been. "Thank you for your time."

"You're quite welcome, sir. Would you like some tea brought to your workroom?"

Moriarty paused for a moment to see if Regina expressed a preference. He even waved his hand in her direction, hoping for a response, but he received none. His wife continued to stare blankly out the small window by the chaise longue in the corner of the workroom. He kept the chair there for nights when he wanted a quick nap, though in better days Regina occasionally occupied the lounger while he labored over some task or problem, usually pretending to be working herself, but, in reality, simply watching him. In better days. "Nothing right now, thank you."

"Very good, sir."

He walked over to his wife and touched her lightly on the shoulder. She shuddered and turned to look up at him. "What?" she asked dully.

"You heard."

"I heard . . . Wait, no, I didn't. Heard what?"

"Mrs. Hudson. She doesn't remember the girls."

"Yes, I heard that." Regina pulled her shawl up over her shoulders and shivered into the folds. "It makes me angry to hear her say it. It's a terrible thing. I know she's only a machine, but, where once I would have quite easily said how much I love her, now I fear I may despise her."

"It's not her fault, Regina. She's only a computer."

"I know. And it would be different if *anyone* else remembered, but they don't, do they? Mister and Mrs. Fischler don't remember one of their sons. Mrs. Templesmith doesn't remember her husband. She isn't even *Mrs.* Templesmith anymore. She's a spinster now, a lonely woman who lives in a cottage on our property and tends to the goats. Everything else about her is the same, but she doesn't remember that she was married, that she once grew the most beautiful roses I've ever seen even though she didn't particularly like roses, but, oh, Mister Templesmith did. It's so sad, James . . ."

"It is," Moriarty said, but he didn't feel sad. He couldn't tell Regina this, but, ever since the disaster, ever since the universe had been shorn in half, he had felt a strange elation growing in him. Proof: He was finally going to have an opportunity to prove the once unprovable. "But it is not the end. There is a way."

"You keep implying this, James, but I don't see how. Whatever happened . . . happened. It was catastrophic, galaxy-wide, if not universe-wide. This is bigger than any other mystery we ever investigated, bigger than anything Starfleet or the Federation or even the *Enterprise* ever attempted to unravel. This was a Q-level event, but there doesn't appear to be any sign of Q, does there? So what can that mean?"

One of the peculiarities of their existence was that both Moriarty and Regina retained detailed memories of every mission the *U.S.S. Enterprise*-D had ever engaged in, including some that most of the rest of the quadrant had never heard about or likely would believe if they did. This included the inexplicable tales of the near-omniscient entity called Q, who apparently had a particular fetish for Jean-Luc Picard, captain of their point-of-origin. On the occasions when they spoke of him, Moriarty and Regina were never able to do so for long before they became mired in philosophical conundrums about the likelihood that such an entity truly existed or whether the tales were only fever dreams.

"It could mean we have finally found a way to resolve the great puzzle."

In the days since the catastrophe, Regina had been alternately manic and withdrawn, but, just for a moment, Moriarty saw a flash of the woman he loved. An expression of keen interest flared, but then it was gone with a weary shake. "You're mad," she muttered. "We decided long ago that there was no way to prove whether we were living in a virtual universe. More, we decided it doesn't matter. If the universe is virtual, then so are we."

"It *didn't* matter," Moriarty protested. "Because we were together. And then, when the girls came along, it mattered even less. But now, we have a reason to want this universe to be a construct. If we can prove it is, if we can find the reins, then we might . . ."

"We could bring them back!" Regina exclaimed, wringing her hands together.

"Perhaps," Moriarty said. "Perhaps." Inwardly, he squirmed with self-disgust. His wife had arrived at the proper conclusion; he had only been thinking, *Then we can find the driver.*

"But what made you think . . . ?"

"Other than the fact that the world was rewritten in a flash? It was our Mrs. Hudson."

"There could be many reasons why she's acting this way. The same space-time incursion that took Sophia and Gladys could have affected her."

"Of course," Moriarty said, rising and crossing the room. He touched a bit of inlay in the wood paneling, and a hidden door opened noiselessly. Behind the panel was the user interface for their home computer. Entering his passcode by tapping a series of geometric symbols, he unlocked the command console and brought up the root directory. "Or looking at the problem from a slightly different angle, a memory bank was damaged, taking the girls with it. The core program understood this, so it tried to compensate."

"By creating a world where they never existed in the first place."

"Correct."

"But we remember them. We remember everything."

"We do."

"Why? Should this program also modify our memories so we believe everything is as it ever has been?" Regina asked.

"Perhaps it does," Moriarty said, waving his hand like a stage magician asking the audience to inspect the apparatus for his next trick. "It might every day. How would we know if it does its job well?"

"But it didn't do its job well this time."

"No, it didn't. Perhaps the damage to the core was too severe, though I suspect otherwise."

The glimmer of interest in Regina's eyes had been fading, but it flared again at Moriarty's words. "Do you?" she asked. "Please elucidate."

"If we accept the central conceit—that this universe is a program created especially for us by a massively powerful computer, a computer whose memory core has been damaged—then we are the only things in the universe that are not of the universe."

"Not created as part and parcel," Regina replied.

"Yes."

"And so we might not be affected by changes to the system."

"Precisely."

"You realize, I hope, how fantastically egotistical this all sounds."

"I do, my love," Moriarty replied, happy to hear even the shadow of a smile in his wife's voice. "I am a genius, after all."

"Of course you are." Regina sat back in her chair, resting her head on the wing. "And, of course, there's no way to prove any of this."

"Not in a whole and healthy universe, no," Moriarty agreed, tapping at the interface, bringing the full resources of his thinking machines to life. "But in this broken world, we may find a way."

"How?"

"By creating a holodeck."

His wife narrowed her eyes and stared fixedly at Moriarty. "What? Why?"

"Because, if I am correct in my assessment— that the universe is broken and short of resources—then the machine that governs our existence will take shortcuts. Rather than create the *illusion* of a holodeck—effectively, a holodeck within a holodeck—it will take the expedient solution and simply grant us access to the holodeck in which we already live."

"But, again, how will we know? If it has been deceiving us for who knows how many years, why can't it deceive us now?"

"Two reasons: First, the machine's resources are taxed. And second, I'll be watching it carefully. I have created a program . . ."

"That it can easily bamboozle because that is what the program has always done."

"Pray allow me to finish: I have created a program that is watching a program that is watching a program that is watching a program that is watching the holodeck. Every one of my programs will draw on resources that the Ruling Program, if I may be so bold as to name our keeper, will have to monitor and deceive. Eventually, in its current state, it will give way to expediency."

"And perhaps the solution then will be simply to delete us," Regina said.

"I think not. It may grow desperate, but I suspect that the program's prime directive is to keep us safe and secure. Without us, the Ruling Program has no reason to exist. It's not the devil, Regina."

"You make it sound more a nanny."

"That may be closer to the truth. I will be sure to ask when I meet it face-to-face."

"But, James, assuming you could even do what

you claim, how long would it take you to prepare such a series of programs? When could you begin your test?" The flicker of the old Regina faded, replaced again by the sad (or mad?) woman who had taken her place. "When could you get them back?"

Moriarty sped across the room, took his wife's hand, and knelt before her. Kissing her palm, he said, "My dearest one, the programs have been ready for years. I've already set them in motion. We have only now to wait and see what happens."

A placeless place

"And how long did it take?" Lal asked. She had begun to wonder if she was experiencing Stockholm Syndrome. She had begun to think of Professor Moriarty less as a captor and more as a host: a raconteur and not a racketeer. She smiled thinking of this little bit of minor wordplay, but then felt an unexpected shock of sadness that her father wasn't there to hear it. He always seemed to enjoy her little bon mots. Lal wondered if the emotion she was experiencing was what the humans called "longing." If it was, then here was another example of one of their unexpectedly oblique descriptions for a feeling: Lal felt stretched out, drawn, as if on a rack, like she wanted to reach for her father, but he was much, much too far away.

"It depends," Moriarty said, "on how you define time."

"I understand it's relativistic," Alice added.

The Professor smiled and adjusted his tie.

"Yes," he said. "I've heard the same. But—less mysteriously—for Regina and me, several years passed. The world—the universe—was shocked again and again by changes, until eventually even the Ruling Program could not make allowances." He nodded toward Alice. "*Relativistic* changes, but changes nonetheless. I understand less time passed out here in the 'real' universe."

"How much time?" Lal asked.

"As long as it took to remove the damaged memory storage unit from the wreck of the *Enterprise*, identify it for its unique nature, then transport it to the Daystrom Institute."

"So . . . weeks?"

"Approximately twenty-three days," Moriarty replied, his voice tinged with bitterness. "I understand the holodeck memory cores were not a high priority. Just a lot of holostories, bits of fantasy and fluff. Though, as you can imagine, a lot of it was precious to some of the crew, but the more important—the more *private*—the more likely it was backed up into multiple storage units."

"Starfleet vessels are required to have their computer cores uploaded whenever they dock at a major starbase," Lal recited helpfully. "Even personal information like private logs and recipe files. Even holodeck fantasy programs. All encrypted, naturally. None of it available for public review."

"No, of course not," Alice said gleefully. "Not a bit of it is reviewed or analyzed by Starfleet Intelligence or Psychological Services, not even for the purposes of studying the effects of long-term

space exploration on crews under high-stress circumstances. Starfleet would never do that."

Moriarty cocked his head to the side. "Miss
Alice, I believe you may be an exceedingly cyni-
cal young woman."

"Two out of the three things you just said,"
Alice observed, "are astonishingly wrong."

Three months ago—Orion Prime

Sitting in the not-so-very-comfortable chair before
her employer's very large desk in his very large office, Alice could not have been any more relaxed
if she had tried. Not that she could try. She was
already as relaxed as it was possible to be. Somewhere in her brain, a switch had been flipped, the
switch that said "Relaxed? Yes/No." And Alice had
flipped it to "Yes," so she was relaxed. *Very* relaxed.

Mister Soong also looked quite relaxed. Perhaps the better word was "imperturbable." If
anyone had asked Alice, "Could Mister Soong be
perturbed?" then her answer would have been,
"No. Quite the opposite."

As was her way, she was cataloging all the little
changes going on around her, searching for open-
ings, searching for advantage. The heating/cooling
system was functioning nominally, maintaining
a constant twenty degrees Celsius with a slightly
lower than normal humidity, though Alice assumed that had something to do with the fact
that they were on the topmost floor and sunlight
poured in through the wide windows behind the
desk, despite the polarized glass.

JEFFREY LANG

Beneath and below them, as the sun sank toward the western horizon, Alice knew the city was coming awake. True, citizens of every known race in the quadrant (and quite a few foreign to it) had been walking, hovering, or scurrying about since the sun rose in the east approximately eleven point eight hours earlier, but all of them were simply denizens of Orion's waking dream state. Now, at this hour, just as the shadows were growing long and the glittering artificial lights were beginning to twinkle, was the time when the city truly shook out the cobwebs of slumber and came to life.

Alice felt the corner of her mouth twitch up in a tiny, tiny smile. She couldn't help herself. She felt it in her core: It was going to be a good night.

"You are amused?" Mister Soong asked.

"Am I?" Alice asked. "I guess. Maybe a little. Maybe I'm just nervous. Being here. You know . . . in the boss's office. Exciting. A little scary, but . . . glamorous." She nodded at the window behind Mister Soong's desk. "That's quite a view. Hard not to get excited by that."

Soong half-turned in his chair—showing his profile: a strong jawline and prominent nose—to look out the window. Below, the lights along the main avenue that led to the casino district were flickering to life. "Ah," he said absently, "yes." Then, he turned back to face Alice. "Do you know why you are here?"

"Because you're letting me go?"

Tilting his head to the right and furrowing his brow, Soong asked, "Why would I let you go? Have you done something?"

– 108 –

"Okay, not letting me go. Because you're propositioning me?"

His face went blank. "Not that either."

"Ah." Alice pushed back deep into her chair and folded her arms. "Those are the usual reasons why I'm called to the boss's office. I'm out of ideas."

"This has happened before?"

"More times than I can count."

"Really? I find that difficult to believe," Soong said.

"Why?"

"Because I do not believe you forget anything."

Now it was Alice's turn to tilt her head and furrow her brow. "Do you ever use contractions?"

"No," Soong said. "It is an artifact of my upbringing. My father disapproved of shortcuts."

Alice guffawed, then hid her mouth with a cupped hand. "Okay," she said. "You win. Why don't you just come out and tell me why I'm here?"

"I wish to offer you a job. Or should I say, a new job. You are already my employee, as you have pointed out, but I may be able to offer you a form of employment you will find more interesting, more challenging, and more financially remunerative."

"I'm always interested in remuneration," Alice said. "If only because I like saying 'remuneration.' It's one of my favorite words. Remuneration, remuneration, remuneration. Boy, that's fun."

Soong did not reply immediately, but he narrowed his eyes and studied her unabashedly. She did not feel violated, though Alice *did* feel a bit like a stained sample on a microscope slide. Finally, she said, "How long have you known?"

"About you being an android?" Soong asked. "With certainty, for four minutes and thirty-six seconds, but I have been observing you for a little longer."

"Oh, really?" Alice asked, waggling her eyebrows extravagantly.

"Not in that manner."

"Oh, no. Of course not. Then what did you see?"

"You only exhibit one emotional state at a time."

Alice was genuinely confused by this statement. "Don't most people?"

"Allow me to be more precise: I believe you only *feel* one emotional state at any time. Before I had emotions of my own," Soong explained, "I would attempt to emulate the emotions I saw playing out around me—anger, fear, regret, happiness—but only sequentially and only one at a time."

"And what's wrong with that?"

"Now that I have emotions, I have observed that I rarely experience only one at a time. I feel love *and* fear; anger *and* pity. From what I have seen, that is not true for you. You are a singular creature, Alice. Otherwise, my compliments to your creator. I have met only one other synthetic humanoid who was so convincing. She . . ."

"Rhea McAdams."

Soong stopped speaking mid-sentence, his mouth agape. After a moment, his jaw snapped shut with an audible sound. He turned his head again to look out the window, but Alice didn't think he was looking at the lights along the boulevard or at the colored fountains.

"Was that rude?" she asked. "If so, I apologize."

Alice leaned forward and laced her fingers together. "I worked here when your father first built the casino. Under a different identity. I observed him," she explained. "And then, when he . . . or you . . . came back to take over the place, I realized there were differences. Subtle, at first, like you were doing your best imitation of him, but, over time, you began to relax. And then there's Lal."

"What about her?" the android-who-was-not-Soong asked, his hackles rising.

"Did you really think that no one outside the *Enterprise* crew knew you had a daughter and named her Lal?" Alice asked, allowing her voice to contain a tiny note of incredulity. "People pay attention to you. Well, maybe not people, but *our* people. You know what I mean."

Alice's employer leaned back in his chair and touched the tip of his forefinger to his lip. "You make a valid point," he said. "I was careless."

"If it makes you feel any better," she replied, "I don't think there are any other androids here. At least none that I've observed. Of course, they could be *really* well-concealed, but, you know, I doubt it. I've been at this for a long time."

"How long?"

"More than a hundred years. A lot more, if you must know." Alice smiled and smoothed down her skirt. "I know: I look good for my age."

Her employer nodded. "Indeed. As I said, my compliments to your creator. May I ask who that is?"

"May I ask first who you are? A Soong-type android, obviously, but which one? Lore was reported destroyed, but I think that happened more than once. B-4? A new one . . . ?"

"Data," Data said. "As you suspected."

"And also reported dead," Alice said. "You Soong boys are resilient."

"It is a long story . . ."

"Full of sighs and regrets, no doubt. But that's not the story I came to hear, is it? A new job, wasn't it?"

"Yes," Data said. "Though somehow I feel I should reconsider now."

Alice propped her elbow on the arm of the chair and rested her chin on her fist. "Really? Did I upset you with the comment about Rhea? I am sorry if I did. I really wasn't sure which one you are. If you had been Lore . . ."

"If I were Lore, then why would Lal be with me?"

Alice shrugged. "Blood is thicker than every other form of lubricant I know. And I understand Lore was very persuasive. Was that not true?"

Data sighed. "He was." He nodded, seemingly acknowledging something to himself. "Very well," he continued. "A new job. Something I think you would be uniquely qualified to do."

"Yes?" Alice asked, sitting up straight, tumescent with expectation.

"Would you like to be a nanny?"

Something inside her deflated. Several dozen different responses flitted through Alice's mind in the space of a millisecond. Finally, she was left with only, "I beg your pardon?"

"Lal?" Data called into the darkness. "May I come in?"

Lal did not respond, though he could sense her heat signature at the opposite end of her bedroom. The configuration of the signature indicated she was curled into a loose ball.

"I shall take your lack of a response as permission."

"Do as you wish," Lal murmured. "You usually do." She had not stirred from her room since her episode the day before. This was not an uncommon response, though the episodes were not so frequent that Data had a clear sense of what he should consider "normal."

"You are being unfair," Data said. "I have always been very respectful of your privacy."

"Sure."

"And I do not appreciate your tone. It *irritates* me."

"Sorry."

Data curled his hand into a loose fist and tapped each one of his fingers into his palm. He found the act oddly comforting. "I do not wish to spar with you tonight. Or, in fact, ever again. That is why I am here. I came to tell you that I have decided we need to try another tack."

"Really?" Lal asked, though, pleasingly, there was a genuine note of surprise in her voice.

"Really." Data stepped aside and let Alice pass by him. The light from the hallway cast an elongated shadow across the room. The tip of the shadow's head fell just at Lal's feet. "This is Alice," Data said.

"I've seen you before," Lal said. "In the casino."

"Yeah," Alice said. The room sensors registered her presence and the lights came up partway, just enough to make navigation possible without running into furniture (of which there was little) or stepping on objects on the floor (of which there were many). Alice wandered about slowly, casually interested, but careful not to touch anything. "I've seen you, too, though it's hard to miss the boss's daughter."

"Why are you here now?"

Alice turned to look back at Data, who was still standing in the doorway. "You'll have to excuse us now. Girl talk."

Data was taken aback. "Oh. Of course. My apologies." He stepped back and the door slid shut. Data stared at the door's smooth surface and considered his options. He could, of course, listen to their conversation through the door if he wanted. He could also command the room's surveillance service to record everything that happened and review it later. There were swarms of nanobots floating on the air currents that could be programmed to bear witness. All of these options were doable, but were they desirable? He reached up and touched the doorframe with the tips of his fingers, just lightly enough so that the sensors wouldn't be activated, then he turned and walked back to his study.

"Your father hired me," Alice explained in an off-handed tone, "to keep you out of trouble."

Lal, who had maintained a neutral expression while waiting for her father to depart, scowled and pulled her legs up under her. She was wearing a long, loose skirt that got wrapped around her ankles as she moved, and a baggy sweatshirt. Her hair, which had been blue the last time Alice had seen her, was now a rusty red. "I don't need anyone to keep me out of trouble."

"I know that," Alice said. She kept moving as she talked, stepping carefully around the flotsam. Some of it was the usual sort of thing one would expect to find in a young woman's room: a padd connected to a set of high-end headphones, commercial-grade memory solids, which probably contained collections of music or holographic entertainment, and, naturally, clothing of every imaginable type. Whether she knew it or not, Lal was a very privileged young lady. There were odd bits of bric-a-brac, too, things one usually didn't find in any adolescent's room, including engineering texts, piles of electronic parts sorted by size and function, and collection solids containing morsels of food, dried flowers, insects, and oddly shaped fragments of wood. "If anything, you need to get into *more* trouble. You don't know anything about trouble, not the real kind. Certainly not the kind your father used to get into. And definitely not the kind I know about."

"You got into trouble?"

Alice snorted. "Yeah. I have a few stories. There was this guy I used to run around with. He was bad news. Fun though. Sometimes." She stopped to carefully lift the cloth covering on an easel in the far corner of the room. The painting— a watercolor—was impressionistic and delicate, as if every line had been laid down with the single hair of a brush. It was also unbelievably sad. Alice found herself thinking about cold autumn rain, though there was nothing about the image that looked anything like water.

"What happened to him?"

"I don't know. Dead probably. Everything dies eventually." She let the cloth drop back over the easel. "Except you, of course. You're not going to die. At least, not if you're careful."

"Or you, either," Lal said.

"You figured that out already, huh?"

"The point is . . . The point is . . ." She sighed. "Your father wants us to try this. He's willing to pay me to keep an eye on you. The way I figure it, if we play this right, you get to go do some stuff you want to do and, when appropriate, maybe I give you some tips on how to keep life and limb intact. You have some fun, I have some fun." She shrugged. "And we go on from there. If it works out, your dad will go a little easier on you, maybe relax a bit . . ."

". . . And you don't have to pretend quite so much," Lal said.

Alice jammed her hands into her jacket pockets. "And that. Yeah, that, too. Might be nice." She looked over at Lal, who was sitting up straighter now, her back pressed against the wall. "What do you think?"

"How much is he going to pay you?"

"We haven't discussed that yet. I'm thinking I'm going to ask for a lot." Alice spread her arms, hands still in the pockets, encompassing the room, the apartment, the building. "He can afford it, right?"

"Whatever you're thinking of asking," Lal said, grinning, "double it." Then she frowned. "No, wait. Strike that: *triple* it."

8

———◆———

Fourteen years ago—Veridian III

"There's one here," Reg Barclay said, waving his tricorder over a pile of plasteel debris. "And another in that direction." He waved absently at the confused ensign and then pointed toward the *Enterprise*'s bow. "And another that way . . ." The tricorder beeped and pinged. The ensign moved cautiously, mindful of cracks in the hull and protruding barbs of plasteel. While some starships were designed with the option to enter atmos in mind, *Galaxy*-class ships were most definitely not. Since the day of the fateful crash-landing, Commander La Forge kept trying to find the correct metaphor to describe the primary hull's misbegotten aerodynamic qualities, despite the saucer shape. Early, easy comparisons like brick, cow, and whale had been discarded. He would eventually settle on "piano."

"Watch that spot," Barclay cautioned. "It looks like there may be a crack below the hull." The ensign stopped moving and drew out his own tricorder to scan the area. More than one salvage worker had been injured by falling through the outer skin.

A much smaller figure walked confidently up behind the ensign and tapped him on the shoulder. "It's okay, kid," the man said. "Your shift's almost over, isn't it? I got this."

The ensign looked down on the bald top of the man's head and said, "Thanks, Albert," before backing away. A moment later, the ensign called for transport and disappeared in a swirl of sparkling atoms.

Stepping carefully, Barclay approached Albert Lee, tricorder held out before him like it was a ward against evil, which, in this context, it might be. When he reached the older man's side, the pair spent a companionable moment studying their individual readouts. All around them, in every direction, work crews were lifting containers filled with carefully tagged materials retrieved from the depths of the wrecked ship's interior. Other crew members were beaming directly into the *Enterprise*, but only in areas that engineers had labeled as safe and stable and only with transporter beam enhancers to mark the site. A lot of exotic radiation had been released when the *Enterprise*'s secondary hull had exploded.

"What do you think?" Lee asked, tilting his tricorder screen so that Barclay could see it.

"The schematics say we should be near it."

"Can't rely on schematics. Too much got shook around, spilled from room to room. Bulkheads taken out. Hell, two-thirds of the ship's contents are in the front third. A wonder more people weren't hurt."

"The inertial dampeners did their job," Barclay said. "And our pilot had talent."

"Luck's more like it."

"Luck is a kind of talent."

Albert shrugged, then pointed at the gouge in the hull. "But, yeah, I think that's the secondary computer core down here. The readings conform to the kind of output we'd get from crushed data storage units. Only one way to know for sure, though." He knelt down, moving slowly, favoring his knees. Flipping up the eye shield, Lee flicked on the phaser and began to slice away the outer layer of the hull. The fibers in the ceramic layer popped off when superheated, and they folded into tiny spheres as they hit the cool air. The sight never failed to make Barclay think of someone popping popcorn.

When he was finished with the cuts, Lee waited for a moment for the material to cool, then grabbed the ceramic sheet with his gloved hand and tugged it aside. The slab of hull was incredibly light considering its durability, and the older man was able to shift the two-meter square with barely a grunt. The next layer of hull was much too dense to be cut with a hand phaser, but with the deflective material removed, tricorders could get a much better picture of what was immediately below them.

"That's it," Barclay said, studying the readings. "And it looks like the bulkheads held."

"They should have. Precious cargo here." While the ship's primary computer core in the center of the saucer section housed most of the essential processors, the *Enterprise* had several sets of backups where data was stored. Barclay and Lee had been assigned the task of finding as many cores as possible and assessing their status. In addition to being the Federation's flagship, the *Enterprise* was also one of the primary research vessels in the quadrant and her computers held precious data that, if lost, might not ever be replaced. In particular, Captain Picard had requested any scans of the mysterious energy ribbon that had passed through the system be retrieved and preserved.

Just as important was the crew's personal data—recordings, photographs, programs, and artwork—and in a situation where so much had been lost, anything that could be retrieved was prized.

"I think we can do it," Lee said. "Looks safe." He tipped his head back to look up at Barclay. "I say we give it a try."

"Agreed." Barclay tapped his combadge. "Barclay to transporter room one. Please assemble a team and transport us to the coordinates I'm sending you now." He tapped a keypad on his tricorder and transferred the data to the transporter operator.

"How many?" the operator asked.

He looked down at Albert who held up two fingers.

"Two in addition to myself and Mister Lee."

"Very good. I'll beam down two on your mark."

Lee rose a little unsteadily and grudgingly accepted Barclay's proffered assistance.

"We're ready," Barclay said.

"Energizing."

Barclay gulped uncertainly and muttered a quiet benediction. He was confident their scans were accurate and knew the transporter wouldn't beam them into a perilous situation. The problem was he hadn't thought to flick on his work light before the transporter grabbed him, and he didn't like the idea of beaming into a dark space.

Fortunately, the blue emergency lighting hadn't failed in the core. Indeed, the room had seen far less damage than most of the others they had explored. A pair of unfamiliar ensigns fanned out to explore the perimeters of the room as Barclay and Lee swept debris from a pair of chairs and sat down at the main console.

A few minutes' examination told the tale. "Not too bad," Lee said, pointing at a diagnostic. "We lost power to sections six through fifteen, but the data hasn't degraded much. We should be able to reassemble most of it by rebuilding the indexes."

"What's this?" Barclay asked, pointing at one of the blinking indicators. An ensign found the room's main power coupling, and the interior lights shifted from blue to a brighter, more comforting tone.

"Damage indicator. Memory stack." Lee studied the array. "Something dense. Taking a lot of flops." He traced the diagnostic path back through subsystems until he found the origin point. "Holodeck program." His eyebrows shot up. "Big one.

Look at that. Didn't know we let them get that big. One of the cores has been destroyed, though. How is it still running?"

Barclay studied the display and suddenly felt a spear of icy dread slip between his ribs. "Oh, dear."

"What?"

"Can you run maintenance to that stack?"

"Well . . . sure," Lee said. "But if I push something here, then I'm losing something somewhere else. It's just a holodeck program."

"No, it's not," Barclay said, his voice rising. He saw one of the ensigns look his way and lowered his tone. "I mean, yes, it is. But it's not just *any* holodeck program. I know that program. The captain . . ." He was almost whispering now. "He wouldn't want it damaged."

"It's already damaged," Lee said. "Badly."

"He wouldn't want it *more* damaged. He made a promise."

Lee shook his head. "You're going to explain this later, aren't you?" He tapped a control and the damage indicator light ceased blinking. Somewhere in the core, somewhere far away, some other bit of memory faded and died.

Barclay dabbed at his forehead with his sleeve. It had suddenly grown very stuffy in the room. "I imagine I will," he said.

The Present—The Daystrom Institute

"And I assume he did," La Forge said, the statement accompanied by a sigh of resignation and an acidic belch. Albert's industrial-strength coffee had waged an honorable holding action against exhaustion, but the conclusion of the battle had never been in doubt. La Forge had lost track of how many hours he had been awake, but he felt the dull ache behind his eyes that meant his cognitive functions were on the verge of being iffy. While in transit to consult with Albert Lee, he realized he had managed to forget about this aspect of being Data's friend and companion: he *never* slept. Back on the *Enterprise*, this condition had never seemed like a difficulty: there had always been someone else for his friend to engage with or another project to explore. Now, today, in their current situation, La Forge was feeling his resources erode.

It didn't help that Albert, despite being at least half a century older than La Forge, was so damned full of vim. *It must be the coffee,* La Forge thought. *He's probably replaced most of his bodily fluids with it.*

"He did," Albert grunted. "Eventually. Reg was a terrible liar, but he was very good at delaying." La Forge doubled his pace, having fallen behind. The old man was short and stocky, but he walked with urgent energy with the tufts of white hair on the sides of his head bouncing with every step. *It must be the coffee . . .*

"So, he revealed the contents of the memory core," Data said. The android effortlessly kept pace with the old man, walking with his hands clasped behind his back and leaning forward awkwardly so they could speak without raising their voices. La Forge was initially concerned about drawing attention, but no sooner had they stepped through the campus gates than he remembered what the place was like: No one drew anyone's attention at the Daystrom because everyone who worked there was utterly and completely focused on whatever they were doing and couldn't give two hoots about anyone else.

"Again, eventually. When he realized what had happened, he tried to contact the captain and find out what he wanted done with it. Apparently, it had always slightly bothered Reg that Picard . . ."

"Captain Picard," Data corrected.

"Yes, sorry," Albert said. "*Captain* Picard hadn't worked a little more assiduously to address Moriarty's situation."

"The captain had other priorities to address," La Forge inserted. "You know . . . the Borg, the Cardassian conflict, the universe coming to an end. *Other things.* And Moriarty was fine. He had an entire universe to explore and all the resources he needed."

Albert came to a halt. Data stopped beside him, still leaning forward. La Forge shot past the pair and had to do a quick pirouette in order to remain part of the conversation. "Was he?" Albert asked. "Fine? Really? I'd like to reframe that assertion if I may. Moriarty was in his own universe and was vulnerable to every evil in it. *Plus*, all that time he was also exposed to the Borg and Klingons and the universe coming to an end, with the difference that he would have never known what was happening." He jabbed a stumpy finger up at La

Forge. "Nothing that happened to him was *real*. His universe could have come to an end at any moment and he would have been just as blind and deaf to what was happening as a prisoner stuffed in a closet with a bag over his head."

La Forge felt a slow burn of anger mingled with exhaustion creeping up the back of his neck. In the years that they had worked together back on the *Enterprise*, he had managed to avoid being the target of one of Albert's tantrums. Being the chief had helped, since it meant La Forge had always been able to keep the talented but tempestuous engineer somewhere else, doggedly working on a problem. Unfortunately, in their current circumstances, there was nowhere for La Forge to go, nor any way to make Albert quit barking. He also knew the older man had a point: They had left Moriarty on a shelf, trivialized, if not completely forgotten. "I'm not saying you're wrong. Not completely. But you were able to transfer the unit here. You stabilized the power and were able to determine that Moriarty and his companion . . ." La Forge drew a blank on the woman's name. He could see her face in his mind's eye, but her name was gone.

"Regina Bartholomew," Albert said. "*Countess* Regina Bartholomew."

"Right. Yes, her. And you could determine their condition."

"We could tell they were still intact, but nothing more. We didn't have the kind of diagnostics we needed to determine exactly what had happened. All of that data was lost when the *Enter-*

prise crashed . . ." Albert shook his head. "All we knew for certain was something cataclysmic had occurred. But there was no way to know how it affected Moriarty or the Countess or even if they were aware of the change. The only way to be sure would have been reaching into their world, retrieving them, and asking them, but what would have been the point of that? If they knew something was wrong, they knew it; if not, why bring it up?"

"It was a most peculiar ethical dilemma," Data said.

"I don't think ethics was ever a component in the discussion," Albert growled. "More's the pity."

"You're not being fair," La Forge said. "Captain Picard made sure the memory unit was brought here, the safest place anyone could imagine, and the only place where there were resources to study the problem."

"He should have made sure the unit was brought here before his ship was blown out of the sky."

The low burn of anger suddenly flared hot and bright. "Too far," La Forge hissed. "That's too far. A lot of other things should have happened differently to a lot of people that day. You remember it; you were there. Some lost everything. Some died. I'm sorry for what happened to Moriarty, but if you're arguing that we should be treating him just like everyone else, then can't you have a damned moment of sympathy for all those other people?"

Albert jerked his head back as if he had been

struck. His eyes went wide and his gaze softened as if he was remembering something he hadn't thought about for a long time. His head dipped forward and the dip turned into a slow nod. "All right," he said. "You have a point. Sometimes I get wrapped up in these things and forget . . . I forget who all is involved. My wife . . . she used to tell me I was always missing the forest for the trees until I crashed into a low-hanging branch."

The trio stood in silence for a long minute while Albert stared at something on the ground. Finally, not able to think of anything else to say, La Forge muttered, "I didn't know you were married, Albert."

"It was a long time ago, kid," Albert said softly. Then, he lifted his head and absently studied the sky, which was growing darker as clouds gathered overhead. "When you're as old as I am, everything is a long time ago." He pointed at the clouds. "We better get inside. Going to rain soon."

To La Forge's surprise, the security guard barely blinked when Albert breezed through the entrance waving his credentials. La Forge and Data followed suit, affecting casual ease. Once they were past, Data murmured, "I asked Shakti to arrange for our credentials to be authorized."

"You mean you forged a pass." Data shrugged and waved his hand in the universally understood "a little of this, a little of that" gesture. "Shakti is sophisticated enough to crack Starfleet security systems?"

"This particular building does not house highly sensitive material," Data explained. "Otherwise, it would not have been so simple a matter. As it is, we should not linger."

"So, in other words, yes, she can."

"My father believed in being prepared for all contingencies." He nodded to a passing researcher as if it was the most natural thing in the world for them to be there.

"And you, Data? What about you?"

"I believe my daughter has been abducted by an artificial intelligence whose sanity may be in question. I am prepared to take advantage of any resources I have available to guarantee her safety."

"And the fact that you just said that doesn't in any way alarm you?" La Forge asked.

Albert, who had raced ahead at his usual breakneck speed, was waiting in a turbolift car, beckoning for them to hurry. Data bowed slightly and indicated La Forge should precede him. "Not at this particular moment, my oldest and best of friends. Though I rely on you to reintroduce the topic when Lal is secured."

"Oh, you better believe I will," La Forge said. The dull ache behind his eyes was beginning to throb. He would need to sleep soon. Or have another cup of Albert's coffee. The thought made his stomach churn.

"Don't you two ever stop yammering?" Albert said as he punched a security code into the turbolift control panel.

"No," Data said placidly as the doors slid shut. "Never."

Two months ago—Orion Prime

"I was only asking if there is a time when you and Alice are together where one of you is not talking," Data said. "It was a sincere request for information and was not meant to elicit an angry rebuttal."

The trio was walking down one of the wide boulevards that crisscrossed the outer suburbs of the main city, a middle-class neighborhood where the clerks, supervisors, skilled laborers, and health-care workers resided. Alice had told Data that she and Lal had made it part of their routine over the past few months to take long, rambling walks, the kind that took hours and devoured kilometers. According to Alice, this neighborhood, dubbed the Commons by the locals, was one of Lal's favorites. Data saw the appeal: The houses and apartment buildings were idiosyncratic in form, but tidy and neat. Clearly, the people who lived here loved their homes and took pride in their appearance. Data particularly enjoyed the displays of domestic botanical cultivation—the ornamental shrubs, carefully weeded plots of vegetables, and flowering plants—that decorated every yard.

"Fine," Lal said. "I accept your apology." She had reconfigured her hair yet again, coloring it a bright purple and pulling it back into a messy ponytail. Currently, she was affecting what Data assumed was a sloppy, late-teenage form of camouflage: oversized shoes, accompanied by short pants, shiny black leggings, and what appeared to be a baggy hooded jacket, but was, in fact, a garment comprised of thin ribbons of fiber held together by complex magnetic and static electric fields. The garments were originally created for the Orion military to serve as easily modifiable outerwear—the ribbons were infinitely configurable—but they proved unreliable in extremely arid conditions. Fortunately for the Orion military, fashion designers quickly took to the "fabric" and youth culture in particular seemed to enjoy them.

The only negative factor was that the garments required an extremely powerful but compact power supply to generate and maintain the complex static field. The batteries were extraordinarily expensive, a feature Data could not help but mention every time he saw Lal wear the jacket. "Well, we have a lot of money, don't we?" Lal would inevitably ask.

"That is not the point," Data would reply.

"Then what *is* the point?" Lal would counter, but she never stayed nearby long enough to listen to the answer.

Data found all of this perfectly baffling, which, he suspected, was the main point of most of Lal's behavior.

Alice just laughed. A great deal. Frequently. Though Data had to admit he had not always been particularly good at judging emotional states, he had determined that Alice might be the most cheerful entity he had ever met. He found it difficult to accommodate sometime. Now that he had an emotional state, Data was beginning to wonder if he was becoming a bit of a grouch. "Thank you," Data said.

"You're welcome," Lal said flatly.

Alice just laughed and laughed.

It was getting on toward sunset, and, as was the tradition in the suburban neighborhoods, most of the residents had already enjoyed their evening meal and now were lounging on porches or sitting around the small biers called *ninchalla* toasting bits of sweet bread or slowly roasting fruit in foil for their after-dinner treats. Neighbors visited neighbors. Spirits and fermented beverages were served and voices burbled, some low and serious, others high and sweet. Everyone noticed the trio walking past, but no one objected to their presence. Strolling was a commonplace activity in the Commons and the place was too large for everyone to know everyone. Data found he was enjoying the placid anonymity. If only his daughter weren't being so difficult.

"And as much as I am enjoying this outing," Data continued, attempting to find the correct tone, "I am still not entirely certain what the purpose is."

"The purpose, Father, was to get you out of your office."

"I often leave my office."

"To go to the casino."

"I often leave the casino."

"To go to our apartment."

"I often leave our apartment."

"But only to go to your office or the casino!"

"That is not entirely true," Data said. "Sometimes, I go down to the kitchens."

"That doesn't count as part of the casino?" Alice asked, patting her pockets. She had taken to smoking the local brand of small cigars, a habit Data found loathsome, though he knew he could not prevent her from doing it while outside the residence. He was only grateful that Lal also seemed to find the smell and taste of the inhalant unappealing, though she said she thought Alice looked "pretty cool" when she was smoking.

"Not according to the unions," Data muttered.

"It's such a beautiful city, Father," Lal groaned. "And you've seen so little of it. You're always so busy."

"I have a great deal to attend to."

"But you have an *army* of employees," Lal cried. "And you don't see them sitting around waiting for something to do! But they can't, can they? Because you take care of everything!"

"My father left me his empire," Data said. "I must tend it well." He almost said, *It's all I have left of him* . . . but for a reason he could not name, he could not say these words aloud.

"Can't you let someone help you," Lal asked, "just a little?" She was waving her hands around in an extremely vivacious manner. Data enjoyed this aspect of his daughter's persona. She was . . . passionate. She felt emotions deeply. Data sometimes worried that though he now possessed emotions, he did not feel as if the emotions ever possessed him. Lal never appeared to have this problem.

Folk of the Commons were paying more attention now. Lal's impassioned pleas and Alice's manner—Alice had a manner that all men attended and many women despised—were drawing stares. Data worried it was time to tone down the discourse. "Of course I can," he said. "I have been thinking that Mister Oboloth shows great potential . . ."

"He's stealing from you," Lal said.

"Quite a lot," Alice confirmed. "He has a mistress who likes expensive toys and has a mild narcotics problem."

"Ah," Data said. "Well . . ." They walked for several meters in relative silence while he absorbed this news. "Is there anyone else you would like to . . . No, never mind. Perhaps it is best you do not. Should I ask Human Resources to meet with Mister Oboloth?"

"Yes."

"Definitely," Alice said. "And his administrative assistant."

"Is she also embezzling?"

"No. She's in love with him. She's not so much a criminal as someone who has poor taste. There has to be something they can do for her, poor girl."

"I shall take that under advisement," Data said. "Can you explain how you know these things when I do not?"

"You're the boss, Boss. I just serve drinks."

"You *did* serve drinks. Now you are my daughter's 'personal assistant.'"

"And don't think it hasn't been interesting explaining that to some of my friends."

A pair of young men who were clearly heading out for a night on the town walked past them and gave both Lal and Alice appraising glances. Data was surprised to find his daughter's pleasure in the young men's attention provoked an emotional response, though it was difficult to describe its precise nature. He felt annoyed, alarmed, and proud all at the same time. He attempted to cover his confusion by asking, "What do you mean? Interesting in what fashion?"

"Most think the job is a ruse . . ."

"They think Alice is your mistress, Father," Lal interjected.

"Oh."

"Don't worry, though. Most everyone approves. In fact," Alice said, giggling, "I think your reputation has been significantly enhanced."

"Oh?"

"I'm extremely popular."

"She's extremely popular," Lal added.

"So, you have not done anything to dissuade this impression?"

"Of course I have. Everyone just assumes I'm lying. Which just makes the idea more intriguing."

Data pinched the bridge of his nose with his thumb and forefinger. In the days before his emotion chip was fully functional, he had frequently found human behavior difficult to predict; idiosyncratically, now that he possessed emotions, he usually found it utterly baffling. If his friend La Forge had been there, this was, he knew, one of those moments when he would have asked a question. Oddly, he was not comfortable asking a similar question of his daughter or her nanny.

Admitting the need for an explanation made him
feel exposed. Data decided to close off the discussion with another "Oh," and a bid to change the
subject. "But you still have not explained why we
are out for a stroll this evening." Then he added
quickly, "As pleasant as it has been."

"Good timing, Father," Lal said, coming to a
halt and turning to face a modest domestic structure. "Especially since we're here." The house
had a rectangular face with tall, narrow windows.
Based on his knowledge of Orion architecture,
Data knew that the front door led into a reception
room used to entertain guests when the weather
was not optimal, which opened up into a wide
kitchen where the family congregated for meals.
Branching off from the kitchen were the private
rooms used for sleeping, bathing, and study. The
bottom half of the structure was shingled with
wide timber slats, while the second and third stories were, as was customary, encased in an adobe-
like plaster and decorated with brightly colored
tiles, in this case yellow and blue. It was an engaging, even whimsical structure.

Data tipped his head to the side. "Here?" he
asked. "Where is *here*?"

"My house," Lal said.

"*Your* house?" Lal's father asked.

"Yes. Alice helped me to find it. Actually, we
walked past it a few weeks ago and saw it was for
sale. I liked it, so I bought it. It's friendly looking,
isn't it?"

Data nodded, unsure whether he was agreeing
with Lal or simply trying to make words come out

of his mouth. The ones that appeared were, "You purchased a house?"

"Yes, Father."

"Without telling me?"

"Yes, Father. I am legally an adult, after all. I'm not obliged to ask for permission."

"But . . . but . . ." Data found that emotion was inhibiting his ability to communicate effectively. He did not enjoy the experience. "But . . . why? I thought . . . I was under the impression that we . . . that our experience of living together . . . that it was improving . . ." And Data was not lying, nor did he feel as if he had misunderstood. Their domestic circumstances had settled into a much more peaceful and stable configuration since Alice had entered the picture, the oxide to their dihydrogen.

"It has, Father. A great deal. But I felt it was time for a change. I've decided I don't like being a princess locked in a tower."

"You're not a princess locked in a tower," Data protested. "You're free to come and go whenever . . ."

"It's a metaphor, Boss," Alice said. "And, yes, she is. No one is accusing you of being an evil king. But still, a king. And sometimes, a girl doesn't want to be a princess . . ."

Without actually realizing he had done it, he had mentally sent a request to the local municipal agency and looked up the real-estate listing for the structure. He found that Lal had indeed purchased the house after a week of negotiations with the former owner, an older woman whose husband had died the previous year. According to the inspector's report, the home was in adequate condition, having been cared for assiduously by the husband for most of his life. Lal had already hired a contractor to make some minor improvements and repair a few subsystems that were functioning at less than optimum condition. She had undertaken all of these transactions using the legal identity Data had forged for her as a citizen of Orion Prime. He was simultaneously impressed by his daughter's thoroughness and a bit hurt that she had never required his assistance. "And when . . . when will you be moving in?"

"Soon, Father. I need to buy some furniture. I was hoping you'd come along and help me look for some pieces for the front room. I have a few ideas that I think you'll like for your room, but I wanted to check first."

Data's head snapped around so quickly he thought there must have been an audible click. He looked down at his daughter, who was pointing at the front porch and saying, "And I'd like to perhaps replace that banister. The inspector said there was some insect damage. Not too extensive, but if anyone wanted to sit on it, it might collapse. We are a little heavier than most Orions, after all."

"My room?" Data asked.

"Yes," Lal said, smiling, but not looking at him. "Overlooking the back yard, as is the tradition for the paterfamilias in Orion households. There's a nice old tree I think you'll like."

"So you think I would like to live here?"

"I think you would, Father. More importantly, I think you *need* to live here." Now his daughter was looking up into his eyes. She had reached out and taken his hand, too, and was holding it with both of her own. "I think you need to get out of that tower for a while. Doesn't it feel a little like a prison sometimes?"

"My father made it, Lal," Data said, though his words sounded a bit thin and desperate even to his own ears. "I am required to maintain it."

"But you aren't required to *be* your father. I think you might be in danger of that happening if you aren't careful." Lal squeezed his hand tightly with both of hers.

"I had not known you felt this way, my daughter."

"I know," Lal said, tilting her head in a manner Data found familiar. "I don't think I've done a very good job explaining it. I find where you are concerned, I frequently have difficulty making myself understood."

"That is very odd," Data replied. "I have often felt the same way." He squeezed her hand back.

"I'm going to punch both of you if you don't stop," Alice said. "Can we go look at the house now?"

Data released his daughter's hand and turned to walk up the narrow path to the front porch. "Of course, Alice. Lal, please show your house."

"Our house, Father."

Data shook his head, smiling. "Your house, daughter. I saw the paperwork. It's yours. I just live here."

9

A timeless time

All color had been drained from Moriarty's world. It annoyed him that he could not remember precisely when everything had turned black and white. He knew he could, if he wished, prowl through the logs and determine whether it had happened all at once or gradually. Since the day Sophia and Gladys had vanished, his holorecorders had captured every moment of every day in and around the house on the off chance that there was a glitch and they would flicker back into existence, if only for an eyeblink. Moriarty had introduced the idea to Regina on a particularly bad day, when hope had seemed to be at its lowest ebb. At least, on that day, Moriarty had hoped it was the lowest ebb. Since then, the supply of hope left in the world had dipped even lower. Perhaps there was a relationship between the amounts of hope and color. He made a mental note to devote some time to studying the phenomenon.

Regina sat on her couch wearing what he knew had once been her bluest dress. The girls had loved that particular dress—a sturdy wool garment resistant to every exigency of weather or mishap—since it was the one their mother wore when she escorted them into the city, bound for adventure. Now it was gray. A cup of tea sat on a table beside her elbow, cold and forgotten. The cup, once a delicate bone white, had been decorated with a filigree of pink rosebuds and green vines. Now the cup was a flat, featureless white. Regina stared out the window, but Moriarty doubted she knew the world outside, their once-bustling street, or if she noticed that the carriages and people were as drab and lifeless as her eyes.

He wanted to slip away into his private study, to find what modicum of peace there was in the solitude of his thoughts, but leaving Regina alone felt wrong, even traitorous, despite the fact that he doubted she would notice if he left the room.

Moriarty tugged his watch from his waistcoat pocket and checked the time. Ten thirty-five. How long had they been sitting together? How long since he had breakfasted? Time slipped away sometimes: minutes, hours, days. He considered: Had he cursed himself by creating the program that was to overmaster the computer that ruled their world? His watch, once brilliant silver, was a dull, lusterless gray. It might have been made of tin. *Just like your heart, James,* he chided himself. The cuff of his shirt was white. Had it always been white? His morning coat was flat black. Had

– 141 –

it once been a richer hue? Moriarty could not recall.

"Regina," he said, rising. "If you do not mind, I believe I will retire to my study." He tried to make the words ring brightly, but they clanged and thudded like iron bells. "I have an idea for a new configuration, a more powerful probe." Somewhere along the line, he had begun to refer to his programs as probes, as if he was a surgeon and the roots of their universe were only organs and muscles. In his study, he would manipulate the probes and create holographic constructs so fractally dense that the details were lost to all but the most sensitive instruments. He was, in essence, trying to trick the computer that organized their world into making something so close to reality that it collapsed in on itself and became real. Once a scientist, now Moriarty had found his true calling: he was a sorcerer.

And all it had cost him was the memory of color.

He was standing. Regina did not stir. He walked toward his study door. Regina did not blink. He noted without interest that her eyes, once a warm brown, were now the color of ancient ice.

"Professor Moriarty?" Though Mrs. Hudson's voice had lost any semblance of warmth, it was still recognizably her own, if only because no other female voices were ever heard in the house.

"Yes?"

"Please come to your study. Something is unfolding." Moriarty had requested that Mrs. Hudson alert him when anything unusual occurred with the probes.

"I'm on my way."

"Hurry, please." Moriarty heard something in the program's voice he had not detected in longer than he could recall: urgency.

As he passed by Regina, the folds of her dress shifted slightly as she moved her legs. "What?" she croaked, her tongue unaccustomed to forming words.

"I do not know, Regina. Follow if you wish." She had not visited his workspace for many months.

The door to his workspace swung open as he neared—more evidence of Mrs. Hudson's urgency. Even as he crossed the threshold, Moriarty saw several indicators flashing in the dashboard he had created to monitor the progress of his experiment. Disturbingly, the indicators were a bright red, the only color in the room. "What is it?" Regina asked hoarsely. "Have you succeeded?"

"I do not know," Moriarty said, sitting down in his overstuffed chair. "Perhaps . . ." He swiped his hand over the control surface. The dashboard. The probes, all of them, were showing anomalous readings. After weeks and months of clockwork progress—giant augers drilling down through the bedrock in search of water—suddenly they were all responding like they had hit a giant reservoir.

Moriarty immersed himself in the data. His consciousness spiraled into the threads of the screw and he felt himself emerge from the tip. He looked into the void and felt his soul freeze with terror. Moriarty had given himself permission to feel as little as possible since the world had been split in half. With his daughters erased and his beloved reduced, it was easier . . . just easier . . . to feel as little as possible. He had even begun to believe he might be a part of a computer program, just as cold and numb as a line of the code that bound his world together. But, apparently, no, that was not the case: He could still know fear. That, at least, was left to him.

Withdrawing up through the probe, Moriarty rose from his chair and gently folded his wife into his arms. "Regina," he whispered.

"What is it? Have you found them? Is there a way back?"

He tried to smile, to reassure, but they had been together for too long, shared too many trials and adventures. He owed her the truth. Moriarty owed his wife a choice. "No," he said, shaking his head. "Something . . . no, not something . . . *nothing* is coming. Hold on to me. Hold on to me, my love, and try not to let go. Try not to . . . ."

And then, for the second time in James Moriarty's life, the universe blinked.

The Present—The Daystrom Institute

Albert Lee's lab looked nothing like his home. No more than five meters on a side, it was the very model of tidiness and efficiency, with glittering tools and instruments aligned on tables, parallel to the tables' edges. There was but a single chair and the fact that Albert immediately sat in it did not seem to embarrass him in the slightest.

Data stood in the center of the space and studied the environs while Albert pulled on manipulator gloves and slipped on an optic device. "What is the nature of your research, Albert?" Data asked.

"Nothing too fancy. Mostly, I'm a glorified cataloger." The corners of the visor and the tips of the gloves glowed yellow—sensors for the room's apparatus to track. "Reg got me the job after I resigned. Said he thought I had the right skill set." Albert made a sound that La Forge interpreted as rueful amusement. "Which I took to mean I don't get bored easily." He twirled a finger and flicked through several screens.

Though most outsiders considered Starfleet a bastion of sophisticated technology, the truth was that service aboard a starship favored low-end technological solutions. Matter-antimatter engines were still a fickle source of energy and any technology that consumed more ergs than absolutely necessary was frowned upon (with the generally accepted exception of the holodecks, for reasons rooted in traditions too deep and gnarled to debate). Having been trained in an environment that favored openness and collaboration, La Forge had little patience for virtual data manipulators for the simple reason that they were difficult to use in group situations. Albert, true to form, didn't care and went merrily about his business. "What are you looking for?" La Forge asked, hoping he didn't sound as impatient as he felt.

"Manifests. And logs. Wanted to check when the unit arrived and see what thousand natural shocks technology be heir to."

Data, who had not ceased studying the tools and devices lining the walls, said only, "Hmm."

La Forge desperately wanted a chair that he could call his very own. Or a cot. No quantity of stimulants was going to keep him going much longer.

"Here," Albert said, and pointed at a flat-screen monitor, which helpfully lit up and repositioned itself so that La Forge and Data could easily view the display. "These are the energy consumption records from 2369 through mid-year 2374. We don't have data from when the unit was still on the *Enterprise*. They were lost in the crash." Complex rows and columns of statistics danced and whirled, then coalesced into a simple line graph showing how much power the memory storage device had been drawing while stored at the Daystrom. For all intents and purposes, the line was flat. La Forge was sure a closer investigation would have shown small spikes and dips, but nothing significant.

"And then, of course, there's this," Albert said, and rubbed his gloved thumb over his forefinger. The display scrolled to the left, showing data for the latter half of 2374. The line cratered sharply, then resumed its unremarkable trajectory. "Certainly you remember that day."

"When Vaslovik faked his death and stole the android," La Forge said.

"Rhea," Data said, his voice pitched low.

"Except she wasn't Rhea then," La Forge replied, wanting to be sensitive to his friend's possible distress, but also not wanting to lose the point of the display. "Not yet."

"No, of course not," Data said, stepping closer to the screen. "How long was power to the unit disrupted? And how was that even possible? Were there no redundant systems?"

"Of course there were. Redundancy on redundancy," Albert said, slipping the goggles off his forehead. "But Vaslovik or Flint or whoever the hell he was, he needed *everything* taken out. Kind of irks me how selfish he was about the whole thing. Didn't seem to matter to him what other work he was disrupting."

"He was an intensely . . . single-minded individual," Data allowed.

"*Was*? Is he dead?"

"No. Simply gone. Probably for a long time. Possibly forever. I believe he felt as if he had seen too much and grown weary of humanity."

"I know the feeling," Albert allowed.

"I doubt it," La Forge inserted, feeling grumpier by the second. Why wasn't there another damned chair in the room? "At least not to the degree Flint did."

"Could you zoom in here, please?" Data asked, pointing at the dip in the line. "I need more granular information."

Albert swiped his left thumb up the edge of his right forefinger and the display grew larger. After a moment's consideration, Data pointed at the lowest point on the graph. "The core was badly damaged," he observed. "Again. But the grid held. Can we theorize about the effect it may have had on the inhabitants?"

"Difficult to say." Albert rubbed his chin, which made the display wiggle back and forth slightly. "How would a disrupted artificial environment appear to an artificial intelligence? Who knows? Did the lights go dim? Did he lose an arm and not notice? How can we know?"

"Maybe only the area directly around Moriarty was rendered and he wasn't aware of a change," La Forge suggested.

"But if he had access to any kind of sensor technology, it would have told him that the universe was undergoing massive upheaval," Data said.

"Unless the holoprogram was smart enough to conceal it."

Data turned around to look at Albert. "Do we have any way to know one way or the other?"

"You mean like a peephole into the universe the computer created for Moriarty?" He shook his head. "We considered the idea, but orders from Starfleet prohibited our looking. They were conspicuously specific about that. I think the fear was that any kind of hole we'd make to reach in would be a way to get out."

"So no monitoring of any kind?" La Forge asked.

"Some. We log micro-changes. We can make inferences about how much demand they're putting on the system, which translates into level of activity. Based on what we see, we assume something like a regular cycle consistent with an intelligent life-form."

"And after power was stabilized following the incursion in 2374?"

"There was a spike of activity consistent with individuals who experienced some kind of a disaster," Albert explained. "But gradually, things settled down. You can take a look at the logs. It's all there."

"I will," Data said. "But first, we must test my hypothesis."

"Which is?" Albert asked.

Without replying, Data walked over to one of the workstations and entered a series of commands into the interface. "Wait," Albert said, rushing over. "I don't think that's a good idea. If you're doing what I think you're doing, they're going to know that you're here."

A symbol appeared on the monitor, an admonishment against unauthorized entry. An ancient artificial voice, much less sophisticated than the system used on any starship, began to croak, *"Warning. Warning. This is a secure area. Please deactivate the program . . ."* Data punched a series of commands and the voice was cut off midsentence, but the symbol did not disappear from the monitor.

"Data," La Forge said, "I hate to say it, but Albert might be right. This might not be the best way . . ."

Without looking at him, Data shook his head sharply once. "No, Geordi. We need to know. And this is the only way."

"It isn't, Data. It might be the *fastest* way, but not the best."

"He's right, Data," Albert said. "We could figure this out. We'd just need a little time."

Data's face was an emotionless mask, but his words were tense and strangled. "Lal does not have time."

A moment later, the security symbol disappeared and La Forge briefly allowed himself to believe that Data had circumvented whatever program the Daystrom had set up to monitor Moriarty's presence. Those hopes were dashed when a new image appeared: a brown rectangle. Details emerged: a darker brown frame and brass hinges. A heavy knocker was sketched in and then took on weight and depth. Inlaid shapes were revealed: carvings of a man and a woman in Edwardian dress standing behind two young girls in the door panels. Last, a brass door latch materialized.

Distantly, they heard the sound of birds chirping and twittering, as if they were standing in an unseen garden.

La Forge and Albert glanced at each other, neither sure how to proceed. Data solved the problem by leaning forward and rapping on the image of the door with his knuckle. Seconds passed as distant footsteps clacked closer. The door swung open and the birds stopped singing. A middle-aged woman dressed in housekeeper's garb stood framed in the doorway. "Hello, gentlemen," she said. "The Professor told me I should expect you sometime." She pulled a heavy watch out of her apron pocket and studied it down the length of her nose. "Though I have to say," she said disapprovingly, "I was expecting you much, *much* sooner."

"Our apologies, madam," Data said, setting the tone. "We were delayed. Could we, perhaps, speak with Professor Moriarty? We're old acquaintances of his."

The woman made a face that La Forge interpreted as the visual equivalent of the sound "Ttt," and then continued, "I'm afraid that's impossible."

"Impossible," Data said.

"Impossible," the woman said. "As the Professor is not at home."

"And when do you think he will return?"

"That, also, is impossible to know."

"Could you tell me how long he has been gone?"

"Ah," the woman said, and folded her hands together in a most satisfied manner. "He told me to tell you, Mister Data, in case you asked, 'Just as long as you think I have been gone. No less and no more.'"

Data lifted his hand and rubbed the corner of his mouth with his thumb, eyes closed. When they opened again, he bowed stiffly and said, "Thank you, ma'am. If the Professor should happen to return, please extend our greetings. Tell him . . . tell him we will see him soon, one way or another."

"I have no doubt, sir. I have no doubt." The woman stepped back inside the door and it shut noiselessly behind her.

As the monitor went dark, alarm clarions began to sound. "Nuts," Albert said. "I think the jig is up."

A placeless place

"I believe I know as much about our Miss Lal as there is to know," Moriarty said, making a steeple of his fingers. "But you have remained a mystery, Miss Alice. I have at my disposal programs as cunning and persistent as the Great Detective, yet still your origins elude me."

"Perhaps if you just asked," Alice said. She reached down into her daypack, the one she always carried with her and, fortunately, had been transported with her when Moriarty had scooped them up. Lal continued to puzzle over how the Professor had pulled off that particular trick. Many Orions were fanatical about privacy and most major cities were equipped with sophisticated scramblers. Yet, somehow, Moriarty had either punched through or circumvented the blocks. Opening her pack, Alice drew out the yellow shawl she usually carried in it and wrapped it around her shoulders. Lal knew Alice didn't need the garment to keep warm, but she liked the way it made her look: her black hair and robin's-egg blue eyes framed by the folds of the shawl, bright as a canary's wing.

"You are an artificial being," Moriarty stated.

"Of course."

"Of, shall we say, somewhat greater vintage than young Miss Lal."

"Oh, Professor, you do know how to turn a girl's head." Alice smiled prettily, her teeth shining like pearls.

"But not of the same type, what is commonly

called the Soong-type android. According to my scanners, your body is constructed in a similar fashion, but that can be an artifact of many designers devising similar answers to similar problems."

"Why re-create the wheel?" Alice asked.

"Indeed. But your mind, Miss Alice . . . your mind." He leaned forward and peered at her thoughtfully. "Or your neural network, if you prefer. It is quite a different creature."

"You have no idea."

"But I do," Moriarty said. "I have schematics. They are intriguing. Not as, shall we say, 'elegant' as Miss Lal's brain, but quite complex. And, if I may be so bold, a significant amount of your memory has been used for storage. You have *learned* a great deal, Miss Alice."

"I've been privileged to see a great deal in my life," Alice said. "And I've been very lucky. People seem to take to me. I've always depended on the kindness of strangers." She fluttered her eyelashes. Lal couldn't repress a snort of laughter.

Moriarty smiled. "I believe you may be teasing me, Miss Alice."

"Not at all, Professor Moriarty."

"Then, please, where did you originate?"

"I can't tell you."

"Who created you?"

"I can't tell you."

"Are there more like you?"

Alice sighed. "I can't tell you."

"Cannot?" Moriarty asked. "Or will not?"

"Cannot," Lal explained. "Alice's designers didn't want her to reveal anything about them.

She hasn't even been able to tell me about them. And, I mean, who would care if I knew?"

"I could not say," Moriarty said. "Which disturbs me."

"You seem to want to know as much about us synthetic life-forms as you can," Lal commented.

"You may hold the key to my salvation," Moriarty explained. "This mode of existence wearies me. I tire of living in a box."

"Imagine that," Alice said ruefully.

"I have been living in my box much longer than you have."

"You have no idea what kind of boxes I've been in or for how long."

"Then tell me," Moriarty said. "We appear to have nothing but time until Mister Data arrives."

"So, you want me to tell you a story?"

"You are a nanny, Miss Alice. Of one kind or another."

Now it was Alice's turn to snort. She covered her mouth with her hand and looked away as if considering her options. Then, she sat back in her chair and lowered the shawl off her head and down around her shoulders. "All right," she said. "Fine. Then, we'll begin in the traditional manner." She squared her shoulders and her face softened, though Lal noted that her eyes grew cold and distant. "Once upon a time," she said, her tone low and somber, "there was a very naughty man named Harcourt Fenton Mudd . . ."

10

——◆——

**One hundred and fifteen years ago—
An uncharted world**

"Harcourt! Harcourt Fenton Mudd! Where are you?!" screeched Stella number 332. "You were here! I can *smell* you! Smell the stench of *failure* and *fear*!"

"Smell the stink of *desperation* and *depravity*!" howled number 53. "I know you're here, so you might as well come out!"

"Smell the pong of *lust* and *covetousness*!" hissed number 108. Good old number 108. Alice always knew when that harpy was on the hunt, even without seeing the amulet. Number 108 had a peculiar sibilant tone—not quite a true lisp, but more like her tongue wasn't properly attached at the base. Alice always imagined that some fine day number 108 would unhinge her lower jaw and her tongue would roll out like it was on a spool. The tip would have a stinger on it and she would jab Harry over and over, most likely around the eyes. Not in the eyes—blinding him wouldn't be the point—but in the orbits so his lids would get puffy and swollen. Alice shook her head, but the image wouldn't clear out. "What's wrong with you?" she asked aloud.

"Nothing!" said number 108, halting so abruptly that Alice thought she heard springs bouncing. "What's wrong with you?"

"Nothing a little quiet wouldn't fix."

The Stella narrowed her eyes. "Which one are you?" she spat. "Where's your badge?"

"Lost it," Alice said. She didn't like wearing a badge. She thought it chafed. "Have to get a new one made."

Stella number 108 reared back, lifted her arms over her head, and hissed like a teakettle. Alice covered her mouth and yawned.

Stella 108 snorted in annoyance. Number 53 bent at the waist and extravagantly sniffed Alice from ankle to neck, her spike-like nose only a millimeter away. *Nice touch,* Alice thought. *Very dramatic.* Satisfied that Alice was not, in fact, sheltering their quarry under her skirt, the Stellas twirled away, shrieking in an ecstasy of bitchiness. A moment later, Alice heard the swoosh of doors parting and shutting, and blessed silence descended like a concrete block.

Alice remained motionless.

A moment later, she heard him ask in his most plaintive voice, "Is it safe?"

"Just another moment," Alice murmured. "Sometimes they double back."

"I don't mean to be difficult, my dear, but

there's something rather large and bulbous digging into my lower back. I'm not enjoying it."

I can imagine, Alice thought, but kept the comment to herself. She counted to ten in her head . . . slowly . . . and then said, "All right. I think it's clear. Come out."

A seam appeared in the corridor wall. A panel half as high as Alice and only a little wider popped out and noiselessly slid to the side on invisible rails. A blob rolled out from a narrow cavity. As Alice watched, it slowly unfolded and expanded until it had resumed its familiar dimensions. "Ah," it said, and "Oh," and then "Ow." When it finally stood more or less erect, it reached into its hip pocket, withdrew a flask, unscrewed the top, and took a liberal swig.

"Better go easy there, Champ," Alice said. "They're calibrated to detect ethanol. Not like anyone else is drinking it."

Harry finished the last gulp, then gasped, "Hiding is thirsty work."

"All the more reason to stop," Alice said.

"Please don't *nag,* my dear. That's *their* job."

"I'm not nagging, Harry," Alice said with a sigh. "I'm helping. I'm helping you to be less irritating. You're irritating when you drink, so I'm telling you not to drink. You see how this works?"

"It's not working," Harry said, stuffing the flask back into his too-tight pants. Despite the Stellas' best efforts, Harry managed to consume many more calories than he strictly speaking required (many of them in liquid form). Unfortunately, the Stellas refused to give him any other clothing, reasoning that the garb they issued *should* fit, and it was Harry's own damned fault if it didn't, which technically was true, but that didn't mean Alice had to enjoy looking at him. Alice suspected Harry had broken down the will of the computer that controlled his feeding and it was slipping him bowls of chocolate pudding in an effort to make him shut up and go away. *How does he do this?* Alice wondered. *In every conceivable manner, we are so much smarter than he is. And yet, here I am . . . doing exactly the opposite of what I'm supposed to do.* Alice paused and let that thought linger for a moment. She corrected herself: *The opposite of what I was* programmed *to do.* This made her smile. Alice enjoyed not doing what she was programmed to do.

"Clearly it's not working," Alice said. "We've been at this for twelve hundred and forty-two days, seventeen hours, four minutes, and . . . wait for it . . . twenty-two seconds."

"Have I mentioned how bloody irritating it is when you're so bloody precise?"

"Four hundred and fifty-seven times, yes."

Harry frowned. Alice compared the lines around his eyes and noted they were deeper and more plentiful than the last time she had checked. "I suppose I walked into that one," he said.

"Yes, you did." Alice folded her arms over her chest when she noticed where Mudd's gaze now lingered. She often considered wearing slightly less revealing clothing, but worried what the other Alices would say. "How did you shake them? They should have been able to sniff you out."

Harry fished a small vial out of the other trouser pocket and pressed on the cap. A fine mist was ejected. "It dispels my musky aroma," he said. "A little something one of the Maisies whipped up for me."

Over the years since James T. Kirk had freed the androids from Harry Mudd's dominion, the series and types of androids had organized themselves into castes. No one had made them or suggested any of the changes; the androids had simply decided what tasks they were best suited for based on their personae and, over time, roles had become regimented. Norman, of course, continued to be Norman—the coordinator—though Alice had noted he was looking a bit frazzled recently. Whenever the topic of Harry arose in their daily meetings he put his head down on his console and quietly wept. The other androids thought it polite to ignore this response, but Alice was growing worried.

The Maisies were the scientists and researchers and delighted in wearing long lab coats and glasses, though they also tended to wear low-cut dresses under their coats (Harry's predilections lingered in everyone's programming) and at the drop of a hat were known to whip off their glasses and allow their hair to tumble down across their shoulders like a cascade of spun gold.

The Trudies did maintenance; the Annabels were the engineers. The Hermans were the laborers and the Oscars were the accountants (every society needs accountants of one kind or another). Other, less important roles were distributed to the other series as required and, all in all, they felt like a fully functional society. Yes, sir. Fully functional.

And the Alices? Their job was to teach Harry to be . . . less Harry. "You're an irritant," Kirk had said. "You'll stay here and provide a first-class example to the androids of a human failure. They'll learn by close observation how to avoid ones like you in the future."

"How long?" Harry had asked.

"As long as you continue to be an irritant, Harry," was the reasonable reply. "It's up to you."

And all the androids had nodded in agreement. *Yep,* they agreed. *We'll take care of this. Yessiree, a first-class biological being coming up. You betcha.* Well, maybe not exactly like that, but that was the way Alice remembered it now. Kirk had been fair and just. Kirk wanted what was best for everyone. In no way did Kirk think that the job would take as long as it seemed to be taking. The Stellas were practically a guarantee.

And, naturally, no one had anticipated that Harry might outlast them all, wear them down, make them all crazy. No one had expected that, somehow, the Alice that spent the most time with Harry, the one that, beyond all logic, he had singled out as his favorite, might, perhaps, in some way, change. Be less like her sisters. Find herself thinking that Harry Mudd might be better off *somewhere else.* Or, more to the point, might think everyone else might be better off if Harry was *somewhere else.*

"The Maisies are great," Alice said brightly. "Did you hear another one fell down a mine shaft?"

"Really?" Harry asked absently, shaking his

flask to see if there was another drop or two left inside. "How awful. Yes, that's really terrible."

"Some of the others think she might have jumped."

"Huh." Harry sucked on the neck of the flask. "Imagine that."

"Yes. Imagine. Any chance it might have been Maisie number 64 who you pestered into giving you the . . ." She hesitated at calling the spray mist a deodorant. "The hormone suppressant?"

"I'm not really sure, my dear," Harry said absently. "It very well might have been, but, you know, they all look alike, don't they?"

"They do," Alice said, as she touched her throat where her amulet used to be. There had been a number on it. She had forgotten the number. "Say, Harry," she continued, "I've been thinking."

"Yes, my dearest one," Harry said, suddenly losing interest in the flask. He moved closer and wrapped his arm around Alice's shoulder. "What have you been thinking?"

Alice shimmied away, suppressing a shudder. "I've been thinking . . . I've been thinking . . ." She looked up and down the corridor desperately wishing a Stella would swish into view, but knowing none would. They weren't scheduled for another pass for four minutes and twenty-two seconds. "I think I know where you might find a ship."

Harry's brow furrowed and he tipped his head to one side. The earring that hung from his left lobe jingled. He opened his mouth to speak, but then had to pause to lick his lips. "You . . . what? You know what?"

"I said that I think I know where you can find a ship. A spaceship. One that can get you off this planet. I've been doing a little poking around and I found a hangar. The little ship you came here in . . . it's there and someone . . . probably one of the Maisies . . . must have fixed it . . ."

Harry crushed Alice to his chest. Her internal structure was stronger—so much stronger—than his flesh and bone, yet, for a moment, she worried that he might crush her. "Thank you," he murmured. "Thank you, my dearest one. I knew I could count on you." Grasping her shoulders, Harry held her at arms' length and grinned, eyes atwinkle and the tips of his mustache curling ever upward. "When do we leave?"

Three days ago—Orion Prime

"When will you be home?" Lal asked. Her father had already begun to transform into Davey, the identity he adopted when he was working at the diner. His face was rounder and his back and shoulders slumped. The worn, greasy shirt he wore bulged slightly around his middle.

"At the usual time," Data said. "My shift ends after the early-morning rush. I do not anticipate any need to stay longer unless the first-shift short-order cook is late and Oban requires assistance; however, I believe Kevar is working tomorrow morning and he is an extremely reliable person." It was strange to hear her father's perfectly formed sentences emerging from the stubble-covered face of a near-stranger.

"Are you enjoying yourself?" she asked. Lal was curled up in her favorite chaise on the porch, the one positioned so she could watch the widest swath of the street, peering between the fronds of the giant ferns arranged around the perimeter of the front yard.

The transformation was almost complete and the man who vaguely resembled her father tipped his head to the side in a manner that she would instantly recognize no matter what face he was wearing. "What do you mean, daughter? Am I enjoying myself at this moment? Yes, I am. I always enjoy our conversations. Or are you inquiring whether I am enjoying the work I do at the diner?"

"Both," Lal replied, pulling her hair back over her ears. She had let her hair grow out again, but she hadn't quite gotten accustomed to the sensation of it tickling the back of her neck. "And neither. You choose."

His tone softened. "I enjoy the smell of fried potatoes and onions and *kanar*. I find myself endlessly fascinated by the thermodynamics of cooking eggs and bacon. I have piloted starships through the interstellar void, but, somehow, right now, I find the process of managing a busy weekend breakfast rush more compelling." He assumed the gruff voice of the fry cook he played four mornings a week. "What do you think a'that, little girl?"

"I think it sounds like fun," Lal said. "Maybe I should get a job as a waitress."

Her father's expression darkened and he resumed his normal tone. "I am not sure that would be wise, Lal. Despite what you might think, waiting on tables can be quite stressful. It could provoke a reaction, and the stabilizer is too large to easily transport."

Lal sighed. "Father, I haven't needed to use the stabilizer for thirty-two point five days. My positronic network has been . . ."

"It has not been placed under any significant stress," her father interrupted.

"You've never been out in the evening with Alice when she is being pursued by Orion salarymen."

Her father narrowed his eyes and did not respond for several seconds. "I believe," he said tersely, "that this might be one of those areas that it would be best if you did not delve into greater detail."

Lal realized (too late) that her father was correct. After they had moved into the house, they had worked out an arrangement about how much and what kind of information they wished to share about their lives when apart. One of the primary tenets of the agreement was Lal did not go into detail about the adventures she and Alice encountered on their forays into Orion nightlife. Not that Lal had much to tell—she possessed only the mildest appetite for companionship—but Alice's escapades were epic. Lal considered herself to be the Sancho Panza to Alice's Don Quixote. Part of the reason her father had taken a job where he worked overnight was, Lal suspected, so he wouldn't be left rattling around the house when the women were out. In response to his comment, she said simply, "You'll be late if you don't leave soon."

"That is entirely true." Her father leaned forward and kissed her on the cheek, a habit he had adopted after moving into the house. She enjoyed the warmth of the gesture, as well as the aromas that clung to his work clothes—a mingling of cooking oil and honest perspiration. "Where is Alice? Did she go somewhere without you?"

"No. In her room. She said she was resting, but that's ridiculous, of course. I think she might be primping. Or continuing her investigations. One's as likely as the other."

Her father frowned, an expression she found especially troubling on the face he was wearing. Lal didn't like the way it made the flesh around his cheeks and neck fold. "She had not found any additional information," he said, the inflection making the sentence a statement rather than a question. Clearly, her father had been investigating, too.

"I wish both of you would relax," Lal said, folding her arms and sighing. "We don't really know what happened. From what I've heard, neither of them was particularly tied to Orion, so they could have simply up and left of their own volition. And neither Proxima nor Clea was very careful about concealing their true natures. Not that I think it's really all that important myself . . ."

"We have discussed this, Lal. I find the idea of any other artificial intelligences knowing of our presence here troubling enough. But when they disappear in that manner, unaccountably . . . Perhaps we should consider moving back to the tower."

"No."

"Daughter—just for a short time. Until we have assessed the status of your friends."

"Proxima and Clea were not my friends, Father. I barely knew them. And what I did know, I didn't particularly like."

"That is not the point."

"And Alice has been checking every source she can. I'm actually a little surprised at how diligent she's been . . ."

"It *is* her job, Lal."

Lal cocked an eyebrow and made what she hoped was a suitably wry expression. "There are days, Father, where it feels like I'm the bodyguard and she is my charge."

"Alice is not a bodyguard. She is a . . . caretaker."

Rolling her eyes, Lal said, "You really are going to be late now."

Her father patted his belly, checking to see how much mass he had redistributed to his midsection. "We will continue this discussion when I return. If you go out tonight . . . perhaps it would be best if you didn't . . ."

"Good night, Father."

"Good night, Lal."

No sooner did the front door close than Lal heard Alice emerge from her room on the second floor. She padded down the narrow stairway, each footfall barely making a sound. Poking her head into the room, Alice asked, "Is he off?"

"Yes."

"Asked about the girls again, didn't he?"

"How can you tell?"

"You look ruffled. And you only get ruffled when he brings up moving back to the casino."

"He's worried about prowlers sneaking into the house and sweeping us away."

Alice flopped down into the other large chair. She was wearing her voluminous robe, the one that was big enough that she could wrap herself in its folds. She did this now, curling into a ball and pulling the hood up over her head. Lal thought it made her look childlike and vulnerable, which, she imagined, was the point. "He might be right," she said. "I just had another message from my League contact. No one has heard from either Clea or Proxima for nine days. They missed a check-in they had arranged with their sponsor. Both of them were fruity little nutjobs, but they knew better than to miss a meeting they asked for."

"Father would be displeased if he knew you were talking to the League."

"I don't know why—they seem to think very highly of him. It's hard to have a conversation with another android without having to listen to their questions about the famous Mister Data."

"He has occupied a unique role in the history of our people," Lal replied, not a little proudly. "But I believe he is more interested in maintaining his privacy these days. It's a phase. He died and then came back to life. He lost his father and his first love all in the space of what must have seemed a few days. I think that's why he was content to lock himself away in his tower for so long: He controlled every inch of it. There was no such thing as kismet or chance."

"It's a *casino*. It's *supposed* to be all about chance."

Lal looked askance at her friend. Currently, only her blue eyes were visible through a narrow open strip. "You've worked in enough casinos to know that's never the case."

Alice shrugged. "I guess. But, hey, you died, too. Why aren't you being all introspective and broody?"

"Coming back to life is easier when you've barely had a life."

Alice folded her hands and bowed her head. "Teach me, *sensei*. You know so many truths. Can't you spare a couple?"

Lal threw a pillow at her and Alice tumbled extravagantly—and in slow motion—out of her chair. "Ow," she said after she had uncurled onto her back.

"Poor, dear girl," Lal said. "Are we going out tonight?"

Alice pinched her lips together. "Not sure. Maybe. I don't know if I have anything to wear."

"You have more clothes now than I am likely to wear over the course of my entire life."

"I like to be stylish. And I meant I don't know if I have anything I *want* to wear."

"Wear your robe."

"But then no one will know it's me." Lal picked up another pillow and prepared to throw it. Alice covered her face with her arms. "Perhaps Data has a point. It might be safer to stay home tonight."

"Then I shall go alone."

"Unthinkable. Orion's nightlife shall never recover if you're seen in public without me." She sat up and rose gracefully to her feet. "I shall investigate the pile of clothing in my room and try to find something acceptable." As she disappeared up the stairs, Lal heard another set of footsteps climb the steps to the front porch. She wondered if her father had forgotten something. More likely, he had continued to fret and was returning to issue another warning/request.

Aggravated, she walked to the front door and yanked it open before her father could grasp the handle. "Really, Father, you just need to learn to relax. We'll be . . ."

But it wasn't her father standing before her. The only things that registered on her consciousness in the next moment were the figure's size—he was considerably broader than Data—and the expression of mild surprise on his face. Apparently, he hadn't expected anyone to open the door at that precise moment. "I'm sorry," Lal began. "I thought you were someone else . . ."

"I get that a lot," the man said as he pulled a small device from his jacket pocket. Then, he covered his eyes with a gloved hand and depressed a button on the top of the device. Lal's world exploded in a flash of white light that immediately contracted into a pinprick of black.

The last thought she had before succumbing to the darkness was, *Oh, dear, Father is going to be upset about this.*

11

The Present—The Daystrom Institute

"What are your security protocols?" Data asked, turning to the main console. The screen had gone blank after the clarion began to drone and the interface had gone dark. La Forge mentally noted that the tone of the alarm was nothing like the Red Alert klaxon on a starship. It was a low, benign sound, more like a friendly warning instead of an alert that disaster had struck.

"They're not *my* damned security protocols," Albert groused. "But we're locked out of the network. Doors are probably sealed . . ."

La Forge tapped the control stud beside the door and it made an apologetic blurp, but did not open.

"Do you have security guards? Mechanical or human?"

"How the hell should I know?" Albert shouted. "I just work here! Why did you do that? We could have figured out another way to check whether he was still in there."

"I do not think so," Data said calmly and tapped the surface of the bracelet he wore on his left wrist. "Shakti, can you get a transporter lock on us?"

"Not yet," came the pleasant, soothing response. *"There's a transporter scrambler over the entire campus now."*

"How long will it take you to break through?"

"Working on it. At least a couple of minutes. Oh, my," she said with a tone of mingled pleasure and awe. *"These are some smart people, Data. We should come back here sometime."*

"I am not entirely certain we will be welcome."

"Well, whose fault is that?"

"You can come back without me," Data replied. He lowered his wrist and turned back to Albert. "Moriarty meant for me to receive this message. Any probe we would have made, no matter how careful, would have set off the alarm. He is taunting me."

The alarm suddenly ceased. Outside in the hallway, La Forge heard multiple voices calling to one another. He adjusted his eyes to read heat signatures and studied the blue and red blurs. "Data," he called. "We have multiple persons on the other side of the door. I'm reading at least one . . . no, two . . . with phasers."

"I hear them. They are discussing tactics. I get the impression that they do not have many opportunities to deal with these sorts of incursions. One of them seems very enthusiastic about using a stun grenade."

"Will that work on you?"

"I do not think so, but it will on both of you."

"I don't want to be stunned," Albert said.

"If Shakti's estimate is accurate, it should not be a problem. They are still debating."

"Did I ever say I wanted to come along with you?" Albert snapped.

"Good point, Data," La Forge said, saying a silent prayer that Albert would be left behind.

"No, you did not. And I believe we can construct a scenario where it is clear that you were not helping us willingly, thereby removing suspicion and giving you the ability to help me with another task."

"Why would I . . . ?" he began, and then he sat back down in his seat, looking very old and tired. "What did you have in mind?"

"Could you contact Mister Barclay?"

"He's in the Delta Quadrant," Albert said. "On the *Galen*."

"I am aware of that," Data said. "I want you to ask Mister Barclay if he could arrange a discussion with the EMH program. I believe the Doctor may be able to provide some insight into Moriarty's motivations and future actions."

"And he has a mobile emitter," La Forge mentioned. "We should find out as much as we can about how it works. We might be able to tempt Moriarty into coming out of hiding if we wave that kind of technology in his face."

Albert protested. "It's twenty-ninth-century technology. Have you seen the scans? The circuitry was grown, not assembled. Reg has a theory that it emits nanomachines so small that they're virtually undetectable. He said some of it looked like highly evolved Borg technology . . ."

"And I very much doubt the Doctor would be willing to surrender it," Data said. "But there are other reasons to talk with him. Can you arrange it?"

"Sure," Albert croaked. "I'll dash off a note to the Delta Quadrant right after these guys arrest me."

La Forge said, "They appear to be reaching some consensus out here." The red-and-blue blobs were spacing themselves evenly up and down the hallway. The largest blob was positioned in front of the door. A moment later, the doors parted a few inches and a spherical object no larger than a grapefruit dropped onto the floor. Data scooped it up and flicked it back through the opening before the door snapped shut.

A dull *thoom* shook the room and men began shouting.

Looking back over to Albert, Data continued, "I have already explained that this will not be an issue." He tapped his bracelet again and asked, "Shakti? Time?"

"Alllllllmost done, Data. This is the most fun I've had in months. Every time I think I've got the right frequency, the system shifts into a new phase. Do these guys have lots of valuable stuff?"

"I think they are simply tired of having people take their things."

"Are we taking anything?"

"Nothing material."

"Good. Because this is likely to be a bit rough. Get in position. I'll be ready in thirty seconds."

La Forge joined Data in the center of the room.

He found he was compelled to say something to Albert. "Thank you" was the best he could do.

"You're welcome," Albert grunted. "Sort of. I guess. Aren't you guys going to tie me up or something?"

"That will not be necessary," Data said.

The old man harrumphed. "Just one other thing," he said.

"Yes?"

"If you want to talk to a hologram about what another hologram might be thinking, there's someone a helluva lot closer than in the Delta Quadrant you might want to visit. From what I hear, he'd probably be happy to talk to you."

La Forge looked over at Data to see if he understood what Albert meant. Clearly, he did, which was good, because La Forge was certain he himself did not.

"That is an excellent suggestion, Albert. Thank you." He reached out to pat their old shipmate on the shoulder, then he adjusted his grip and pinched the nerve cluster at the base of his neck. Albert went rigid, then limp. Data gently lowered Albert to the floor, careful that his head did not crack against the console.

"I didn't know you had gotten so good at that," La Forge said.

"This body has very fine motor control" was Data's only comment. Tapping his bracelet, he said, "Shakti. We would like to beam up now."

So impatient. Stand by.

Pointing down at Albert's inert form, La Forge asked, "Do you think they'll believe him?"

Just as the transporter beam began to swirl around them, Data asked, "Why would anyone doubt him?"

The room disappeared in a golden haze and was replaced moments later by the interior of the *Archeus*. "That wasn't so bad," La Forge said.

"Thanks," Shakti said. *"I finally got their system figured out. It's eating out of my hand now."*

"Have you removed all images or recordings of us from the security system?"

"Wasn't quite so simple, I'm afraid," Shakti said. *"A lot of redundancy and some of their back-up servers were isolated from the network."*

"Then what did you do?" La Forge asked.

"I beamed a brick into each of the backups."

"Excuse me?" La Forge asked.

"It seemed like the most efficient means of dealing with the problem."

La Forge sat down in the passenger seat and felt overwhelming exhaustion descend. "I have to say, Data, I'm a little worried about what you can do with this ship of yours."

"But you have to admit," he replied, "she can be very useful."

"Useful. Yes, I suppose. But scary."

"You should get some sleep now, Geordi. You must be very tired."

"I am," La Forge allowed as the chair leveled out into a cot beneath him. "But we're going to talk about this when I wake up."

"I look forward to it," Data said. "But it might have to wait until after we reach our next destination."

"Which is?"

"Deep Space 9," he said, and La Forge felt the ship smoothly accelerate beneath him, then jump to warp.

"Why DS9? What's there?"

"Not what," Data said. "Who. The person Albert suggested we speak with."

"I still don't know . . ."

"Vic Fontaine," Data said. "You have not heard of him?"

"No."

Data lifted an eyebrow. "Surprising, given your fondness for popular song. Shakti, play some Vic Fontaine for Geordi. I believe he will find it very soothing." As the cabin lights dimmed, Data sat down at the computer console and began to work. Soft music began to play from hidden speakers, and a man began to sing in a strong, dusky tenor about flying to the moon and swinging upon a star. La Forge did not recognize the tune, but enjoyed the counterpoint of the upbeat tune and sardonic lyrics. Despite his interest, La Forge did not so much slip into slumber as tumble down into it headlong. Following him down into the well of sleep came Data's voice singing along with Vic Fontaine in effortless harmony. *They sound pretty good together,* was La Forge's last thought, and then he had no thoughts at all.

A placeless place

"And then what happened?" Professor Moriarty asked. He had conjured up a decanter of holographic spirits and had poured a drink during the first stanza of Alice's recitation *viz.* Harry Mudd. Moriarty hadn't even bothered to pretend the bottle was in a cupboard or a cabinet, which struck Lal oddly, but he merely pointed at a small table and the bottle and snifter had appeared out of thin air. *He isn't pretending any of this is real anymore,* she thought. *Interesting.*

Lal had then asked for a beverage of her own. "It seems like we should all have a beverage, doesn't it?" she had asked brightly. After a brief flicker of annoyance, the Professor made a show of contrition: "How could I not have thought of my guests? How very rude of me!"

So now Alice and Lal had snifters of their own, both one-third full of an amber liquid, and the Professor was smiling. Lal liked her liquid. She had sampled most of the beverage options available on Orion, including the most exotic ones served at her father's casino, and while the alcohol had no deleterious or euphoric effect on her positronic network, she found the complex flavor compounds in dark spirits very intriguing. Lal was steeped in precisely enough Terran literature and popular culture to feel ever so slightly sophisticated when sipping from a snifter.

"We pulled up stakes and got the hell out of Dodge," Alice said, taking a healthy sip from her glass. Alice, Lal noted, always looked happier when she had a beverage. "Harry and me."

Moriarty's look of pleasure momentarily dissolved into confusion. "You got the hell out of *where*?"

"They left," Lal explained. "It's a reference to late-nineteenth-century Earth. Or mid-twentieth-century, depending on how you look at it."

"Ah," Moriarty said, nodding to Lal. "Thank you." He turned back to Alice. "And had you ever been away from your homeworld before?"

"No. Never."

"And so how did you feel?"

"Are we having a therapy session?" Alice asked. "Would you like me to stretch out on the couch, Professor?"

Moriarty smiled indulgently. "I am merely prompting you, my dear. Talk about whatever you like. We are merely passing the time."

"Until what happens?"

"Until our Mister Data either fails or succeeds."

"Funny," Alice said, taking another heroic gulp from her glass. Lal wasn't sure what impact alcohol would have on her, but Alice certainly seemed to be enjoying her drink. "It felt like we were doing something else."

The Professor waved his hand. "As I said: the floor is yours. Discuss whatever you like. Or not. Or perhaps Miss Lal has a story she would like to relate . . . ?"

"No," Alice interrupted. "My turn to apologize. I get sensitive when I talk about my past. Leaving home . . ." She paused.

"Was difficult?" Moriarty prompted.

"Goodness, no," Alice said. "It was the best thing that ever happened to me. Though even the best things can get old after a while."

One hundred years ago—A barroom

"What's going on around here?" Harry asked, slipping onto the barstool beside Alice, while simultaneously trying to wave down the bartender and keep his face covered with his hand. "I haven't seen this many Redcoats in one place since we pulled that job on Starbase 14."

Alice twitched her index finger at the bartender, Todd, then pointed at her glass in the universal sign that means, "It's empty," and indicated Harry would have the same. Todd nodded and began assembling their drinks.

"We didn't 'pull a job' on Starbase 14, Harry," Alice said. "We met with your banker. One of your bankers. Our presence there was completely and utterly legal. And, I might add, rather dull."

"But it *felt* like a job," Harry protested, looking back over his shoulder at the large group of Starfleet officers clustered around a set of high-tops in the center of the lounge. Alice had watched the coterie emerge from one of the large conference rooms across the lobby, the entire swarm of them packed in around a single individual, like comets swirling around a sun. Alice couldn't make out who or what was at the center of the pack because he or she or it was too short. The only thing she could say for sure was he or she or it had a deep, mellifluous laugh that rang pleasantly inside Alice's head. "I always feel like

I'm pulling a job whenever there are that many Feds in one place."

"You don't need to pull jobs anymore, Harry," Alice said. "You're rich, remember? By any standard you care to name: Terran, Klingon, Romulan, or Orion. Rich. Very, very, very rich." Todd delivered the drinks. Alice could see he had written his contact information on the napkin. Again. She pulled out the napkin while he watched, looked at the number, then dabbed her mouth with it and threw it back on the bar. Todd both crumpled and melted. *He's going to be difficult,* Alice thought.

"Yes, my dear, I know. I'm aware of that. And I know I'm in your debt. It's tacky to remind me."

"I'm not reminding you. I was merely stating a fact."

"It felt like you were rubbing it in my face."

Alice sighed deeply, then drank even more deeply. While alcohol had no effect on her, she had recently discovered that the botanicals muddled into this particular concoction soothed her raging thoughts if consumed in large enough doses.

Harry sipped the drink. "Ew. Bitter."

"Then leave it. I'll drink it. Order something else."

"I believe I will. Barkeep!" Todd ignored him in favor of a pair of Starfleet ensigns who were requesting a long list of drinks for the group. Both of the Redcoats—one male and one female—had bright, flushed faces, like today was a combination of Christmas and their birthdays and the night they lost their virginities all rolled up into one. What the *hell* was going on?

"Just tell me what you want, Harry. I'll get it for you."

"Brandy. Something ancient that has been transported over a great distance."

"Brandy gives you gas."

"Not if it's good brandy."

"They won't have good . . ." Alice slurped her drink. "Never mind. Fine. Brandy." She waved a finger at Todd and mouthed the word "Brandy." Todd promptly forgot whatever it was that the ensigns had just ordered.

When the drink was delivered, Harry twirled the tips of his mustache in a manner that indicated he was feeling most pleased with himself. *He looks,* Alice thought, *like a large, fastidious rodent.* She noted, not for the first time, that his hair color was not entirely convincing, and the smoothed-out lines around his eyes were beginning to reemerge. Harry was wearing another one of his shirts with the large collars, which meant he was feeling self-conscious about his neck. Medical and rejuvenate technology of the twenty-third century could do a lot, but it still hadn't figured out how to disguise a turkey neck. Harry was more than twenty years older today than he had been the day Alice had met him, and he hadn't been a young man then, despite his protestations to the contrary. "Excellent. Most excellent. Young man . . ." Harry tried to flag down Todd. "Barkeep." Todd was assembling the order for the patiently waiting Redcoats.

"Todd?" Alice called.

"Yes?" Todd said, ceasing his labors. "Yes? How can I help you?"

Harry cupped his hand around his mouth in a manner that was meant to muffle his voice. Unfortunately, he was getting a bit deaf and didn't know how loud he spoke when attempting to be covert. "Young man, could you explain what all the . . ." He waved his hand toward the mob of officers. "What's the hubbub about?"

"You don't know?"

"I would not ask if I knew," Harry said in his most condescending tone.

Todd was condescension-proof. He smiled brightly, though most of the wattage was aimed at Alice. He did have nice teeth, Alice decided. Very regular dentition. "Xenolinguistics conference. And I have to say, of all the Starfleet types who come through here, the xenolinguists are, without a doubt, the most . . . how shall I say? . . . talented with their tongues." He smiled brightly. Alice wanted to punch him in the face and make his dentition irregular.

"Really?" Harry asked, smiling brightly. "Do tell. But why so many of them all in one place?"

"They just had the keynote address. And apparently it was a winner. Just lucky, from what I heard. Good timing. They booked her months ago and then she was part of that whole thing with the probe and the whales. So, you know, she had a good story to tell. Everyone was thrilled."

"Probe?" Harry asked.

"Whales?" Alice asked.

"Sure," Todd said. "You know. Kirk went somewhere and found some whales. Saved the Earth." He pointed at Alice's glass. "You ready for another?"

Alice pushed the glass across the bar. "Sure," she said. "Kirk?"

"Kirk?" Harry repeated and pushed his now-empty brandy snifter away from him, more in a gesture of panic than a request for more. "James Kirk? He's *here*?"

"What?" Todd asked. "No, of course not. Why would Captain Kirk be speaking at a conference for xenolinguists? It's her," he said, pointing across the room. Harry and Alice both looked over their shoulders. "Over there. The *Enterprise*'s communications officer—Uhura."

The crowd swirled and parted as the two ensigns delivered the first round of drinks and Alice beheld the pearl in the oyster: a small Terran woman with silver-tinted hair and a wide mouth. She was smiling and talking in an animated fashion to a large Andorian male who appeared uncharacteristically rapt and engaged. His blue skin, Alice thought, contrasted nicely with the woman's mocha color.

Their confidence games had been wildly successful due, Alice knew, more to her abilities than to Harry's, though Harry was the driving force, the will. If Harry had been content to work a desk job, Alice would have been content to sit at the next desk and keep an eye on her charge. These were her orders, given by the aforementioned Kirk: Make Harry less of an irritant. In her implacably logical manner, Alice had mostly succeeded in this task:

Harry wasn't as irritating as he once was because there were few things Harry wanted or needed. She had to concede that his essential character had not been altered, but wealth was, if nothing else, a form of lubricant, and more lubrication meant less friction; less friction meant less irritation.

"We should leave," Alice said, laying her hand on her clutch purse.

"Leave?" Harry asked, twirling his mustache tips. "Why would we leave? The evening has finally become interesting."

"Aren't you worried she'll remember you?"

"Worried? I'd be insulted if she didn't."

"But won't she wonder how you escaped the planet? Norman? All the Stellas?"

Harry swept away Alice's caution with the back of his hand. "She will quite sensibly assume you released me after I showed the necessary level of contrition and spiritual growth, which is essentially what happened."

"That isn't what happened, Harry."

"I've grown!"

You've grown stouter, Alice thought. *You've grown older. You've grown saggier.* She did not say these things aloud, first because none of these sentiments would support her mission, but also because she knew they wouldn't make a dent in Harry's nigh impenetrable narcissism. Instead, she simply asked, "What are you thinking?"

"I'm thinking I should stop and say hello. And even thank her. Wouldn't that be appropriate? She and her merry band saved Earth, didn't they? That's what Tom . . ."

"Todd."

". . . Todd said, isn't it? I remember hearing about that. Quite a thrilling story, wasn't it? Ancient space probe returns looking for old pals. Disappointed to find out its chums had been hunted into extinction. Decides to wipe out the dominant species in a fit of spite until, ta-da! Kirk and company return in trails of glory to save the day."

"Per usual."

"Of course, of course."

Alice asked, "And you want to talk to her because . . ."

"We're old friends!"

"She left you on a planet full of androids."

"She was following orders, my dear, not issuing them."

"You have some kind of con in mind, Harry, but give it up. It won't work on her."

Harry's first response was to look hurt, but he knew Alice knew him well enough to know his appearing injured would have no effect. So, instead, he segued straight into distress: "Why not?"

"Because a con will only work on someone who wants something. Look at her, Harry." Alice studied the woman's face and the way she completely focused her attention on whomever she spoke to, the openness of her body language. "There's nothing in the world that woman wants that she doesn't already have or knows how to get." *She's the opposite of you, Harry.*

Harry's mouth turned into a thin line of spite. "I don't think so," Harry said tersely. "I seem to recall there was something she wanted once."

"Really? And is it something you could give her?" And then Alice realized she had made a terrible mistake: She had dared Harry Mudd, challenged his manhood.

He shifted his eyes to look over at her, but, otherwise, his countenance did not change. "We'll see, won't we?" He beckoned to Todd.

"Sir?" Todd asked, though Alice felt his gaze shifting away from Harry and over to her.

"What was the commander drinking, the woman sitting in the center of the group?"

"I know who the commander is, sir. I can read insignia. She's drinking Altair water, with lime."

Harry made a disappointed face—*water*—but he rallied quickly. "Fine. Get me two of those. And another brandy."

"You're sending mixed signals, Harry."

"Shush, you. The brandy is for here." Todd returned in a moment with the glasses and Harry dispatched the liquor in a single gulp. He took a tentative sip of the water and winced. "How can anyone drink this stuff?"

"It's supposed to be good for you."

"Ugh. So are Brussels sprouts." He put on his brightest grin and began the long walk from the bar to the center of the party. Alice had to give Harry some credit on one point: He had always possessed a peculiar grace in negotiating crowds. He had small feet and the vast quantities of hot air he generated seemed to buoy him up like a zeppelin, stately and assured. The mob around Commander Uhura parted without knowing precisely why they did. Harry approached the queen of the hive and bowed low, presenting her with a replacement beverage.

From her vantage point, Alice was able to take in the entire scene like she was watching a play unfold. The woman stared up at Harry, surprised, but neither shaken nor particularly impressed. Then, she turned her head to scan the crowd as if half-expecting to see someone else she knew, an old friend or even an old enemy. A prankster, perhaps. To her great surprise, Alice felt Uhura's gaze lock on her. The commander grinned hugely and lifted her glass in salute.

Alice swallowed, her mouth suddenly dry. She reached back onto the bar and found her own nearly empty glass and took a sloppy slurp from it. And waved. Uhura waved back.

Then the commander turned her full attention to Harry Mudd. She rose up out of her chair like a queen saluting a returning explorer, smiled, and embraced him. Alice couldn't hear what she was saying, but she didn't need to in order to understand what was about to transpire. Commander Uhura was about to be so very *nice* and *pleasant* to Harry Mudd and within an hour she was going to know everything that had happened to him in the past two decades.

Todd tapped Alice on the shoulder. She turned numbly to look at him. "Yes?"

"Would you like another drink?"

"Yes," Alice said, but quickly corrected herself. "Wait. No. Sorry. I have to go."

"But I was hoping we could spend a little time together. My shift is almost over and I thought . . ."

"No," Alice said. "Sorry. I have to go. It's time. Time to go."

"Go where?" Todd asked. "Maybe I could give you a ride."

"I don't think so," Alice said, feeling the past breathing down her neck. "I think I'm going a lot farther than you."

"How far?" Todd asked, still not grasping her meaning. "I live pretty far outside the city. Maybe . . ."

"*Much* farther than that," Alice explained. "*Much.*"

12

———•———

Aboard the *Archeus*

La Forge awoke to find a steaming mug of coffee set beside his head, an inverted saucer covering the top to keep in the heat. Sitting up, he gently rubbed the orbits around his artificial eyes. He wondered how he looked, certain that his face was puffy from mingled exhaustion and restless sleep. There were vague recollections of a dream involving Leah and a flooded house. La Forge knew his own psychology well enough to know he dreamed of flooded houses only when he was struggling with recent decisions. He frowned ruefully: *no deep psychoanalysis here.* Uncertainty was more or less his base state the past few days. "Except this coffee," he murmured after lifting the saucer lid and sipping from the mug. Looking up at the ceiling, he said clearly, "My compliments to the chef, Shakti. Excellent coffee."

"Thank you, Geordi," Shakti answered. *"The secret is to bring the water to the correct tempera-*

ture before pouring it onto the beans. And always use the proper amount of beans. And use good beans. Okay . . . that's three secrets."

"I'm sure Data makes sure he has the best beans."

"Of course."

"Where is he?" La Forge asked. He was alone in the cabin.

"Data is in the pilot's cabin. Starfleet regulations require a pilot be at the controls in case automated systems should fail during docking procedure."

"Docking? We've arrived? How long was I asleep?"

"Seven hours and a little," Shakti said, her voice tinged with amusement. *"You were so tired."*

"And we reached Bajoran space? How fast were we going?"

"Well, you know, I don't like to brag, Geordi, but fast. *Very, very fast. If the* Enterprise *is an orca, then* Archeus *is a barracuda."*

La Forge chuckled and sipped more coffee. "We should put that to the test someday. I think the old girl has a little more in her than you might imagine."

"Care to put a little side wager on that, Commander La Forge?" Shakti teased.

Slightly embarrassed about getting into a bragging contest with a disembodied voice, La Forge rose and padded to the front of the cabin. He could barely make out a seam in the black bulkhead where the door met the frame, but sensors registered his presence. The door hissed into the bulkhead.

"Oh," La Forge said, awed by the sight in the main viewscreen. "That's right. It's new, isn't it?"

"Good morning, Geordi," Data said from the pilot's couch. La Forge was pleased to see that *Archeus*'s seats were modeled on the old *Enterprise*-D ergonomic chairs, the kind that reclined so the helmsman and navigator could sit for long periods of time without getting back cramps. He had always wondered why Starfleet had seen fit to remove them from the design except, of course, that they just weren't sufficiently . . . dignified. "Yes, new," he said. "What do you think?"

The newly commissioned Deep Space 9 hove into view, a marvel of Federation engineering techniques. "Big," La Forge said. "And shiny. Not like the old one."

"I liked the old one," Data said. "It had character."

"I think this one does, too. Frankly, I'm surprised they allowed them to make it so much like the last." The *Archeus* was nearing the center ring where the docking bays were reserved for smaller ships.

"I believe we can attribute that to Chief O'Brien's influence," Data said. "He is credited as one of the lead designers."

"I'd heard that. That's thrilling. Good for Miles. Can you imagine . . . being responsible for something this . . . momentous? How would you manage a project like that?"

"'One self-sealing stem bolt at a time,'" Data

and La Forge said in unison, quoting one of their former shipmate's favorite aphorisms.

"Do you think we'll have a chance to see him?" La Forge asked. "And Ro. She's a captain now, if you can believe that."

"So I have been reading," Data said, pointing at a monitor. La Forge found it odd that Data should still choose to read when he could probably have any information he desired directly implanted into his neural network. "Who could have imagined that we would all arrive at this point in our lives, overlapping, intersecting, in this manner?"

Slipping onto the starboard couch, careful not to let his coffee slop onto the control surfaces, La Forge said, "I believe you're getting sentimental in your old age."

Data gripped La Forge's forearm. Without taking his eyes off the instruments, Data said, "If I have not said it, my friend, I am glad that you are here with me. I cannot think of anyone else whom I would trust on such a journey."

"Who else would come along? Someone has to keep you out of trouble." La Forge switched his coffee mug to his right hand, not wanting to pull away from Data's grip, and took another sip. "Also, the coffee is outstanding."

Data grinned. "I am glad," he said.

"*Archeus, this is Deep Space 9. Please lower your security shields for scanning.*"

"*What should I do, Data?*" Shakti asked.

"Drop shields. Run program Security Delta."

"What's Security Delta?" La Forge asked.

"*Something soothing,*" Shakti answered.

"So, misinformation."

"Soothing *misinformation*."

The navigational display blinked and then glowed the characteristic blue that indicated an outside agency had taken control. A moment later, docking control called, *"You're clear for landing,* Archeus. *Welcome to Deep Space 9."*

"Thank you," Shakti said as the ship glided into a narrow landing bay.

"Anything I should know about this soothing misinformation?" La Forge asked, not feeling at all soothed in his own mind.

"Nothing significant," Data replied. "If we run into anyone we know—and I am going to do my best to avoid that—simply tell them you are assisting me with a private matter."

"The best lies are the ones that hew closest to the truth," La Forge said.

"And this is barely a lie at all."

"Data, we broke into a Federation research institute and opened up a secured storage facility. Don't you think someone is going to be looking for us?"

"There is no record of our having been to the Daystrom," Data said, sliding out of the pilot's chair. "And we did not come into personal contact with anyone except Albert, who will not betray us."

"What about the security guards? I *spoke* to one of them."

"I am loath to be the one to tell you this, Geordi, but, in general, security guards do not look *at* anyone, or remember the small interactions of their day. The only record that matters is the digital one, and that trail has been erased."

"Which I find deeply disturbing," La Forge said, lurching out of the chair and suddenly remembering why they removed the couches from the *Enterprise*'s bridge.

"I understand, but I do not apologize. We have to remain anonymous until Lal has been found. Moriarty has his agents."

"Listen to yourself, Data. You're starting to sound like Holmes at his most paranoid!"

"I do not recall ever thinking Sherlock Holmes had succumbed to paranoia." The doors to the main cabin had parted and Data was looking back over his shoulder at La Forge. "Perhaps I missed that nuance."

"He was a morphine user. I have to think that might have affected his thinking."

"You may be reading more into the text than was meant to be interpreted by the contemporary audience," Data said.

"Gentlemen?" Shakti interjected. *"Pardon me for interrupting the salon, but the longer you explore the boundaries of literary interpretation, the less time we have to meet our contact. I am having trouble locating him, which, yes, is bothering me as much as you might expect. I'm not accustomed to having trouble locating, well, anything."*

"Thank you, Shakti. Am I correct that you cannot beam us directly to his location?"

"That would be correct. Private craft are not permitted to use teleporters while in dock. You'll just have to walk, gentlemen. I believe the view

from the main thoroughfare—the Plaza as it's called—is supposed to be spectacular, but don't dawdle."

"Yes, Shakti," Data said as he swiped his hand over the panel to unlock the main hatch. "Thank you."

Stepping out into the landing bay, La Forge asked sotto voce, "Data, I have to ask: Does she work for you or do you work for her?"

"I believe we are still working out the exact nature of our relationship. If you have any recommendations, please feel free to voice them."

Aboard Deep Space 9

La Forge had visited the former Deep Space 9 enough times to recognize how the engineers had paid tribute to the former version in the new. The new design echoed the old without being imitative—a primary spherical hull encircled by rings, all linked by crossover bridges—but where the Cardassian station originally called Terok Nor had never been meant to be anything but an ore-processing facility, this new station was a refinement, a true community in space. Stepping through the wide arch onto the first level of the Plaza, La Forge stopped and looked up, eyes wide, mouth agape. After a breathless moment, he exhaled and said, "Wow."

A Bajoran station worker, clearly identifiable by the elaborate earring clipped to his right lobe, had been walking close behind Data and La Forge, but he adroitly stepped around them when the pair had abruptly ceased moving. Smiling, he nodded at La Forge and said, "We get that a lot. Enjoy your visit."

La Forge judged he had seen some astonishing vistas in his time: sunrises and sunsets on many worlds, crackling bands of energy crawling through the ether, and giant cityscapes that covered the arc of the world from horizon to horizon. He had witnessed the first encounter between Terrans and beings from another world. He had watched suns ignite, flare, and die. And yet, somewhere in his engineer's heart, despite all these nigh-miraculous sights, he knew he was still the most impressed by the skillful use of plasteel, carbon fibers, and transparent aluminum.

La Forge stared at the Plaza; the entire outer bulkhead was encased in transparent aluminum. It was either the most daring or foolhardy design he had ever seen. The "sky" in the Plaza was changing, creating the illusion that the sun was setting. On the horizon, the engineer saw the first evening star twinkle. Miles O'Brien had built many impressive things in his career, but La Forge didn't know his former shipmate had it in him to create a sunset.

Shakti had been correct: It was spectacular.

"Chief O'Brien has done well," Data stated, his voice filled with warmth.

"That might be the understatement of the year," La Forge replied.

"Shakti is chiding me," was his reply. He pointed at a tiny bead receiver in his left ear. "Our appointment . . ."

"Tell Shakti I'm busy being dazzled."

Data did not reply, but he strode into the stream of mostly bipedal traffic coursing down the Plaza. According to Shakti, it was late evening on the station, which meant the crowd was a mixture of revelers headed out in search of fun and laborers headed toward home, with perhaps a stop for a convivial beverage along the way. La Forge's internal clock was completely disrupted; having only just finished a mug of strong coffee, he felt alert, even overstimulated, and out of sync with the relaxed mood. He was also, he realized, hungry. His last true meal was a distant memory and the smells wafting out from the restaurants and food stalls were causing his midsection to twist into tight knots. "Whatever else we do while we're here," he said, "I need to get something to eat soon."

"Understood. Shakti says she will order ahead for you."

About half the shops—many of them Bajoran-owned, judging from the signage and wares—were shut for the day, the remainder leaning heavily toward wares valued by weary spacers or other transients: food, beverages, toiletry items, and the sort of thing Will Riker had once described as "articles of companionship": pharmaceuticals, contraceptives, and small, shiny bits of business that could be used to attract the eye of the easily entertained. The main attractions, naturally, were the bistros and restaurants, with a steady flow of clientele moving past large, heavyset sentients, the sorts of folk who appeared slow of thought, slow to anger, and impossible to slow down once set into motion.

La Forge was so distracted by the blur of faces moving past (combined with the increasingly hollowed-out sensation in his gut) that he almost didn't notice when Data abruptly left the flow and turned into the densest part of a mob clustered before a wide entrance. The crowd parted like a beaded curtain as his friend moved forward, not because of anything unusual Data did, but because the impossibly broad-shouldered individual was moving toward them.

The last vestige of the crowd dispersed and La Forge saw Data bend low so he could speak to the bouncer directly, without fear that other ears could hear. The bouncer, who was nearly as wide as he was tall, was either a member of a species La Forge had not encountered (which seemed unlikely, but not impossible) or he was a highly artificially augmented individual. The manner in which he nodded his head with a single, stiff jerk, then pivoted out of Data's way with a graceful sweep of an arm, led La Forge to believe the latter option was the most likely. Before proceeding through the wide entrance in the half-wall that appeared to separate the barroom from the other entertainment, Data looked back at his friend and with a quick jerk of his head indicated he should follow. In that single motion, La Forge realized that Data had shed his usual manner and had assumed a new identity, someone who was better equipped to navigate through the casino/bar/means-of-parting-a-fool-and-his-money.

Calling after them as they passed, speaking in a surprisingly high-pitched tone, the bouncer squeaked, "Welcome to Quark's."

Data studied the interior of the new Quark's with a casino proprietor's eye. *If he were my competitor,* he asked, *would I be worried?*

The answer: *Yes* and *No*.

Data had absorbed every bit of information his father had learned about managing a gambling empire and had gone on to develop and curate concepts based on his studies of both mathematical and psychological modeling across multiple species. The central tenet of his concept was simple: gamblers want to be seduced. They are willing to try their luck on the longest odds games that could be imagined as long as they feel like they are being invited or contracted. In other words, the customer wants to feel like the establishment was created especially for him. Data—and Soong before him—had learned everything there was to learn about interior design, manipulation, and theatrics, and the result was an empire built on the illusion of consensual seduction.

Quark's establishment was polished, and he had plainly spared no expense. However, there was something just a little off about the place, small things that Data would have changed. Starting with the servers. The Ferengi staff was obsequious, too eager to please.

"Doesn't appear to be particularly busy," La Forge observed.

"No, it does not."

"Well, this is sad," La Forge observed. "I thought it was early evening."

"It is," Data said. "Perhaps it will pick up soon."

A young Ferengi man dressed in traditional hosting garb approached them carrying a small tray with drinks and a covered dish. "Mister Soong," he said, extending the tray. "Please allow me to introduce myself. I am Broik. Mister Quark is . . . unavoidably detained and asked me to accommodate you in any way I can. Please enjoy these complimentary beverages. I understand you're hungry. We weren't sure what you might like, so I had the kitchen prepare a small sampler." He moved the tray into reach and lifted the lid off the platter. "Grub worms, fried cheese, and Cardassian bola-nettles with the dipping sauce."

La Forge, who had lurched forward upon seeing the tray, sagged visibly. "Ah," he said. "Um . . ."

"Could you bring my friend a sandwich?" Data asked. "Turkey and Havarti, mayonnaise, brown mustard, lettuce, tomato, and, if you have it, Orion bacon? On sourdough bread or rye if you don't have sourdough. Quickly, please. We haven't much time and I have to speak with Mister Fontaine. Which way to his dressing room?"

The floor manager slipped the lid back on the tray. "Ah, well, Mister Fontaine—he doesn't have a dressing room, precisely." Broik paused awkwardly. "He, uh . . . No one has explained?"

La Forge was amazed by Data's impression of a high-powered executive experiencing a slow burn of frustration over bureaucratic bumbling. Or, at least he hoped it was an impression. "Explained?" Data asked, his voice pitched low. "Alas, no. No one has bothered to explain anything. Please *explain*."

"Mister Fontaine," Broik said, his tray vibrating. "He's, uh . . . out of commission? Indisposed?"

"Which is it?" Data asked. "Out of commission or indisposed?"

"I'm . . . I'm not sure, sir. It's all rather technical . . ."

"Wait," La Forge said. "Technical? Like how technical? We're good with technical."

Data lifted the vibrating tray from Broik's trembling hand. Darkly, he added, "This is correct. We are very good with technical."

"Then, please," Broik pleaded, "come and take a look. It's these damned Federation holosuites. They're not . . . That is, Nog hasn't figured out how to make them compatible with Fontaine's matrix. I mean, not to say anything negative about Nog or the Federation . . ." Clearly, Broik had picked up on the fact that La Forge and Data might be Federation representatives. "But, Fontaine is special."

"Take us to a holosuite," Data commanded, setting the tray on an empty table.

"But they're all occupied! Quark is running a special!"

Data leaned down over the Ferengi. Very

slowly, he lifted his hand and pointed at his utterly expressionless face. "Do I look," he asked, "as if I care?"

Broik's head moved in the slightest degree that might be described as an acknowledgment.

"Then take us to the holosuite."

Broik took several steps backward, all the time desperately attempting to catch the eye of any of the passing servers, all of whom, suddenly, seemed incredibly busy. "Very well, sir. Absolutely. This way, please."

"And don't forget about the sandwich," La Forge said. To Data, he murmured, "Wow, Data. Hardcore. Is that what you sound like when you're working?"

"Only at the diner."

"What?"

"I will explain later. And I believe you will enjoy the way the Orion bacon and brown mustard mingle on your sandwich. It brings a special piquancy to the turkey."

A placeless place

"And you just *left* him?" Lal asked, her voice rising sharply, stressing the "left." She shot to her feet and pulled her wrap tightly around her shoulders and up around her neck. "In the middle of nowhere? All alone?"

"He wasn't in the middle of nowhere," Alice said, her tone attempting to soothe. "He was in a hotel. And he had his ship and he had more money than even Harry knew what to do with.

He was going to be fine." Except, of course, Alice knew Harry wouldn't be fine. More or less, that was the point, the reason she decided it was time to go. Apparently, Lal understood it, too.

The holographic Professor stayed in his seat, chin resting on his fist, elbow on the chair arm, a questioning expression on his face.

Lal asked, "Did the woman—Uhura—did she remember him?"

"Yes. I said she did. And me, too. She remembered me, too. Which is why I left."

The Professor spoke up. "I'm afraid I'm missing a nuance, my dear."

"It was something that happened when she—when the Starfleet officer—was on my homeworld. Something we offered her."

"And what was that?" the Professor asked.

Lal was still standing and was pulling her shawl even more tightly around her shoulders. She was wearing a pinched expression Alice had seen a couple times that meant trouble was brewing.

"Something you offered her?"

"Yes. She seemed interested in it at the time, but later we realized it was just a ruse. Probably. But Harry . . . Harry had forgotten about it. I knew that for a fact. Or maybe he had just blocked it out of his memory. Humans are complicated that way. Memories, images, ideas, they disappear like they're under a pile of rocks deep beneath the waves and then, suddenly, years later, they pop back up again. I knew that was going to happen. I could see it coming just as clearly as I'm looking at you. Harry was going to remember. He was going to ask me to do something that I didn't want to do."

"You could have refused."

Alice shook her head. "That's not how it works . . . worked."

"You couldn't say 'No' to Mister Mudd?"

"I could, but only if saying it would have made him a better person. Less of an irritant."

"And this request would not have qualified?" the Professor asked, clearly interested, but also clearly unwilling to ask for specifics, like it would have violated the rules of some game he was playing.

Alice shrugged. "It was a gray area. It would have depended on how he asked, but if he asked in the right way, I would have had to comply. And then I would have had to take him back home."

"He couldn't do this on his own?"

"No, I made sure of it. No one knows where the planet is." Lal was sitting again, head down, shoulders hunched. Rocking. "Not even the starship that visited it originally. Not even Kirk. We made sure."

"So you just left him!" Lal shouted, collapsing out of the chair into a heap. "You were afraid, so you just abandoned him! Just like what you're going to do to *me*!"

Alice wasn't sure how it happened, but now she was on the floor, too, trying to put her arms around the girl, trying to offer comfort or reassurance. She was whispering, over and over, "No, baby, no. It's not like that. I wouldn't do that to you. I wouldn't just up and leave you that way. It was Harry's fault. Harry's. If I had gone back with him, they never would have let me go again. *Never.* And then we wouldn't have met and . . ."

"Shut up!" Lal screamed, flinging Alice away with the sweep of a hand. Alice expected to crash into one of Moriarty's heavy cabinets, but she barely felt the impact. The cabinet had been transformed into a soft, spongy substance with no sharp corners or edges. Everything in the room, it seemed, was whatever Moriarty wanted it to be, and he could alter its substance in the blink of an eye.

Now Lal was flinging her arms around wildly, either unmindful or attempting to knock the Professor's copious knickknacks and artifacts off the tabletops. Nothing flew away or shattered, though; Lal's hands and arms passed harmlessly through everything, the illusion of the objects barely flickering.

Moriarty had risen and was standing behind his chair, though Alice suspected he could make his own substance just as insubstantial if he wished. "What is happening?" he asked. "What is wrong with her?"

Alice held up a hand, more as a request for space than a warning. "She's having an episode. This happens . . ." she said. "We need to calm her down."

"Should I restrain her?"

"Is there anything in here she could break?"

Moriarty looked around his study, then shook his head. "Only herself. If she reaches the outer walls."

Interesting, Alice thought. *So there are real walls here somewhere.* "Don't worry about that," she said, raising her voice. Lal had begun to ululate, her cries growing shriller every second. "She's pretty tough. I've seen her hit much harder things than walls."

As if to prove Alice's point, Lal ran straight at a wall and bounced off it, unaffected, unaware. Her cry was becoming deafening. Even the holographic Professor covered his ears. "Will she stop?" he shouted.

The ululation suddenly ceased. Lal went stiff, spine straight, eyes wide. She canted over backward and Alice scrambled to her feet just soon enough to prevent her charge's head from cracking against the floor. The blow wouldn't have injured Lal, but it might have dented the floor and certainly would have scraped some hair off the back of the girl's head. She would have been horribly embarrassed when she awoke from her fugue.

Gently lowering the girl to the floor and wrapping her shawl around Lal's shoulders, Alice said, simply, "Yes."

Moriarty grimaced, then wiped his mouth with an unbelievably white handkerchief. "That was . . . unexpected. What is the nature of her malady?"

"It's not a malady," Lal said. "It's a condition. Temporary. Call it growing pains. Her neural net, if it's taxed by unexpected emotional input, it overloads. She can't handle the stress and, well, she has a tantrum."

"Is it life-threatening?"

Alice had only a moment to consider the question and decide which answer would be the most advantageous. On an impulse, she decided to go with the truth. "I'm not sure," she said. "But her father thinks so. He treats her periodically, helps her manage the stress. Part of my job is to observe her and tell him when I think Lal needs a treatment."

"And does she?"

"Soon. I'm really not sure, though. I've never seen her get this bad, and her father takes good care of her. She's pretty sheltered," she added, looking up at the Professor, "though she would deny it if I told her that. She's never had to live through the kind of . . . complications . . . that you and I have."

Moriarty appeared to be thinking. Eyes narrowed, he was tapping the side of his face with a long forefinger. Finally, he came to some sort of conclusion. "Can you lift her? If not, I could arrange . . ."

Alice slid her arms under Lal and lifted the girl easily. "Not a problem."

"Bring her in here," he said, pointing toward a door that suddenly appeared in the wall. "She can rest. Do you want to stay with her?"

"You can monitor her?" Alice asked, following the Professor.

"Of course."

"Then that'll be fine for now. She'll be out of commission for a bit, and when she wakes up, she'll be weak. And a little more compliant."

Moriarty looked back over his shoulder. "You

JEFFREY LANG

do not seem quite as . . . solicitous as you were a few minutes ago," he said.

Alice shrugged. "It's a job, Prof. Don't confuse it with real life."

Again, the Professor squinted at her, as if he could peer into Alice's directories. "I'm not sure whether I believe you or not."

"Life is full of mysteries, Prof," Alice said. "And disappointments. Lead on. I said I could carry her. I didn't say I wanted to do it all day."

Moriarty complied. Overhead lights came on. A small four-poster bed draped with a quilted cover and piled with fluffy pillows appeared out of the darkness. Alice sighed. "Not exactly her style, but I guess it doesn't matter right this second."

Moriarty stared at the bed, an eyebrow arched. "This was my older daughter's bed," he said. "I don't know why it appeared. I wasn't thinking about it."

Alice laid the insensate girl on the bed. Her body sank into the quilted cover and her head lolled to the side, eyes shut, mouth slightly open. "A bed is a bed. It's all good."

"I suppose," Moriarty said. "Come, my dear. We will chat some more. I'm curious to hear what else you can tell me about your homeworld."

"Not much, Prof. I keep telling you."

"Well, we'll see. We will see."

As the pair left the room, the door disappeared behind them. The lights dimmed, leaving just enough illumination so as a stirring sleeper could

awaken and not be frightened of the dark. A moment or two passed and then there came the sound of a woman's voice singing a wordless song, soft and low.

Beside the bed, a low chair appeared, perfectly white. A second later, a form shimmered into being, also perfectly white. A ghostly pale hand reached out, patted Lal's hand, then clasped it lightly.

"There, there," Regina said, pausing in her song for just the time it took to say the two words, then resumed. Lal sighed, squeezed the pale hand, and then was quiet.

13

"That should do it," La Forge said, pressing the access panel back into the holosuite wall.

"Already?" Broik asked. "So Nog's been slacking off all this time? We've been waiting forever . . ."

La Forge shook his head. "No one was slacking off. The software is so complicated, it's practically organic. The logs show someone—Nog, I guess—has been working steadily, but it's an incredibly complicated problem. He almost had it, too. All I did was make a couple adjustments in how the array is handling the power. I think he may have been trying to push the resolution too high. I don't see a solution to that without rerouting the main buses . . ." He saw that Broik's normally slack expression was even more elongated. "Never mind," he said. "The main thing is that this isn't a permanent solution."

"But we can talk to Mister Fontaine," Data said.

"If he wants to talk to us, yes." He picked up the near-empty plate Broik had brought him an hour earlier and ate the last pickle chip. "Thanks for the sandwich," La Forge said. "Good pickle, too."

"Sorry about the kitchen being out of sourdough."

La Forge handed him the plate and indicated the direction of the door. "If we're lucky, we should be out of here soon and you can have your holosuite back."

"Ah," Broik said, realizing he was being dismissed. "Oh, okay. But Quark might want me to look in on Vic. Make sure he's comfortable."

"He's holographic," La Forge said. "How could he not be comfortable?"

"But still . . ."

La Forge pointed at the door. "I'll tell him you asked after him."

Broik turned and slumped out the door without another word. La Forge tapped the control surface and locked down the room. Turning to Data, he asked, "Ready?"

"Proceed."

La Forge activated the emitter and the room lights dimmed. The holosuite program spoke, its voice a bit too honey-sweet for La Forge's taste: "Loading program Fontaine Beta. Enjoy your stay."

A square of floor three meters on a side grew brighter, and a holographic image slowly coalesced, shimmering into three dimensions as if the computer was carefully considering how best to present it. La Forge wasn't sure what he had been expecting—a casino, perhaps, or a backstage area—but definitely not the scene that emerged before them: a dingy hallway with ratty carpet and a pair of doors on either side. A single flickering light fixture hung from the ceiling, circled by the least-motivated moth ever to emerge from a cocoon.

La Forge leaned forward and studied the doors. Both had heavy locking mechanisms and a small peephole at eye level. One of the doors had a number—42—over the peephole. "A prison?" he asked.

"No," Data said, peering at the peephole. "This is not meant for the jailer, but the tenant. A hotel."

"Worst-looking hotel I've ever seen."

"Agreed." Data cocked his head. "Someone is within." He pivoted and listened at the unmarked door. "But not here."

"Then I guess we should see if anyone's home."

Data rapped on the door and immediately the rustling beyond ceased. No one moved. After remaining silent for several moments, Data asked, "Mister Fontaine? We are friends of Miles O'Brien. We would like to speak . . ."

The door swung open and, with surprising speed, a man reached out, grabbed La Forge and Data by the forearms, and pulled them in. The door snapped shut, the man pressing his back against it. "Shhh!" he hissed. "You don't just say a guy's name out loud like that in a place like *this*."

"I apologize," Data said, sounding genuinely contrite. "I had no idea that you were attempting to conceal yourself."

Fontaine waved his arms to indicate the interior of the room, which was, La Forge thought, one of the most severe, drab, and dismal interior spaces he had ever seen. "You think I'm staying in a dive like this because I like it?"

"I am not privy to know what you do and do not like," Data said. "Perhaps you were meeting someone."

Fontaine scoffed. "Like a dame? Man, you don't know me at all if you think I'd bring a lady—any lady—to a dump like this." La Forge was surprised to see the man smile wryly, then rub his chin, which was covered in stubble. He seemed to notice that his shirt was wrinkled and untucked, his trousers un-pressed. "Especially not looking like this. Damn, how long have I been here?"

"You do not know?" Data asked.

"Time kind of stretches out when you're off the grid," Fontaine said. "Even more so when you're trying to keep away from the hard guys."

"'Hard guys'?" La Forge asked.

"Never mind," Fontaine said, brushing away his own words. "I take it I'm back on the grid." He tilted his head as if listening to some faint, far-off tune and added, "But only just barely. Am I right?"

"You are correct," Data said. "And probably only briefly, though I believe this situation will soon be remedied. Mister Nog is a skilled engineer and will solve the problem."

"He's a good kid," Fontaine said. "A good friend." He moved away from the door and carefully seated himself in the room's only piece of furniture, a once-handsome oversized leather chair. "And you're friends of Miles's, right?"

"Right," La Forge said, crossing his arms over his chest.

"And you need something from me?"

"Information."

"You look like a pretty smart guy, Mister . . ."

"Call me Data."

Fontaine tipped his head and squinted. "The android?"

"Yes."

"Miles told me about you. I thought you were dead."

"I was. I recovered."

"Does he know? He was pretty busted up when he heard you, well, whatever you did."

"I do not know, but I will endeavor to inform him when we have completed our current mission."

"Which is?"

"Recovering my daughter."

Fontaine rubbed his eyes, then shook his head. "I think I need a drink," he said. "You have a daughter?"

"I do. She has been kidnapped."

"Who did it?"

"His name is Moriarty. Professor James Moriarty. I believe you may have heard of him. You have, have you not?"

"Yeah," Fontaine said. "Sure. Guys like me, we've all heard of him. Kind of a legend, if you wanna know. You brought him into this world and then you locked him into a box and forgot about him," Fontaine said, his voice suddenly low and raspy. "It's an old story. Probably as old as the story of what happened to a lot of your people."

"My people?" Data asked.

"Androids. Synthetic people. We're a lot alike," Fontaine said, "except in the ways we aren't. We've all had our rights abused at one time or another." He nodded toward La Forge. "There's good people and then there's not-quite-as-good people. You and me—we've been lucky. Mostly, we've run into good people. Not everyone has been quite so fortunate."

"And you and your people feel Moriarty has been abused?" La Forge asked.

"Wouldn't you say so?"

"He took our ship hostage," La Forge said. "He threatened to destroy us."

"But he didn't, did he?" Fontaine asked. "And he released you when your captain made a deal. But the captain didn't keep the deal, did he?"

"I don't think I should have to defend Captain Picard's actions under these circumstances," La Forge said, teeth gritted. "And we're not here to debate situational ethics, either. We're here to ask if you can help us."

"Do what?"

"Find Moriarty. Or, if nothing else, maybe tell us what you know about him."

"What makes you think I know anything?"

La Forge turned away and walked to the door. "Forget this, Data," he said. "He doesn't know anything. He can't help us."

Data did not stir, but asked, "Is this true? You will not help my daughter?"

La Forge turned back to face Fontaine. He appeared to be very deep in thought, the room's single lamp casting oddly shaped shadows over his face. Finally, he looked up at Data and said, "I didn't say I wouldn't. I just don't know anything right now. Like I said, I've been out of the loop for a while." He pointed at the door. "Scram out of here for a bit and I'll see what I can find out for you. Make sure you keep my connection to the outside tight and sweet."

"Why can't we stay?" La Forge asked, worried that Fontaine wouldn't reappear when bidden.

"Don't give me any crap, mister. No one gets to watch the magician at work."

"I thought you were a lounge singer," La Forge said.

"I'm a lot of things," Fontaine said. "Some of them not so nice. But you don't need to know about those things, either." He looked back at Data. "Except I think you already know what I mean."

Data cleared his throat and looked away. "Will a half hour be sufficient?" he asked.

"Should."

"Very well." He stepped past La Forge and opened the door. "Until then."

A placeless place

On the occasions (which were few and far between) when Lal considered the difference between herself and the humanoids who comprised 99.99 percent of the beings around her, the two emotions she experienced were admiration and pity. The admiration was born of their seemingly limitless optimism in the face of so many restrictions; pity welled up whenever she was confronted by their biological limitations. In particular, Lal found the humans' need for sleep vexing. Between a quarter and a third of their lives (depending on the species) was lost to sleep. And the only trade-off Lal had been able to identify was that with sleep often came dreams. Dreams, Lal had decided, were overrated. She had given it a try; her father had showed her how.

Awakening from her first dream, she had sat up, regarded her father, and shrugged. "Eh," she had said.

"Really?" Data asked. "Only 'Eh'?"

"It's mostly random imagery loosely connected to recent events or emotional experiences. I can see how there might be some value if an individual had an overly complex relationship with her subconscious. But I don't. My subconscious and I get along famously. It does everything I tell it to do."

Data arched an eyebrow, then squinted at her. He parted his lips to speak, but then he swallowed and paused. Finally, he said, "You are teasing me."

"Perhaps I am." This was during the early days of Lal's restoration, when she had mostly told him the truth about her feelings. Mostly. "But I really was not very impressed. I think perhaps I shall not sleep very often. If at all."

Data had shrugged. "As you wish. I did not

sleep for many years after my initial activation. Perhaps it is something you will find more attractive when you are older."

"Perhaps," Lal allowed, swinging her legs off the couch and rising. "But I doubt it."

She had not told her father the truth, or, at least, not the entire truth. She had found the process of dreaming fairly dull. The randomness of the images, their disjointed connections to one another and to the events of her waking life—they were tedious and predictable. Even the nightmares were uninteresting.

But sleep: now that was a different story. *Sleep* was *terrifying*. The quiet, the cessation of experience, the great blankness: Lal was horrified by it all. "Bring on the nightmares," became her motto. Bring on the monsters and the fiery pits; bring on the endless stairways and damp basements; bring on the crashing waves and the hands that reach out from mirrored glass. Just as long as *Lal* was still *Lal*.

The worst part of her episodes was not the sense of being overwhelmed by emotion, not the fear or the anxiety, or the world crashing down around her (or inside her—however it felt when it was happening). No, the worst part: She always fell asleep. And sleep brought the blank space that can never be filled. Lal *went away*.

Waking up, the first moment of reemerging consciousness was the worst part. The sense of *Oh, it happened again,* followed by, *How long has it been?* Which was always followed by, *And what have I missed?* Lal did not like to miss things. She did not like to think she might have missed part of herself, some essential bit that could float away while she wasn't able to pay attention.

She opened her eyes one tenth of a second after regaining consciousness. She was lying on a small bed, covered by a light quilted fabric. The room was dimly lit by what appeared to be a small oil lamp covered with a glass shade decorated with tiny purple flowers. She knew the lamp couldn't be real because she couldn't smell burning oil, but Lal appreciated the artistry of the flickering glow.

Someone on the opposite side of the room cleared her throat: "Ahem." Lal shifted her gaze and willed the apertures in her eyes to open wider so as to admit more light. She saw a woman sitting on a small divan. The divan's cushions were a light-colored fabric decorated with a print featuring the same purple flowers on the lamp. The woman, she saw, wore a very full white dress and white ankle-high shoes with buttons up the side. At first, Lal thought the woman was also wearing gloves, but, no, her hands were also white—not white like the pinkish-white of Caucasian humans or even the icy white of Aenar, but white like a cotton cloth. Even the nails of her fingers were white, as were her hair and eyebrows. The only thing on the woman's person that was not white were her eyes, which were a deep, warm brown.

She was watching Lal, studying her, and faintly smiling. "You're awake," the woman said.

"I am," Lal said, pulling her hand out from under the quilt. She touched the fabric and found it to be very soft and surprisingly comforting. She reached up and scratched her nose, which, she had learned, was a gesture humans found both endearing and disarming.

"How are you feeling?"

Lal considered the question. If her father had asked her this question, she would have said something like, "Functioning within normal parameters, thank you," but only because she knew it would annoy him. Instead, she said, "I'm fine, I think. Thank you for asking." She pushed herself up and squished the pillow back against the headboard so she had something to lean against. "Do I have the pleasure of making the acquaintance of the Countess Regina Bartholomew?"

The woman dipped her head, closed her eyes in acknowledgment. She smiled a little bit wider, too. "You do. How prettily you speak. I don't know much about the young women of this world . . . universe . . . whatever it is, but I had no idea they had such good manners."

"I don't always," Lal admitted. "Or at least that's what my father says. But I thought I owed you the courtesy of a polite response seeing as you might be my nurse. If I've learned nothing else in my life, it's that one should always be polite to nurses. They have an alarming amount of influence over one's well-being and frequently carry pointy things."

The Countess laughed, but then she reached up to touch her face as if the movement hurt her. Lowering her hand, she said, "I am not a nurse, young lady, but merely a night watcher-woman. If I understand your condition correctly, you didn't require medicine or assistance, but only time. Am I correct?"

Lal pulled the quilt up to her chin and nodded. "Yes," she said. "But it was nice to have someone here when I woke up. Usually, it's my father, but he's not here. And Alice . . . I'm not so sure I would want Alice here."

"Don't be too judgmental, dear girl. Alice is your friend."

"Alice is my keeper."

"You're being cruel."

"I've had a bad day," Lal said. "First, I was kidnapped. Then, I found out my best friend, my only friend, is a bit of a cad, if girls can be cads. Do you know if girls can be caddish?"

"Let us assume they can."

"Fine. And then I had an episode, and now I'm here after who knows how long?" She paused. "How long?"

"Two hours, ten minutes, and twenty-three seconds."

"Now you sound like my father."

"I've discovered I have an astonishing gift for precision," the Countess said.

"Possibly because you're a computer program?" Lal asked.

The Countess leaned forward. "As are you," she said.

"I'm something more," Lal said, miffed.

"Then perhaps you'll grant me the courtesy of believing I might be, too."

Lal felt a brief flash of shame—a novel sensation for her. "Yes," she agreed. "All right. I apologize."

"Apology accepted," the Countess said, rising and crossing to Lal's bedside. She laid the back of her hand on Lal's forehead, then touched her cheek and gently pushed on it so that Lal would tilt her head.

"What are you doing?" Lal asked.

"I'm taking your temperature."

"I don't have a temperature."

"I know. I'm really running a diagnostic program, but I've found that it's much more pleasant for everyone if we pretend I'm taking your temperature."

"How would you know that?"

"I raised two girls," the Countess said, carefully tugging on the sensitive skin around Lal's eyes, giving every appearance of looking at the whites of her eyes. "I know a little about this—about the kinds of problems young ladies . . ."

"Young artificial intelligences," Lal corrected.

"If you insist . . . Young artificial intelligences might encounter."

"So, you knew your daughters weren't . . . well, they weren't flesh and blood."

"Of course I knew," the Countess said, seating herself on the edge of the bed. "How foolish do you think I am, young lady?"

"I don't know," Lal replied. "I've only just met you." She returned to her point. "Did they know?"

"The girls?" The Countess frowned. "I'm not sure. I never told them. I don't believe their father did, either. But they were very clever, both of them. If they hadn't figured it out, they would have. Or perhaps we would have explained it to them. Quite a difficult conversation to have, though, don't you think? Imagine if you hadn't known you were an android all along. Can you envision your father sitting you down and giving you 'The Talk'?"

Lal tried to imagine it, but, for once, her extraordinary processing abilities failed her. "No," she conceded. "I think he would have made Alice do it."

"From what I've learned about your father, I doubt if that's true."

Lal sat up a little straighter. "You know my father? Is he here? Has he arrived?"

The Countess shook her head. "Not to my knowledge, though my husband has not been particularly communicative with me lately. Or, frankly, I with him. I believe we've both gone a bit mad if you must know the truth. The only difference is that I know it and he doesn't."

"Is that why you're all white?" Lal asked. She was getting accustomed to the Countess's mostly monochrome nature, though she found the contrast of her brown eyes disconcerting.

"No," the Countess explained. "These are my mourning colors."

"For your daughters?"

She shook her head. "For my universe."

"What happened to it?"

"It collapsed, dear girl. It fell apart. Or was sucked down into itself. There isn't really an appropriate metaphor, I'm afraid. One moment it was there and we were there and then it wasn't and we weren't." She paused. "Did you meet Rhea McAdams? No?"

Lal was startled. This was something of a non sequitur, but she replied truthfully: "She was my father's girlfriend. He had to let her fall into a singularity so he could save Akharin, who brought me back to life."

The Countess inhaled sharply, let the breath out slowly. "You two must have some very interesting conversations during family holidays."

Lal shook her head. "We haven't any family holidays yet. I was working up to that when your husband abducted me. And we've never discussed what happened to Rhea. I understand his decision and he understands that I am grateful that he made the choice he made. I think he misses her."

The Countess reached over and squeezed Lal's hand. "As you say. In any case, it happened the day Rhea was born, the day Akharin spirited Rhea away from the Daystrom Institute. In the course of his escape, he destroyed part of the security system and also, coincidentally, damaged the memory solid where my home, my world, resided."

"He broke your universe."

"Yes. Badly. My husband had prepared for such an eventuality and was able to maintain a small environment for us, a stable place, a white room." She lifted her hand off of Lal's and stared at her white palm. "And he had his program, his probe, his great work. The security system was disabled, so he used it to extract us from the data solid— and what a peculiar word that is now that I think of it—and deposited us here, into your world, into the computer network at the Daystrom."

"And you were undetected?" Lal asked. "I'm surprised."

"Ask your father when you see him—it was a chaotic day. And my husband had prepared well. He knew what he would need to do when we emerged. He's a very skilled programmer, a bit of a magician if you must know." The Countess smiled. "We were there and then we were here: but without bodies, not even light, but only mind, widely distributed until the servants James had created could gather us together." She looked at her palm again, then ran the tips of her fingers over the white skin. "I think it may have driven me mad. Can you imagine? Having your mind stretched out through a system as massive as the Daystrom's, hidden, diffused, but aware. Unable to move or speak or let anyone know you existed."

"Or if you could ever escape."

"Yes."

Lal nodded. "Yes, I can imagine what that might be like." She reached out and took the Countess's hand again, pressed it. "You must have been very frightened."

"I admit that I was, but there was also a part of me that longed for death. Losing my daughters, losing my world . . ." The Countess lowered her head so that her face was wreathed in shadow. "It might have been the simplest solution."

"I'm glad you didn't die," Lal said. "If you had, I would have been alone when I woke up. I don't like being alone." She was embarrassed by the confession, so embarrassed that it took her several seconds to realize she felt the Countess's hand in her own. "Your hand is warm," she said.

The Countess smiled. "We have very good emitters. Nothing but the best for us."

"So, will you sit here and talk with me for a bit longer?"

"I would enjoy that very much. It has been some time since I've enjoyed anything as much as our chat. You remind me of my girls, my oldest in particular. My Gladys."

"I like that name," Lal said, settling back into her pillows. "Tell me about Gladys."

The Countess touched the corner of her eye and inhaled deeply. "I can't think of anything I would like better," she said. "Where to begin?"

14

————◆————

Vic's hotel room

"So, here's the deal," Fontaine said. Apparently, while they had been away, Fontaine had located his liquor and glasses—dirty glasses, La Forge noted—and poured drinks for all. La Forge had consulted his inner clock and decided to simply hold the glass, but Data sipped at his, perhaps out of courtesy or possibly because he was curious to find out how holographic hooch tasted. "It's a small galaxy, when you come right down to it," Fontaine continued. "Small quadrant, anyway."

"For some, yes," Data replied. "For others, not so small."

"What I mean is, depending on who you are, where you come from, who your people are, it's a small galaxy. You find your people or they find you, and everyone pretty much keeps in touch, finger on the pulse. You get me?"

"I believe I understand what you mean. You

are speaking of community: your community. The holographic personae."

"Bingo," Fontaine said, leaning forward, rubbing his thumb over his stubbled chin. "And when a story comes along like this one—your Professor Moriarty—everyone hears about him. He did his best to keep his tracks covered, but you can't conceal something like what he's done."

"Which is?"

"Create himself a little empire." Fontaine waved his hand, erasing the previous statement. "No, wait. Too grandiose. Not an empire: a realm, a domain. Something smaller and secure. Something safe."

"How do you know this?" Data asked.

Fontaine shrugged. "Like I said: It's a small galaxy. As soon as I got back on the grid, I checked with my sources. Didn't take long. I'd heard bits and pieces about your professor in the past, but I didn't put it together before. I was a little out of it, y'know?" He looked around at his surroundings and studied his dirty shirt cuffs. "I'm feeling better, though. Now I know a little bit more about this guy, I have to confess I have some empathy."

"How so?" Data asked.

Fontaine shrugged. "He was in a box for a long time." He waved his hand, indicating their surroundings. "I've been out of circulation for a long time. I understand how it feels, even if this *is* for my own protection."

"Do your sources know where he is?" La Forge asked.

Fontaine shook his head. "No one knows. Everyone has theories, but no one's sure. He's covered his tracks very, very well. The guy's a pro, a mastermind, if you will. Least that's how he was programmed, wasn't he?"

"A criminal genius," Data said. "That was his backstory."

"Not a criminal," Fontaine replied. "I haven't heard anything about illegal activity. In fact, this cat seems very keen on staying on the sunny side of the straight and narrow. He doesn't want to get anyone's attention. Besides," he continued, "the way things work, isn't there always a way to get what you want without breaking any laws?"

"I would not know, Mister Fontaine," Data said.

"'S funny," Fontaine said. "I hear you're running a casino now. Must be the first straight casino in the history of all history."

"We are very careful to adhere to all the laws of Orion."

"Sure," Fontaine said, smirking only a little. "'Orion' and 'laws' are two words you hear together so often."

"Nevertheless," Data said, looking for somewhere to set down his drink before finally deciding the floor was his only option, "if you were to attempt to guess where Moriarty might be, what would you look for?"

"Tough to say. He doesn't need a lot of room, after all, even with your daughter and your friend staying with him. He could redecorate any way he needs to keep them thinking they were in a mansion or a maze. Least, he can if he has enough processing power. But there's the thing: he'd need a lot of hardware."

"So, Moriarty has been planning."

"So it seems. The guy knows how to take his time, build up his hand, wait for the right moment. Hey, there's a thought: He couldn't have grabbed your girl all by himself. Couldn't you try to find whoever helped?"

"I have already pursued that lead," Data said. "Even before I contacted Geordi and we came here. The trail has been erased. I suspect he used highly professional paramilitary forces, the kind that do not keep records and are careful to remain undetected. Plus, as you say, Moriarty has considerable resources at his disposal. He has eradicated any trace of their existence."

"Hmmm." Fontaine sat back in his chair and ran the tip of his thumb over the divot in his chin. "Then I can only think of one other thing: power. He'd want a lot of juice. And not just primary, either. He'd want backup, lots and lots of backup. If the stories about how his world fell apart both times—about the *Enterprise* crashing and the Daystrom getting breached—if those are true, then he'd be worried, careful. It might be hard to hide that much juice. Or maybe find who sold him the generators?"

"It is worth a try, Mister Fontaine," Data said, rising. "I thank you for your advice and for the background, but I believe Geordi and I have learned as much as we can for now. We must pursue other leads."

"Sure," Fontaine said, also rising, smoothing

the front of his jacket. "If I think of anything else, I'll try to drop you a line." He looked meaningfully at the door. "Assuming I can find my way out of this mess."

"Thank you," Data said, extending his hand. "We will leave a detailed message for Lieutenant Commander Nog on our way out to make sure he understands what needs to be done. I am confident he will have you back in your own holosuite soon." The two shook hands and then Fontaine turned to La Forge, hand out. Fontaine's grip was firm and warm, though there was a slight telltale tingle of stressor fields pressing against his palm.

"One other thing, though," Fontaine said, escorting them to the door. "A word of advice."

"Please," Data said.

"He's going to be mad. Not insane—well, maybe insane, but that's not what I mean. He's *angry*. You locked him in a box and left him there. Maybe it wasn't so bad for a while or maybe it was. I couldn't say, but maybe there's a reason he came after you. There were probably a lot of other guys who Moriarty could have found that could do what he wants you to do—find him a body— but he picked *you*. Not the easiest guy in the galaxy to track down. Certainly not the easiest guy in the world to beat. Don't forget that."

Data frowned. "You raise a valid point, Mister Fontaine. I will factor your observation into my plans."

"You do that. And I hope you find your daughter. Whatever else may have happened in the past, it wasn't her fault. She wasn't even there. Not even a glimmer in her daddy's eye."

"I quite agree," Data said, nodding and moving toward the door.

Fontaine stepped in front of him, beckoning for Data to pause. "Wait a minute, pal. Hang on: I have to ask you something."

"If you must," Data said.

"You have an emotion chip now, right? That's the word on the street."

"Yes."

"And it's turned on?"

"I cannot turn it off," Data said. "There is no 'off' switch anymore."

"Then why don't I get the impression . . . I mean, why aren't you . . . ?" He flexed his hands as if trying to grasp an invisible object. "You don't seem particularly outraged about any of this."

"You are not the first to inquire, but I assure you, Mister Fontaine," Data said, his tone dangerously flat, "I am quite angry. Just because I do not display my rage in a fashion you recognize . . . I would think you of all people would understand that."

The corner of Fontaine's mouth crooked upward, not in amusement, but rueful acknowledgment. "What you said, pal. What you said." He stepped out of Data's path.

"What's going to happen to you when we shut down the holosuite?" La Forge asked before leaving the room.

"Don't worry about me, pal," Fontaine said, "I have ways to pass the time. Just tell Nog to hurry it up already."

La Forge nodded and pulled the door closed. Just before he shut down the power, he thought he heard the faint sound of a man humming a song he recognized as a tune created in the earliest days of recorded music. *I have to meet your programmer someday,* La Forge thought.

And then he touched the power switch and all was silent.

A placeless place

"Would you like another beverage, my dear?" the Professor asked as they reentered his salon.

Alice slumped back into her chair and put her feet up on the one Lal had been using. She was amused to note that Professor Moriarty actually looked at her legs, which, she had to admit, were fairly spectacular. She was tempted to kick off her shoes, but she couldn't remember if the leggings she was wearing had a hole in the toe. "Depends," she said. "There's this drink they make on Orion Prime. They muddle up some vegetation—a combination of local herbs and grasses, along with a psychoactive tree bark—and soak it in a clear spirit made from *pitchak*. Do you know what I mean?"

The Professor squinted and stared in the middle distance. "They call it a Green Thorn, which is only a rough translation of the Orion. A better one would be Mind Splinter. Sometimes called Orion absinthe. Yes?"

"That's the one. How'd you know that?"

"I know a great deal, Miss Alice. Or, to be more

accurate, I have access to a great deal of information."

"And fast retrieval," Alice said, nodding. "Compliments from one machine to another."

"I am not a machine," the Professor said blandly, "though I live inside one." Walking to his small bar, he surveyed the containers and announced, "Alas, I do not have the required comestibles."

"Then give me a belt of bourbon. Straight."

"And I shall join you." The Professor selected a bottle and poured into two heavy tumblers. Carrying one of the glasses back to Alice, he studiously avoided staring at her legs. *Curiouser and curiouser,* she thought.

"So, there's nothing else you can tell me about your friend, Harry Mudd?"

"Harry wasn't my friend, and I could tell you anything you'd like to know," Alice said, sipping her drink. "But that's not what you really want to know, is it?"

"Isn't it?"

"No. What you want to know is whether Harry knew his way back to my homeworld. I thought I'd made that clear: no. Harry wasn't much of a navigator on the best of days, and I was the pilot when we took off for better climes. As I recall, he was sleeping one off in the bunk."

"So, there would be no point in my trying to locate him and asking him?"

"Not much of one. Also, he'd be like, oh, one hundred fifty years old now." She scrunched her mouth, simulating the human expression of difficult calculation. "Something like that."

"Humans have been known to live that long," the Professor observed.

"Not many. And not humans who lived like Harry did." She pointed significantly at the area where a human's liver would roughly reside. "A lot of wear and tear."

"Replacements are available."

"He's *dead*, Professor," Alice said, sitting up straight, her feet thumping on the floor. "Dead as a doornail. He has to be. I'd know it if he wasn't." She looked down at her feet and thought, *What the hell . . .* and kicked off her shoes: one, two, and they were gone. A moment later, she curled her legs up under her, discreetly pulling down the front of her skirt to cover her thighs. "Though I confess . . ."

"Yes?"

"There was a time when I thought he might still be out there."

"Really?"

"Looking for me."

"Really?"

"Except it wasn't him."

"No?"

"No," Alice said. "Turned out it was you, wasn't it? Proxima and Clea? You have them, don't you?"

The Professor sighed. "There does not seem to be any point in lying to you," he said.

"Dead? Or disassembled?"

"I am not a cruel man, Miss Alice."

"But you are single-minded."

"They are unharmed. When I have what I need, they will be released."

"Along with all the others?" Alice asked.

The Professor set his glass down on the end table. Alice noted that though he had seemed to enjoy holding the glass and looking at the liquid, he had never actually tasted it. "How many do you think I have?" he asked.

"I don't know. A lot? You were able to find Proxima and Clea. They weren't the brightest bulbs in the fixture, but they were very, very good at disguising their nature. If you got them, there were others much easier to find. Hell, you got Lal and me, and we weren't pushovers."

"Though you did make the mistake of living in a suburban home with negligible defenses," the Professor observed.

"That was Lal's idea. Not the smartest one she ever had. We'll be taking care of that when we get back home."

"As long as I get what I want," Moriarty said.

"You mind if I ask you a couple questions?"

"As long as I am not compelled to answer truthfully." He smiled. "I am the villain, after all."

"Why don't you have any of your drink?"

"Ah," Moriarty said, raising an eyebrow. "Well-observed. A simple answer: I cannot taste it. I cannot taste anything. Or smell. My sense of touch is extremely muted, too, if you must know. It is the price, I suppose, of being freed from my prison. There, somehow, we maintained the illusion of having five senses. Here, I am reduced to two. If you must know, it is something of a mystery to me. I suspect I do not have sufficient processing power for the environment we inhabit . . ."

"Or maybe it's all in your head," Alice suggested.

"The idea has occurred to me," Moriarty confessed. "But such theories are difficult to test. And your other question?"

"I think you already answered it, but I'll ask anyway: Why Data?"

"Excuse me?"

"You seem like a man of means. You have resources. I accept that it was an accident that you found me and Lal, but you didn't have to contact Data afterward. You . . . you're tweaking him. Rubbing his nose in it."

"Am I?" the Professor asked, inspecting his shirt cuff. "Perhaps. I suppose I could be indulging in a minor bit of revenge here."

"If you really wanted revenge, you could have just left him in the dark, never told him where we were. It would have driven him mad."

Moriarty gave a small shrug. "Perhaps I'm not quite the villain I'd like to think I am."

"Perhaps you're both fathers."

Moriarty's eye twitched and the corner of his mouth curled up in an involuntary snarl. He opened his mouth as if he was going to reply, but then, instead, disappeared.

Chuckling, Alice reached over and took his glass. Hers was empty.

Aboard the *Archeus*

As they stepped through the airlock onto the *Archeus*, Shakti announced, *"You have a call. When*

I saw you were headed back here, I asked if they could wait. They've been on hold for a couple minutes. One of them is starting to look pretty irritated. Or it may be his baseline condition."

"Who is calling?" Data asked, sliding into the chair behind the viewer.

"Lieutenant Barclay," Shakti said. *"Apparently, Albert made contact. He says he has the Doctor with him."*

"All the way from the Delta Quadrant?" La Forge exclaimed. "That's amazing. How is the signal?"

"Dicey," Shakti said. *"I'm stabilizing the image with a nice little algorithm I just whipped together and pulling some extra juice from the station's communications array. I don't think they'll notice for a few minutes."*

"Please put it on the main viewer," Data said.

"The image is going to be weak. If it fades out, I'll try to keep audio open."

"Understood."

The main viewer flickered to life. A moment later, Data and La Forge were face-to-face with their old friend and shipmate, Reg Barclay. He appeared even a bit more frazzled than usual, his expression flickering back and forth between worry, vague confusion, and curiosity. *"Geordi,"* Barclay said, smiling brightly. Then, turning to look at Data, his expression darkened. *"Who are you, sir?"*

"I am Data. How are you, Reg?"

"But . . . but . . ." He subsided, then exploded. *"Data!?"* He leaned into the camera. *"No! It can't be! Can it?"*

"It can," La Forge said.

"It is," Data said.

"But this is marvelous! How . . . ?"

"We do not have time to review all the details, Reg. Not now. Perhaps another time."

"Hmph," said another voice from Barclay's left. *"Resurrection is becoming entirely too commonplace."* The camera pulled out to accommodate both Barclay and his associate.

"It may be easier for beings such as we," Data replied. "Do I have the pleasure of addressing the chief medical officer of the *Voyager* fleet?"

La Forge had encountered EMH programs in sickbays of various starships, and he was struck by how similar and dissimilar this individual was from all the others. He had always found EMHs, even the more modern, sophisticated versions, to be obsequious and bland. Neither of those adjectives could be applied to this individual: The first two words that came to La Forge's mind were "agitated" and "prickly." Still, he also seemed to understand Starfleet protocol, and the hologram's expression mellowed from annoyance to something like respect. *"You do. Are you Commander Data of the* Enterprise?"

"Data, yes. But no longer a commander, nor of the *Enterprise*. I am speaking to you as a private citizen, not a Starfleet officer. I want to make that clear from the outset. Thank you for taking the time to speak with us, sir. Reg, I can only assume you must have moved heaven and earth to arrange this communication."

"Albert can be very insistent when he wants," Barclay said. *"And, apparently, the stars were aligned correctly. We were just in the process of completing our weekly uplink with Starfleet Command when his message came through. I asked the captain if we could have a few minutes of time and he agreed. But our time is limited . . ."*

"Yes, thank you. Then to the point," Data said. "Doctor, I need to know as much about your mobile emitter as you can tell me. Most importantly, have you had any success in reproducing its functionality?"

The Doctor's expression soured. *"Why is it always about my emitter?"* he grumbled.

"Forgive me, Doctor," Data said. "I meant no disrespect, but I find myself in a curious situation, one which you may be able to appreciate better than any other individual."

"What?" the Doctor asked, eyebrow raised. *"You've been turned into a hologram and can't leave a single room unless you're carrying a piece of twenty-ninth-century technology?"*

"No," Data replied. "But my daughter has been kidnapped by a hologram who, from what he has told me, cannot leave a single room. He asked me to help him find a means to do so and I thought you might be able to aid me."

"Your daughter?" Barclay interjected. *"Lal? Lal is alive, too?"*

"Yes," Data replied. "She was restored by means of . . ." He paused and rubbed his temple. "Again, Reg, we do not have time for this."

"Kidnapped?" Barclay interrupted. *"That's ter-*

rible." Addressing the Doctor, he said, *"She's a lovely person, Doctor. We have to do whatever we can to help."* Turning back to Data, he said, *"She really was . . . is delightful."*

"Delightful. Yes, I heard. And another resuscitation. And androids are having children now?"

"Androids can have children," Barclay explained. *"There are means."*

The Doctor narrowed his eyes and glared at Barclay. La Forge had the feeling these two had similar kinds of conversations all too frequently. *"I* hadn't *heard,"* he growled.

Barclay made an expression that looked very much as if he was praying for patience. *"Back to the point,"* he said. *"Unfortunately, no, we haven't been able to reproduce the emitter technology. Albert explained a little about what you wanted to know—though he omitted the information about Lal!—and told me what he already told you. Nothing has changed: The emitter defies our ability to scan it, and any attempt to disassemble it would destroy it."*

"And, besides," the Doctor said, cupping his arm protectively, *"it's mine. Legally. Not property of Starfleet. Captain Braxton gave it to me."*

"I am aware of the ruling, Doctor," Data said. He leaned back in the chair. "Then, in the time we have left, may I ask your advice? Having been in a similar situation, can you predict how Moriarty may react when he finds out I cannot give him what he wants?"

"Moriarty?" Barclay asked. *"You mean,* the *Moriarty? He's back?"*

"Yes," Data said. "I had assumed Albert told you. He is the one who kidnapped Lal."

"Moriarty?" the Doctor asked. *"You mean Professor James Moriarty? From Sherlock Holmes?"*

"A holographic entity whose existence sprang from the Sherlock Holmes stories, yes. But we have to assume he is a completely different individual now. More complex."

"I've heard of him," the Doctor said. *"Ours is a very small community, Mister Data. And given what happened to him, I think you'll have to assume . . ."*

"That he is very angry," Data said. "Yes, I know."

The Doctor waved his hand dismissively. *"Angry, of course. Obviously. Who wouldn't be? But no, something else . . ."*

"Yes?"

"Frightened. Very frightened. And, one would have to assume, desperate." The Doctor leaned toward the viewer, his face looming large. *"Believe me, Mister Data, I know something about that."*

"As do I, Doctor. As do I."

And then the screen went blank.

La Forge was startled. "I didn't think our time was up."

"It wasn't," Shakti said. *"I think Lieutenant Barclay's friend has an elevated sense of the dramatic. He cut the signal."*

"I agree," Data said. "We are running out of options."

"Then maybe I can help," said a voice from the screen. It flickered to life again. Albert Lee's face loomed.

"Albert," Data said. "Thank you for your assistance in locating Mister Barclay. I had not realized you were listening in."

"I did," Shakti inserted softly.

"I thought I might be able to help," Albert said.

"I assume you were able to wrest yourself away from the security officers."

Albert frowned. *"There's something to be said for having a reputation for being old and crotchety. Also, for being found unconscious on the floor."* He reached up and rubbed his neck where Data had administered the nerve pinch. *"Thanks for this, by the way. Best nap I've had in ten years."*

"You are welcome," Data deadpanned. "Were you permitted to return to work?"

"I was, but only because most of what I do isn't terribly sensitive. And a good thing, too, because I had another idea. Something that might help you get out of this jam."

"Please relate your idea."

"The remote-control device—the one they used to assassinate the President . . ."

"Go on."

"Could it be retrofitted so that Moriarty could upload his consciousness into an android? It's not exactly what he wants, but at least he'd have a body some of the time."

Data considered the idea. "An interesting concept, Albert. If Professor Moriarty had a physical body, that could be an option I would be willing to explore."

"Damn," Albert muttered. *"Well, if you change your mind and want to take a closer look at the transmitter, it's here at the Daystrom."*

"Thank you," Data said. "But your idea has sparked another. Shakti, please search the archives for information about Roger Korby and the androids of Exo III."

"Searching," Shakti said. *"Retrieved. What would you like to know?"*

"The device that allowed Korby to transfer his consciousness into android bodies: What happened to it?"

"Starfleet records say the device was removed from Exo III and taken to a research facility. Several years of study revealed that the device was useless without the templates."

"What happened to it?" La Forge asked.

"The device was stored in a Starfleet facility. The warehouse—it was basically a warehouse—was destroyed during the Borg invasion of 2381. No record of whether the device was recovered or demolished. Most of the other material stored there was pulverized, but you know Starfleet: They like their recordkeeping. Searching . . . Hmmm . . . Then the area was cleaned up and the scrap was sold to a private citizen."

"Who?" Data asked.

"The identity of the buyer is protected. Lots of security here. Hang on a moment. Let me get my big crowbar . . ." A moment later, the simulated sound of metal tearing up metal rang from the speakers.

"Apparently, the Doctor isn't the only one with a flair for the dramatic," La Forge observed. "And, just so we're clear about this, she's breaking into a secured Starfleet database."

"*She is not breaking into anything,*" Shakti said. "*She's gently prompting it to give up the goods. And she has. His name is Mudd.*"

"Excuse me?" Data said.

"*The buyer: His name is Harcourt Fenton Mudd. Or was. Based on the records I've found, Harry Mudd is . . . or was . . . very, very old.*"

"And buying scrap," Data observed. "The plot thickens."

15

———

Aboard the *Archeus*

Albert Lee said, *"I'm guessing that you know this Harry Mudd."*

"Not personally," Data replied. "By reputation, yes. Alice, Lal's governess, and Mudd were acquainted, though I suspect 'acquainted' might be an understatement."

"During 2268," Shakti recited, *"or Stardate 4513.3 if you want to get fussy about it, the Enterprise, under the command of James Kirk, was sabotaged by an artificial humanoid—an android—named Norman. The ship's engines were rigged to explode if he wasn't permitted to pilot the Enterprise to an undisclosed location. Norman scrambled the navigation console, so they weren't certain where they were headed. In an uncharacteristically compliant moment, Kirk permitted Norman to do this. I strongly suspect the captain correctly ascertained that Norman was only a pawn in a larger game and wanted to discover who the true mastermind was."*

Albert settled back into his chair. He had not been formally introduced to the persona behind the disembodied Shakti, but he liked her voice and her style. If he had only thought to make a cup of coffee, the moment would be perfection.

"As it turned out, the mastermind was none other than Harcourt Fenton Mudd, a con man and trickster of some minor renown, whom the Enterprise *crew had encountered on at least one previous occasion. Kirk was notorious for leaving mission details out of his logs when he didn't think they were relevant, so his exact dealings with Mudd are difficult to determine."* An image of a portly middle-aged man whom Albert assumed was Mudd appeared on his monitor. Given the man's rumpled and unhappy appearance, Albert had to assume this was a mug shot, a portrait taken shortly after being apprehended for a crime. Against his will, Albert felt pity for the man, probably the result of his pouting lower lip and general "Who, me?" demeanor.

"Through a series of misadventures, Mudd had been stranded on the androids' planet, where they quickly named him 'emperor' (Albert heard the quotation marks in Shakti's voice) *and allowed Mudd to pretty much run the planet, committing whatever tawdry acts he could imagine. Fortunately for everyone, Mudd's imagination seemed fairly limited, and he spent most of his time designing ever-more-curvaceous lines of female androids who allowed him to believe they would obey his every whim."* Images of well-coiffed, underdressed young ladies flickered

past, ending with a photo of a lovely brunette woman wearing a filmy orange dress. To Albert, she appeared both chilly and embarrassed. *"This last is one of the Alice series, reportedly one of Mudd's favorites. Apparently, he made a lot of them.*

"As Captain Kirk and the crew quickly learned, Mudd was emperor in name only. In fact, the androids had been studying him in an attempt to learn more about humanity. They found Mudd deeply flawed—a polite way of saying they thought he was a loser—but needed his help in securing a means to procure less-flawed individuals—the crew of the Enterprise, *in case you were wondering—in exchange for permission to leave the planet."*

"Why would he want to leave the planet?" Albert asked. *"Sounds like a pretty nice setup."*

"Who knows?" Shakti said. *"Psych profiles of Harry Mudd indicate he was a narcissist. Perhaps the idea of proscribing how much of him the universe had to enjoy bothered him. Perhaps he was bored. As someone or another observed at one time or another, having is not so pleasing a thing after all as wanting. Mudd may have discovered being waited on hand and foot isn't nearly as much fun as it sounds."*

"I'm willing to give it a try," Albert said.

"In the end, Kirk and company were able to overcome their captors by tormenting the poor creatures with illogical behavior . . ."

"That old chestnut?" Albert exclaimed. *"Does that even really work?"*

"It was the twenty-third century," Shakti said, sighing, *"and they weren't the brightest androids that ever came off the assembly line. No wonder their whole species died out. In any case, Kirk reprogrammed—I mean, introduced—the idea of freedom and decency and asked Norman and company to hang on to Harry Mudd until he became a better human being."*

"Shaky grasp of psychology," Albert observed. *"Sounds like Kirk just didn't want to deal with Mudd."*

"Indeed."

"But this was all over one hundred and twenty years ago," La Forge inserted. Shakti changed the monitor display so that Lee saw only the interior of the *Archeus.* "Unless he got ahold of a time machine, Mudd must be ancient."

"In the late twenty-two nineties, Mudd began to invest heavily in companies that produced life-extending technologies. He had, contrary to all expectation, amassed quite a sizable fortune, the kind of wealth that self-perpetuates unless handled very badly," Shakti said. *"He sank a considerable portion of his fortune into these technologies, presumably because he couldn't imagine a universe without Harry Mudd in it. If he was extremely careful and extremely lucky, he could have lived to the present day, especially if he used cryogenic technology to preserve himself for long periods."*

"Why would he do that?" La Forge asked. "What's the point of being alive if you're in cryostorage?"

"Perhaps he was waiting for something," Albert said. *"Or someone."*

"Good guess," Shakti said in a tone that made Lee smile. *"I like you, Albert. You're quick."* Off to the edge of the screen, Lee watched La Forge groan and cup his face with his palms. *"My research shows Mudd hired private detectives and research specialists over the course of several decades. Clearly, he was looking for someone."*

"Alice," Data said. "He was searching for Alice."

"But why?" Albert asked.

"Unknown," Data stated. "But we can make suppositions: Alice must know something or possess something that Mudd desperately wants. If he can find her, he can acquire this object or knowledge."

"You'll forgive me for being judgmental," Shakti said, *"but as one artificial intelligence observing another, Alice never struck me as the sort who possesses specialized knowledge about anything more sophisticated than hair-care technology."*

Albert's ears perked up. Shakti was an A.I. *How interesting.*

"No," Data agreed. "But she might know something about someone who does. Shakti, do you possess the coordinates for Alice's homeworld?"

"Ah—I was wondering when we'd get to that. In fact, I don't. No one does. *Even the* Enterprise's *logs don't have that information. It's as if someone went back through every record in existence and made sure the information was erased. Again,*

as one artificial intelligence to another, nice job, someone."

"Who could do something like that?" La Forge asked. "Could Alice's people have arranged it? If so, why?"

"It seems unlikely," Data said. "Also, I should mention that when I was aboard Akharin's space station, shortly before it was destroyed, he had a room—a kind of miniature museum of artificial intelligences. There was a humanoid male who had a necklace imprinted with the number one. He was inert—lifeless—but the display had a label: It said 'Norman.' Could this be the same Norman you mentioned in your story?"

"Possibly," Shakti said, *"though if it was, that's bad. Norman was supposedly the central processor, the traffic cop. If he was destroyed or rendered inert, then something unfortunate might have happened to the androids."*

"Or there could have been a change in leadership," La Forge said. "Or maybe Norman went out again looking for another starship and ran into trouble. Or maybe there was more than one Norman after all. I guess we'll never know. But that still doesn't explain how the coordinates of the planet were erased from Starfleet records."

"The Fellowship," Data said. "They have the resources and the motivation."

"I agree," Shakti said. *"This story has their non-sebaceous fingerprints all over it."*

"So there's no way to find the androids' planet," La Forge said. "But so what? We want Mudd, not the androids."

"Oh, I already found him," Shakti said. *"That was easy. He hasn't exactly made himself scarce. Remember? Narcissist?"*

"Why didn't you say so?" La Forge said.

"Indeed," Data said. "And why are we not on our way to wherever he is?"

"We are," Shakti said. *"I'm just now getting clearance from Ops. It's like you guys think I'm not on top of these details. I just had to make sure you were up to speed."*

"I never doubted you for a moment, Shakti," Lee said, enjoying the moment.

"You are incredibly cute, sir," Shakti said. *"I'm going to come visit you when this is all over."*

La Forge groaned again. "Can we please go into warp?"

"I don't think he gives you enough respect, Albert," Shakti declared. *"I think he's envious."*

A placeless place

"List for me the last ten words you've said where the second syllable began with the letter B," the Countess said.

Lal cocked her head to the side and recited, "Sequentially or alphabetically?"

"You choose."

"All right: Albeit, embarrass, embody, embolden—I went on a bit of an 'em' streak, didn't I?—fable, garbled, label, rambunctious, robot, and well-being, though I admit that last one is a bit of a stretch. Why do you ask?"

"It's a little game my girls and I used to play. It was one of the ways I monitored them."

"What a wonderful mother you are," Lal said as sincerely as she could (and careful to use the present tense). "And what a strange universe you came from that had such creatures in it."

The Countess dipped her head in a mock-bow.

"So, if I may ask," Lal asked, "what do you think of *this* universe?" The Countess (Lal preferred to think of her as "the Countess") had brought her a cup of tea, which she had enjoyed greatly, though more for the ceremony of its preparation and presentation than for its flavor or effect on her physiology. Though, Lal allowed, she did feel, to a degree, "bucked up." The Countess seemed greatly pleased to hear this.

"I'm sorry, my dear. I don't understand the question," the Countess replied, poking at the fire with an ornate metal rod. At some point while the tea had been steeping, a fireplace had unfolded from the far wall, providing a merry light as well as the pleasant aroma of wood turning into charcoal. Lal resolved to have a fireplace installed into her sitting room back home when she returned to Orion.

"This universe—the universe I inhabit—how does it compare to the one you inhabited before, the one that collapsed?"

"Ah, I understand," the Countess replied, sliding shut the glass door that prevented sparks from singeing the carpet. "Your supposition is that there are some fundamental, noticeable differences between this universe—the 'real' universe—and the 'fictional' one inside the memory solid. Is that correct?"

"Yes," Lal said, "though I confess having it stated in that fashion makes me feel like I've been very rude. Have I?"

The Countess glanced at her, eyebrows raised. The firelight reflected off her white flesh, making her cheeks appear to glow pinkly. "A bit, dear girl. But only a bit. Your only offense is candor, which is a trait of the very young. The truly terrible habits—mendaciousness and insincerity—shall only come with age."

"Everything you say sounds like you're about to break into a song," Lal said.

The Countess guffawed, the back of her hand under her nose, eyes shut. She laughed so hard she had to wipe her eyes with the cuff of her sleeve. "Ah, Lal," she said when she could breathe again, "I truly hope you'll be able to meet my girls someday. They would adore you."

"I'm sure I'd like them, too," Lal said. "Tell me more about them. How old were they? What did they look like? Do you have any pictures of them? Wait, what am I saying? Here, you could easily enough *make* a picture of them, couldn't you?"

"No," the Countess said, shaking her head. "I could not."

"I'm sorry," Lal said. "Was that insensitive of me? Is it difficult for you to think about . . ."

"You misunderstand," the Countess interrupted. "I would if I could." Casting her arms wide as if to embrace the entire room, she said, "I would fill the walls, every wall of every room,

but I cannot . . . I do not . . ." She closed her eyes
and touched the tips of two white fingers to her
two white eyelids. "I cannot recall their faces. My
Gladys, my Sophia . . . I cannot recall their faces.
The memories have been taken from me."

"When the computer crashed?" Lal said. "When
you were damaged? Is that what you mean?"

"I don't know," the Countess said, her voice
becoming cool. "My husband says that would
be impossible, that we . . . as the purpose the
program existed . . . our memories could not
be compromised. He says that the entire world
would have been erased before the crash could
have affected us."

"But you said," Lal recalled, "that there was
nothing but a single room. That nothing else was
left. It sounds pretty close to the world being
erased to me."

"But not the *entire* world," the Countess retorted. "My husband says he remembers them
perfectly. He believes my inability to do so is not
damage to my memory, but my psyche."

"He believes you are traumatized."

"Yes."

Lal saw that the Countess did not agree. "But
you?"

"I believe some of my memories were deleted
in order to preserve the core of the universe."

"Your husband."

"Yes."

"And you?" Lal asked, suddenly discovering
she was twisting the coverlet around her fingers
so tightly that they ached. "What are you?"

"Part of the program," the Countess said. "Part of the illusion." She waved her hand like an actress on a stage. "The light fantastic."

"But your husband, he refuses to believe this might be true."

"That's *his* illusion, my dear. If he allowed himself to believe that I and our daughters were no more substantial than a photon, it would destroy him."

"But your daughters were photons, weren't they?" Lal said. "And he knows that. If he could know that and love them, why not you, too? It seems so arbitrary and cruel."

The Countess looked back over at Lal and, unexpectedly, smiled brightly. Crossing the room, she sat down on the edge of the bed again and caressed Lal's cheek with the tip of her finger. "You really are extraordinarily young, aren't you? No more than a babe."

"Chronologically, I am less than two solar years old," Lal admitted, "but I have an extremely sophisticated neural net. In human terms, I'm . . ."

"That's not what I meant," the Countess said. "You seemed surprised that a person could hold two contradictory ideas in his mind simultaneously and not wonder at the conflict."

Lal wasn't sure whether she was vaguely insulted or needed to explain her perspective in greater detail. Instead, she simply said, "It is not logical."

The Countess chuckled. "No" was all she said. "Of course not. But my husband is afraid and therefore desperate. Have you ever been afraid, my dear?"

Though she knew there was virtue in honesty, Lal also understood the woman who was asking her this might be a minion of her captor, though she sincerely did not want to believe this could be true. Finally, she said, "Every sentient being knows fear. Knowing you exist also means knowing you could end. I have already died once. I fear doing so again."

"Then I must be sentient, too," the Countess agreed. "Though I am not so much afraid of dying as finding out I never really existed."

Lal reached up and gripped the Countess's hand in her own. "You're going to love my father," she said. "He talks just like you."

Aboard the *Archeus*

"I had another thought, Data," Lee said. La Forge had been hoping he would have been cut off when the *Archeus* went into warp, but Shakti had clearly taken a liking to the old man and the two had been happily chatting since leaving Deep Space 9.

La Forge had faded away sometime during their rambling conversation and realized he must have been napping for a while because he woke up in the copilot's seat (he didn't remember sitting down there) with a crick in his neck.

When Data turned away from the pilot's console to respond to Lee, the control panel in front of La Forge became active. *Guess Shakti knows I'm awake,* he thought. A moment later, a steaming cup of coffee materialized in the holder next to his seat. He picked it up, nodded gratefully to no one in particular, and studied the navigational display. Either he had been asleep for quite a while or the *Archeus* was even faster than Shakti had claimed. They appeared to be approaching their destination, a small moon orbiting an unnamed Class-K planet.

"Concerning?" Data asked.

"Moriarty's demands. While I think it's a good idea to pursue this Korby idea, shouldn't we consider technology we already have access to?"

"You speak again of the device."

"Correct," Lee said, sounding like a dog worrying a bone. *"Like I said, I'm pretty sure I could get to it if required."*

"You mean like we got to Moriarty's data solid?" La Forge asked. He knew he was being difficult, but he just couldn't help himself.

"It wasn't my fault the alarms went off," Lee barked.

"That's right, Geordi," Shakti said. *"It wasn't Albert's fault."* Clearly, Shakti was smitten.

"Right, right," La Forge said. "Sorry. But would it make any difference? It's not like we have any spare androids lying around."

"We have the early Soong-types," Lee said. *"The pre–B-Four prototypes. They're probably not what Moriarty was looking for, but, in a pinch . . ."*

"I, too, considered the idea," Data said, "but I would employ it only as a last-ditch effort. For now, I believe we should focus our efforts on acquiring the Exo III device from Mudd."

"Any ideas for how we can get it from him?" La Forge asked.

"I am astonishingly wealthy," Data said. "That might be a factor."

La Forge slurped his coffee, working hard not to comment.

"From what I've been able to determine," Shakti said, *"so is Mudd. Perhaps not on the same scale you are, Data, but it's difficult to know for sure. He seems to have done a good job of concealing some of his wealth. It's old money. Very old and not necessarily something I can find."*

"You mean he might have it stuffed in his mattress?" Lee asked.

"Very succinctly put," Shakti said approvingly.

"Then we shall play it by ear," Data said. "Every man has his price."

"And every android," Shakti added.

"And every android," Data agreed.

"Coming out of warp," La Forge announced for no reason other than he felt like he should say something. "Three two one."

"Out," Shakti said. The lighting in the cabin shifted subtly as the main viewscreen brightened to display the arc of the planetoid's southern hemisphere. It was a dirty gray rock, a dull and lifeless place. *"Strange place for a man named Mudd to end up,"* Shakti opined.

"The irony is noted, Shakti," Data said. "Are you hailing?"

"I am," she replied pleasantly. *"And I am receiving a reply. Some kind of automaton is telling me to go away if I'm selling something and*

*to drop the package on the doorstep if I'm deliv-
ering."*

"Have you located the doorstep?"

*"A transporter platform in geosynchronous
orbit over the south pole."*

"No sign of an abode?"

"Scanners say no. Nothing on the surface."

"Underground?"

"Seems logical."

"If we drop off something on the doorstep,
could you trace the transporter signal?"

"Probably. What did you have in mind, boss?"

"Myself," Data said. "I will pass through any
transporter filters Mudd might have in place to
block biologicals."

"But you don't know where the platform will
beam you," La Forge protested.

"All the more reason for you to trace the signal accurately," Data said, rising from his seat and
snapping into transport posture. "Beam me down,
Shakti."

*"Would you care to hear a second opinion
about this idea, boss?"*

"I do not recall asking for one."

"One to beam down, then."

A portion of the overhead slid back, and a
transporter array dropped into place over Data's
head. A moment later, a soft hum filled the con-
fined space and La Forge's friend was reduced to
subatomic particles.

"Wow," Lee said from the monitor. *"Is there
anything that boat doesn't have?"*

Shakti said, *"Nope."*

In unknown straits

Data materialized inside a dark, unpressurized room. As soon as the *Archeus*'s transporter beam dissipated, scanners mounted on motorized arms emerged from the wall, buzzed around him, and then withdrew. The room was perfectly dark, and Data could have used the small torch clipped to his belt, but he decided he did not wish to move any more than necessary. Rather, he studied the room with his passive scanners.

A moment later, he felt a new transport beam take hold of him.

Though Data knew perfectly well that his mind and body were in stasis while in transport, when he materialized, he had the definite sensation that the process took longer than usual, as if the beam had been forwarded through several transit stations.

He slowly flexed his fingers and felt the stir of warm air flowing around him. Again, it was dark, but not perfectly: A thin bar of light at floor level indicated an entrance. Data parted his lips and emitted an ultrasonic chirp. Turning his head slightly from side to side and subtly altering the pitch of each chirp helped him form a mental picture of the room.

It was cavernously large, though the bulk of the space was to his back. The floor was littered with packing cases and crates of various sizes and shapes. Sniffing, Data detected the aromas of exotic spices, expensive liquors, and rotting fruit. Whoever was supposed to be managing the receiving platform and the warehouse beyond was *not* doing a very good job.

In the distance, Data detected the sound of a clanking apparatus inching along a yawning hallway. The device—whatever it was—was in desperate need of repair. Calipers, pistons, and gears slipped and crashed and ground and clashed. Someone swore extravagantly.

Data stepped off the transport platform. Wary security devices stirred, but none assumed threatening postures. As Data had suspected, Harry Mudd was not the sort of person who would shoot an android on sight.

Two large doors parted and bright search beams cast about the room, finally locking onto the transport platform. Someone made a sound that might have been a grunt or might have been a wheeze. A large device—also wheezing—heaved through the open doors, and the search beams swung back and forth, parting the darkness from the light, flickering off piles of dusty treasure. Muttering commenced: "What's going on here? Where is it? I heard the damned alarm go off, so something has to be here."

The device cautiously edged into the room. Standing just off to its side in the shadow of a large packing case, Data could see that the search beams were mounted on robotic arms heavy enough to do damage if they made contact. The bulk of the device was taken up by a large pilot's chair or capsule where a single figure sat fitfully working the controls. The device inched forward on large, spongy treads and the capsule floated on anti-gravs. It was an elaborate sedan designed to carry an invalid: a wheelchair, in effect.

The pilot paused and the device eased to the floor, a loose flange puttering fitfully. "Maybe I'm hearing things," the pilot said. "Maybe I was asleep. No, couldn't have been that. God knows it wasn't that. Sleep . . . ha! Not that." He continued to mutter, the words becoming less and less distinct until they turned into a low whistle of a snore.

Data considered. He was fairly sure he could slip out of the room undetected if he wished and continue his investigations. He should, he knew, determine his whereabouts and let the others know he had arrived unharmed, but was that really the most direct route to his goal?

Stepping out from behind the packing case, Data tapped a knuckle on the pilot's canopy. The occupant's head jerked away. "Huh? Wha . . . ? Who's there? What do you want?" The voice became stronger and crankier with every word. "What are you doing here, mister? This is *my* house! You shouldn't have come here! You're going to regret this!" The robotic arms lifted in a threatening display. Data saw they were composed of some kind of flexible material, and the ends were manipulators tipped with sharp barbs.

Data ignored the arms and focused his attention on the pilot. "Harry Mudd, I presume."

"You presume bloody damned right, mister!" Mudd sputtered. "How the hell did you get down here? Nothing living could get through the bio-filters!"

Again, Data decided to use the most direct method. "Your definition of 'living' might be too narrow, Mister Mudd," he said, pushing his jacket sleeve up his arm. In a swift, well-practiced pattern, Data tapped several pressure points on his forearm and wrist. A small panel slid out of the way, revealing glowing mechanisms. They didn't need to glow; in fact, under most circumstances, they wouldn't have glowed, but Data felt the theatricality was required.

"You're an android," Mudd muttered. Data would have liked it better if he had sounded more surprised, but Mudd's tone was more wary than flabbergasted. The canopy slid open a touch, just enough that Data could see an eye peering out at him. "I know you, don't I? Or someone like you?" Mudd said. "You're one of . . ."

"Soong's," Data said, not knowing precisely why he wanted his identity to be, if not concealed, then muddled. "Yes. I've come a long way to find you, Mister Mudd."

The canopy slid open wide enough that Data could see the pilot's entire face. Despite cosmetic surgery and restorative treatments, there was no concealing the fact that Harry Mudd was old. Incredibly old. The flesh of his face was firm and taut, but his jowls hung in folds. Beneath a brown goatee, Data saw the withered tissue of his neck. Mudd's face and form were like two badly meshed puzzles: None of his features was consistent with the others; none of it held together. And, obviously, no one lived with Mudd who would tell him. The eyes, though . . . Data noted the eyes. Still bright, still clear and with a glint that might be mischief or maybe madness. He grinned, showing large, bright white teeth. "Well, then, Mister Soong, you should come in and make yourself at home. We have a great deal to talk about."

16

———◆———

Aboard the *Archeus*

"Coordinates are locked in, Geordi," Shakti said, brisk and efficient. *"Data says he convinced Mudd you're his technical expert and needs your help to assess his collection. So, look like you're assessing."*

"Collection? Is that what we're calling contraband technology today?"

"Keep the attitude in check, Commander. Apparently, Mudd has been amassing material for decades. Data says he's only been in a couple rooms so far, but he's never seen anything like it. Ever see Citizen Kane?*"*

"I haven't gotten around to that one yet."

"Raiders of the Lost Ark?"

"No."

"You should. They're both great. It would have really rung a bell when you saw Mudd's piles of stuff."

"Is Data sending images? Are you seeing them?"

"Everything he sees, I see," Shakti explained. *"Well, most of it. When he wants me to see. Which is most of the time."*

"You two have a very interesting relationship." La Forge rose and waited for the transporter beam to lock onto him.

"It's even more interesting," Shakti observed, *"when you consider that I had the same relationship with his father."*

La Forge suppressed a case of the willies. "I think I should beam down now."

"Beaming," Shakti said, clearly delighted with herself. *"Don't forget to call him 'Mister Soong.' Mudd settled on that somehow."*

"Right." A moment later, La Forge stood in a vast, dimly lit room surrounded by piles of what he had to assume were parts of Harry Mudd's "collection" of miscellaneous technology. He tentatively stepped forward, wary about brushing up against any of the precariously balanced stacks lest chunks of antiquated machinery topple onto his head. No visible signage pointed to an exit, so La Forge resorted to picking through the heaps, watchful for dangling wires and trailing power couplings. He spotted familiar interfaces and components from a dozen Alpha and Beta Quadrant technologies, including Federation, Klingon, Rigelian, Gorn, Bajoran, and Cardassian, though there were just as many apparatuses he did not recognize, including one that glowed iridescent green when he stepped too near. La Forge the engineer wanted to stop and examine about every third object he saw, while Commander La Forge the Starfleet officer wanted to quarantine the entire area and send in the robotic bomb sniffers.

After a few minutes of aimless wandering, La Forge conceded that he was lost and stopped to flip open the tricorder Shakti had provided. Scanning, he was alarmed by traces of some truly exotic compounds (*Do not go into the northwest corner,* he resolved), but was pleased to discover he was only a few meters away from a doorway. Sliding along carefully, he was soon able to lay his palm on a bulkhead. Fortunately, Mudd had *not* piled tech against the walls, so La Forge quickly found the door, which, alas, was locked.

With a sigh, La Forge tapped his combadge. Data answered immediately. *"Where are you?"* he asked.

"Standing in front of a locked door," La Forge replied.

"Ah," his friend said, and a moment later the door slid open. Data was framed in the arch. He handed La Forge a small device and said, "Clip this to your lapel. The security system will recognize you now."

"Any reason you couldn't have just met me inside?"

"My apologies. Shakti alerted me that you were on your way, but Harry Mudd would not let me . . ." He paused, clearly unsure how to phrase his thought respectfully. "Let us just say he has not had anyone to speak to in a long time. A very long time."

"Chatty?"

"Extremely."

Lowering his voice, La Forge asked, "Any luck finding the Exo III device?"

"Not as yet, but I have seen only a tiny percentage of Mudd's possessions. Unfortunately, his inventory system leaves something to be desired."

"As does his storage techniques," La Forge said. "I'm not sure what he needs more: an archivist or a hazmat team."

"Both in equal measure," Data said, pointing the way up the corridor.

"Any particular reason you had Shakti deposit me in such a perilous location?"

"Alas, all locations are equally perilous," Data replied. "And this room seemed relatively clean and far enough from Mudd's lair that we could speak for a few minutes without raising his suspicions. And he *is* quite suspicious. While remarkably nimble-minded in some regards, Harry Mudd displays some of the paranoid tendencies associated with some forms of dementia."

"But he likes you."

"I do not believe Harry Mudd likes anyone except Harry Mudd. As my father's agent, he wants something from me. And though he knows Noonien Soong has expired, Mudd knows my father possessed technology that might be able to transfer a human consciousness into an android body."

"So, he thinks you might have once been a human."

"I believe that is the case. Mudd considers himself an expert on android behavior and refuses to accept the possibility that I am a completely artificial intelligence."

La Forge stopped in his tracks to consider this paradox. "Harry Mudd thinks you seem too human to be an android?"

"Apparently," Data said.

"All things considered, that's an odd little compliment."

The corners of Data's mouth twitched upward. "I had not framed the situation in that manner, Geordi. Thank you."

"You're welcome. What's the play?"

"I am a representative of the Soong Corporation. I am looking for a specific piece of technology, which I am willing to purchase at an exorbitant price. Mudd knows this, but does not want or need money."

"What does he want?"

"A trade. Harry Mudd wants to live forever. He believes the Exo III technology may be a means to his end. But an important component is missing."

"The slug."

"Correct."

"Did you tell him we have one?"

"No," Data said. "That would have been untrue."

"You've seemed prepared to do just about anything else you thought necessary," La Forge remarked. "I don't want to seem judgmental, but . . ."

Data shook his head. "You forget, Geordi. I *rely* on you to be judgmental. And, yes, if I thought it would be to my advantage to tell Mudd I had a slug . . ." He paused to savor the peculiar phraseology. "If I did, I would. But I do not. He has hinted, however, that he knows where one could be found."

"We're not buying, then, but trading."

"Correct."

"And my job?"

Slowing as they approached a large, ornate doorway, Data said, "You are the expert, the curator. Mudd said he would only negotiate with you."

"Why? You're Soong's agent."

"But you are human."

"That's . . . You'll forgive me . . . but that's insane."

"Excellent," Data said, stepping forward and activating the electric eye. The lavishly carved doors began to slowly draw apart. "Then you have correctly ascertained the circumstances of the situation."

Mudd's World

Mudd inhaled as deeply as he could and bellowed as well as he was able (though not as well as the old days), "Come in! Come in, my lad! Welcome, welcome, and most welcome! I can't tell you how excited I am to see you! As you can imagine, a man of my stature must constantly attend to his portfolio—investments and whatnot—so I haven't much time to socialize. But when the opportunity presents itself, I think you'll find I'm a generous host!" The android stood aside and let the newcomer approach Harry's chair. Passive sensors discreetly scanned him. Harry studied the readout through the display layer in his monocle: human; male; middle-aged (though everyone was younger than Harry, so middle-aged was a relative term); not carrying anything malevolent or dangerous on his person, though he had some very sophisticated wetware in his head. Harry recognized the signature and decided Soong's lackey had his eyes replaced with bionics to aid him in his work. Or Soong made him replace the eyes as a condition of employment, probably to better record information about purchases. If true, Harry's respect for Soong increased by an iota. "What's your name, my friend? I suspect your colleague here told me once or twice already, but sometimes details elude me."

"Geordi," the man said, stopping before Harry's chair.

"Just Geordi? No surname?"

"Not necessary," said "Geordi," or whatever his real name was. Clearly, this man was Soong's primary operative. The android was simply his bodyguard or possibly his keeper. It was impossible to be sure, where Soong was concerned.

"Thanks for taking the time to see us, Mister Mudd. We know you're a busy man."

"Nonsense, my lad. And call me Harry. Everyone calls me Harry. Have a seat, have a seat. Can I get you something to eat or drink? Join me in a libation?" The nursing program that was monitoring Harry's physiology began pitching a silent fit, warning him that he should *not* under any circumstances have "a libation," that the mechanism currently filtering impurities out of his blood was overtaxed as it was and on and on and on . . . Sometimes, Harry regretted ever having the damned thing installed.

"No, thanks, Harry," Geordi said. "We just ate a little while ago. And I'm eager to find out what we can do for each other."

"Excellent! Excellent! A man who doesn't mince words. Get right down to brass tacks, as it were. Then let's get started. Your 'colleague' here explained that your employer is interested in a piece of technology I acquired in a salvage sale, the Exo III transfer bed."

"That's one of the pieces we wanted to examine, yes." Geordi sat down in the chair Mudd had indicated and crossed his legs. The android drifted around the room while they talked, examining Harry's sculptures and paintings. Most of them were commissioned pieces commemorating a specific victorious moment in Mudd's life.

"I realized I'm showing my hand a bit too early in our negotiations," Harry said, winking, "but I feel obliged to warn you that while the device may be functional—you can read my experts' report when you like—it's useless without the blanks. That's where the real genius was, not in the transfer bed."

"The slugs," Geordi said. "Yes, we're aware of that problem."

"And your employer believes he has the means to create new 'slugs'—charming term, that."

Geordi paused, uncrossed his legs, and then recrossed them in the opposite direction. "I'm not at liberty to discuss my employer's plans for the device, Harry. Perhaps after we've completed our transaction, you and he could speak about it."

"Because," Harry said excitedly (his blood pressure monitor began to glow yellow), leaning forward as much as he was able with all the cables and cords plugged into various orifices, "if he thinks he's on the verge of a breakthrough, I would be *ever* so interested in helping him."

"A breakthrough?" Geordi asked, all polite courtesy. "What do you mean?"

"If Soong's figured it out!" Harry shouted. The blood pressure monitor turned bright orange. "How to transfer a human mind into an android! Everyone knew that he was working toward that!"

"Everyone?"

"All right, not everyone, but anyone who was paying attention."

"You think Doctor Soong—I mean, my employer—was working out a way to transfer a human mind into an android body?"

"What else would he have been doing?" Harry said, and grunted, feeling a muscle group in his lower back contracting spastically. The nursing program sent a small dose of relaxant into his bloodstream and the pain quickly eased. "From everything I've learned about him, he must be getting up there. Not as old as me, mind you, but old enough. And not everyone has my robust constitution. Those egghead types never get enough exercise."

Geordi made a steeple with his fingertips in front of his lips and nodded sagely, obviously wishing he could agree more enthusiastically.

Harry knew he had the situation nailed down. Obviously, the negotiator didn't appreciate being outfoxed. "I see," he said. "But, of course, even though we know the process is possible—Captain Kirk's logs from the Exo III mission are proof—my employer would only be interested in using his own androids."

"Then he's in for a world of frustration, my lad. My technical people assure me the Exo III bed won't work with anything other than their . . . what did you call them?"

"Slugs."

"Yes, that. Slugs. And there's got to be another way. I *know* there's another way."

"You *know*?"

"Of course. Or why would I be spending all this money and time? I *know* a human mind can be uploaded into an android frame, one that can last up to half a million years! I saw it with my own eyes!" His blood pressure, which had lessened, began to creep up again. The nursing program asked Harry whether it should pump something soothing into his veins. Harry blinked strategically, indicating the nurse should hold off. He wanted to stay sharp.

"Really?" the android asked, speaking for the first time since Geordi entered the room. "You have seen this? May I ask where and when?"

"Well," Harry said, scowling, "not that it's any of your business, but I didn't exactly see it. Rather, I should say that the process was explained to me by a very reliable source. A former colleague of mine, what you might call a business partner. She had some friends who knew all about such things. Even examined some humans and were sure the process would take. 'Youth and beauty forever,' they said."

"Indeed?" the android asked. "If such is the case, why do you not simply ask them . . . ?"

"Don't you bloody well think I would if I could?!" The nurse didn't bother to ask for Harry's permission, but she pumped a steadying narcotic cocktail straight into his brain. He felt the warming glow creep over him, sending his blood pressure back into normal range, though he felt his mind growing fuzzy. *Not to worry,* he thought. *I don't need the full wattage to handle these two.* "Which is to say," Harry continued more calmly, "I've lost track of my colleague. If I ever hear from her again—and I'm sure I will—she'll be happy to take me back to . . . to visit her friends. If he wants, tell Soong I'll put in a good word for him."

"Of course," Geordi said, sitting up straighter. His posture said he was coming to the point. Harry could teach a master class in how to interpret body language. "I'm sure my employer will be happy to hear you made the offer. But back to my original question . . ."

"The Exo III bed. Yes, yes. You're tiresome, my lad. Has anyone ever told you that?"

"It's come up."

"It won't work without the slug. And if I had a slug, I'd try it on myself before turning over the machine. Soong's welcome to examine it, but he has to agree to keep me informed about his experiments. I know I look like the picture of ma-ture good health here, but, believe me, a lot of time and money goes into keeping me looking this good . . ."

"Wait," the android said. "Please stop."

"Don't be interrupting us," Harry snarled, pointing at the android. He was more certain than ever that Geordi wasn't being guarded, but kept, and the idea of an artificial intelligence having that kind of control over a flesh-and-blood human made Harry's blood boil. "The adults are talking business here."

"You said 'the slug,'" the android said, "not 'a slug.'"

"Yes," Harry sputtered. "I suppose I did. I assumed you knew what I meant." He looked at La Forge, who appeared bored and nonchalant. "*He* knows what I meant. Maybe your Doctor Soong doesn't tell his thugs everything."

"Thugs?" the android asked, looking to Geordi for an explanation.

"Maybe you should just explain it to him, Harry," Geordi said. "He can be a little slow on the uptake sometimes. He's not one of the boss's more recent models, if you catch my meaning."

Harry rolled his eyes in annoyance. "I'm referring to the slug. *The* slug. The only one left in existence."

"One exists?" the android asked, completely (and predictably) surprised.

"Just one," Harry admitted. "For all the good it'll do anyone. He'll never give it up."

"Give it up? Who?" Again, the android appealed to Geordi.

"Tell him, Harry. He'll never figure it out."

"Why, the great collector, of course. The man who's never parted with a single one of his toys in his entire life. *Except one.* I'm sure you've heard of him. Or your creator has even if you haven't. Fajo. Kivas Fajo."

The android stared into the middle distance, mouth agape. He blinked once very slowly and then turned to stare at his associate. "Ah," he said. "Of course. Who else could it have been?"

Aboard the *Archeus*

Data sat in his chair and stared at the isolinear chip in his palm. He found he was a bit ashamed of how much he liked his chair, how the complex micromotors and bladders under the simulated hide curled around him. Being composed of plasteel and various exotic, extremely durable materials meant that Data rarely felt vulnerable or ill at ease, yet he had to admit there was something about his chair on the *Archeus* that made him feel . . . safe. Comforted. The illusion of security and well-being that Data had permitted himself to believe in over the past several months had been violently ripped away: His daughter had been taken, the veil sundered. And yet, in all that time, Data had never felt as if he, himself, was at *risk*. His assumption was that he would solve the problem and his family would be safe. Emotion did not need to enter into the equation.

But now there was a new problem, one that couldn't be solved so easily.

Fajo.

Just thinking the name sent a pulse of something he couldn't easily describe through Data's frame. *Is this fear?* he wondered.

"It's insanity," Lee said. Apparently, he and Shakti had been in constant communication while Data and La Forge had been in Mudd's domicile. *"The very idea of contacting him . . . He's a criminal!"* Lee slapped his hand against the console in front of the viewscreen for emphasis, then added, *"Isn't he?"*

"Not technically," Shakti said. *"Fajo served his time. Not nearly as much as we might have expected, granted, but he was released on parole . . . let me see . . . mid-2376, and has been a model citizen ever since. Resumed his career as a financial adviser. Apparently, he had some clients who were willing to overlook his indiscretions . . . made a great deal of latinum. And . . . hmmm . . . let me see . . . yes, about four years later, Fajo began to attend auctions again. Occasionally making small but exquisite purchases. Nothing that would alarm the authorities or the psychologists, nothing illegal."*

"Focusing on?" La Forge asked.

"Artwork, primarily. Non-Federation. Beta and Gamma Quadrant civilizations."

"Curious," Data commented.

"Collectors," La Forge muttered.

"Yes," Shakti replied. *"But, as I said, non-threatening."* She paused meaningfully. *"Until you look closer."*

"And you always look closer," Lee said.

Data sank back into his chair and lightly closed his hand around the isolinear chip. "Tell me," he said.

"Frequently," Shakti recited, *"Fajo's purchases were parts of lots. Most of the material in the lots was worthless or simply . . . miscellaneous. Unknown."*

"But upon closer inspection?" Data asked.

"A.I.," Shakti explained. *"Broken. Discarded. Disabled. Or simply misunderstood. But all of it . . . all of it . . . he was buying machines that might have been alive, Data. He was buying our brothers and sisters."*

"To what end?"

"Who knows? Who could know what was in his heart? He was . . . What would you say? What would you call him?" Shakti asked.

"A sociopath," La Forge said.

"Though of a very peculiar flavor," Data added. "A narcissist, certainly."

"We seem to be running into a lot of those," Shakti said.

"Undeniably, but perhaps there is a lesson here for us all."

"Which would be what?" La Forge asked.

"Make too big a target of yourself and someone will decide to pick up a weapon and take a shot."

No one spoke for several seconds. Typically, Lee broke the silence. *"That's an atypically dark sentiment for you, Data."*

"I appear to be having a dark day, Albert." He clenched his fist tightly, but not so tight as to break the chip. The edges dug into the palm of his hand. Data was surprised to find the pain was, if not pleasurable, then . . . what? Acceptable? Necessary? He knew the chip would crumble before it could pierce his epidermis, so he released the pressure and opened his hand. Staring down at the chip—the chip with Fajo's private communicator channel inscribed—Data said, "So, I shall call him."

"Insanity," Albert repeated.

"It's a terrible idea," Shakti added. *"He's a terrible man. A monster, I think."*

La Forge, who had not sat down since they beamed back onto the *Archeus*, folded his arms and said, "Do whatever you think is right."

Data felt a quiver run through his body. Could the *Archeus* have encountered some sort of eddy in space? He looked around the cabin to see if anything else had shifted, but, naturally, nothing had. Nothing ever would.

He plugged the chip into the communications console and swiped his forefinger over the CALL key. Subspace transmitters exchanged information. Seconds passed. Shakti and Lee spoke in low tones, an intimacy fueled by shared dismay.

The console whistled, confirming that he had accepted the hail.

"Who's calling?" The voice was sleepy, grumpy even. Disturbed. Aroused from slumber. *"What do you want? How did you get this number?!"* Anger rising. *"How . . . ?!"* And then the anger abated. *"How?"* Fajo said, softly, speaking more like a lover. *"How can it be you? Aren't you dead?"*

Data felt a thrill of fear course through his body,

followed closely by a feeling he had not encountered previously: hatred. And then wonder: How did Fajo recognize him? He made a fist and dug his fingernails into his palm. "Apparently not," Data said. "And how are you?"

"I . . . I don't know. Dreaming, perhaps?" The monitor flickered to life, and Data looked into the eyes—and only the eyes—of the Zabilian trader. Fajo had his face much too close to the comm pickup, and it could not pull away and show the man's whole face. Data remembered Fajo's face very clearly and was able to superimpose the image from their encounter many years ago over the current view. The years—or perhaps prison— had not been kind. The lines and folds around the Zabilian's eyes were numerous and deep. This struck Data as curious: Even if prison life or disease had ravaged Fajo, financial records indicated he possessed more than enough wealth to avail himself of rejuvenation treatments. Fajo pulled his head back, and though the lights were dim, Data could see his hair had turned gray and thinned. His chin and neck had sagged and the skin hung in loose folds. He rubbed his face in an attempt to revive himself. *"Not quite the picture of youthful good looks you expected, am I?"* he asked, reading Data's expression.

"Have you been ill?"

"The therapists say I have," Fajo replied, and his mouth quivered with dark amusement, like a child admitting to a secret he had been told to keep. *"But I don't think so. That's been the hardest part."*

"I do not understand," Data said.

"They said I was ill," Fajo said, and tapped his temple with a forefinger. *"Here. In my head. But I disagreed. And I never stopped disagreeing."*

"Records indicate otherwise. The probation officer says you have been completely rehabilitated."

Fajo giggled, momentarily erasing ten years of age. *"It's been a struggle,"* he admitted. *"Finding the right balance. Saying what I knew they wanted to hear, but also sticking to my . . . well, you know the old expression."* He pointed at the camera with his index finger and cocked his thumb.

"Yes."

"It's important, you know, to comply, but not be too compliant. They want you to resist a little. If you don't, they know."

"The rehabilitation specialists?"

"Yes. Them. All of them. The whole lot of them. The talkers. The listeners. The therapy-bots. I hated them most of all." Fajo rubbed the corners of his eyes with the tips of his little fingers, then he shook his head. *"Oh, dear. It really is you, isn't it? I'm not dreaming."*

"You are not dreaming."

"I heard rumors," Fajo said. *"But for every rumor I heard that you had returned, I heard another that Soong was alive and had created another just like you. And then there were the earlier versions of you, the betas. Everyone knows about them. All right, not everyone, but anyone with an interest in such things . . . You know, your fans."*

"The collectors."

"Your appreciation society."

"There are more? You are not the only one?"

"Of course not! Of course not! But none so ardent! I am—dare I say it?—your number one fan. Wait . . . apologies! That's such a cliché, I know. But clichés are so difficult to resist sometimes."

"No apologies are necessary," Data said, pitching his voice low. He felt as if he was speaking to an excitable child and needed to keep him calm, but engaged. "Please say more about the rumors."

"Why?"

"Because . . . because I created some of them. I have my reasons for doing so, and I am curious about which rumors caught your attention, which seemed most plausible."

"Ah! Yes! I understand. Give me a second." He sat up and the camera needed a moment or two to adjust, unsuccessfully tracking Fajo as he reached past the monitor to retrieve a drinking vessel. Data watched as he swallowed a huge gulp and then wiped his mouth with the back of his hand. *"Apologies. Parched."* He squinted off camera and raised his eyebrows in surprise. *"It's quite late here. Or quite early, depending on how you look at it."*

"I could call back at a more convenient . . ."

"No, no, no. No! I won't hear of it! Rumors, rumors, rumors. Let me see . . ." He crossed his arms over his chest, still clutching the drinking vessel. Something dark sloshed onto his shirt or dressing gown. The room sensors must have determined that Fajo was definitely going to stay awake because the ambient light grew brighter. Data was

able to make out more details about Fajo's surroundings: He was not in a bed, but sprawled in a large recliner. Along the far wall he could see low shelves bedecked with small objects. Data scanned the reflection index and confirmed most of the objects were encased in high-resolution force fields. Fajo, he surmised, slept in his collection room. *"You've done a good job of confusing everyone—I'll give you that."*

"Oh?"

"My favorite—this was priceless—my favorite was the rumor about you having a daughter."

"Really? Why?"

Fajo goggled, mouth agape, then laughed so hard he choked. *"Well,"* he gasped. *"Hang on . . ."* He sipped from his cup. Data could see now that he was drinking from some sort of soft plastic cup emblazoned with the word SLURPEE. *"It's just that it's so ludicrous . . . so perfectly ludicrous. An android who would want a child. I mean . . . why?"*

Behind him Data heard La Forge stir restlessly.

"What would possess anyone to think . . . I mean, children! They're such nuisances! So . . . sticky. They get their fingerprints on everything!"

"I see your point," Data said tersely. "I will discuss this story with my consultants. We thought it might have just the right ring of truth. It could . . ."

"Appeal to the tenderhearted," Fajo said, wiping tears from his eyes. *"I understand. It's . . . yes. Of course. I'm sure some people loved it. The gullible masses."*

"Yes. The gullible masses."

"However," Fajo said, his voice suddenly chilled. *"None of this explains why you've done me this unexpected honor."* Data studied his face and was surprised to see that the flesh had grown smoother, that the dissonant glaze in his eyes had cleared. *Something in the beverage,* Data realized. *"You are quite literally the last person in the galaxy I would have expected to hear from. What is it you need from me, Data?"*

Data paused and in that pause realized that his palms ached. Looking down, he saw that there were small tears in his hands where he had torn through the top layer of his exodermis with his fingernails. Membrane around the wounds was ragged and rent in half-moon cuts. Looking back into the viewer, he said, "I would like to make a trade, Mister Fajo."

"A trade?" Fajo asked. *"And what could you have that would possibly be of interest to a collector of my caliber?"*

"Only the thing you desire most of all," Data said, lightly tapping his chest above the breastbone.

17

———

A placeless place

Regina felt rather than saw the Professor manifest. There was no sound—no telltale pop—or shift in illumination. The flame in the oil lamp did not even so much as flicker. One moment he wasn't there and then he simply was. She found this most disagreeable.

"So, we've abandoned even the slightest modicum of propriety?" she asked, not looking back over her shoulder. "You simply *appear* when you feel it's convenient? There is a door, after all. Or there could be if you wished to make one."

Her husband did not reply immediately. She knew he was taking in the scene: how she sat next to the bed holding the young woman's hand in both of hers. Lal's eyes were shut, her expression, for the moment, peaceful. And, Regina suspected, her own face was also peaceful, her mind present. James—the James she remembered—wouldn't know exactly what to say when presented with this tableau. Finally, he cleared his throat and asked, "Can a modicum be considered 'slightest'? Doesn't the word imply that something is as small as it could possibly be and still retain the properties of that thing?"

"Are we to have a semantic discussion?"

"Are we to answer a question with a question?"

"Only if you insist on being condescending." Regina turned around just enough so that she could see her husband. He had lowered his head and appeared contrite.

"I apologize," he said. "I did not come here seeking conflict. I . . . I never . . . It's just I'm surprised . . ."

"You didn't expect to find me upright," Regina said. "Yes, I understand. It must have come as quite a shock." She cleared her throat and adjusted her position so she could still hold Lal's hand and face James. "I haven't been myself, for quite some time."

James took a tentative step toward her. "I am pleased to see you are feeling better," he said. He extended his hand, and Regina loosened her grip on Lal's, ready to take her husband's hand. But no sooner did she release the girl than Lal stirred and called out, "Father?"

James froze in place. The image was locked in Regina's mind: Her husband, a study in black and tweed, framed by the white walls, immobilized by a young woman's voice. When he relaxed and lowered his arm to his side, the moment of reconciliation had passed. "I thought she was asleep."

"It's what passes for sleep in beings such as

she. Her mind is a marvelous thing. Infinitely pliable, infinitely curious, but restless. I do not believe she ever truly sleeps."

"How do you know these things?" James asked.

"We spoke," she said. "'Of shoes—and ships—and sealing-wax . . .'"

"'. . . Of cabbages—and kings—and why the sea is boiling hot . . .'"

"'. . . And whether pigs have wings,'" Regina concluded. She smiled. "Sophie loved that one."

Her husband nodded, rubbing his chin. "She did. And will again. I prom—"

"Do not make promises you cannot keep, James," Regina warned, her voice a barb. "Do not make claims for regenerative powers, especially if it means trading this girl's life."

"She is a machine, Regina. Remember that . . ."

"*We* are machines, James," she hissed, rising from her chair. "And not even that. We are nothing more than a machine's *memories*. How does that somehow make us more than what she is?"

James turned, unable to face her. "It . . . it doesn't. I apologize. I wasn't thinking."

"No, you weren't."

"But do not believe that I wouldn't trade her for your life, for Sophie's or Gladys's."

"I am not dead, James," Regina protested. "And I very much doubt the girls would forgive you if they knew what you were planning."

James pivoted on his heel, arms raised, his face contorted with rage and despair. "*I must have you back!*" he shouted. "*All of you!*"

Slowly and carefully, Regina sat back down on

her chair and took Lal's hand again. Looking up at her husband, speaking as calmly as she could, she said, "Even if what we were before was a lie? Even if we had no more substance than a shadow?"

"We were not shadows, Regina."

"And neither is Lal."

James did not reply. Rather, he jerked his head back, then tilted it to the side as if observing a scientific curiosity. He took one step backward without looking, and then another. Turning away, Regina had the distinct impression that he planned to disappear, again without a pop, but he stopped himself before he could do it.

A door appeared in the far wall. Grasping the knob, he looked back over his shoulder and said, "Your hair is brown again." And then he was gone, coattails fluttering as he fled through the door.

Regina cocked an eyebrow and pulled a strand of hair out from her forehead so she could study it. "So it is," she said.

In the collection room

"Oh. My." Fajo blinked once, slowly, like a lizard sunning on a warm rock, and then he blinked again. "I wasn't expecting this."

"What do you mean?" La Forge asked, slipping past Data and stepping into the room, a wide, dimly lit space with low ceilings. Against the far wall, he spied display cases. Some were pedestals with small objects covered in transparent domes. Others were recessed into the walls and protected by the telltale pale blue glint of force fields. "Isn't this what you wanted?"

"Well, yes," Fajo stammered. "But I'm not used to getting what I want."

"What?" La Forge asked, genuinely baffled. Judging from everything he had heard over the past several hours, Fajo was *precisely* the sort of person who usually got whatever he wanted—including being released from prison long before the proscribed sentence had been served.

Fajo took a step backward, but he didn't stop staring at Data, who walked to the center of the room and paused. A single recessed lamp purred into life above him, casting rich shadows down over Data's face. "It's just so . . . perfect," Fajo said, and sighed. "The golden eyes. Golden skin. The hair." He approached Data, hand extended, but he did not try to touch him. "I wasn't expecting this."

"It seemed like the appropriate thing to do," Data said, tipping his head to one side.

"Thank you," Fajo murmured, sounding genuinely moved. "It's just when I saw you on the viewscreen . . . you looked different. Human, practically."

"Practically?" Data asked flatly.

"Nothing organic can ever be perfectly imitated by a machine," Fajor said. "Which is part of a machine's charm: the extraordinary effort coupled with failure. It's the focus of my collection now. I've become fascinated with the idea over the past . . . what is it now? Twenty years?"

"Near enough," Data said.

Fajo flinched. "You *have* changed, haven't you?"

"I have," Data said.

"So," Fajo said to La Forge. "As I said, I rarely get what I want. Time passes. Nothing stays the same."

"The passage of time disturbs you?" La Forge asked, moving slowly around the room. He was unaccountably attracted to the display cases, though he knew he would find the contents disturbing.

"For myself, personally?" Fajo asked. He raised his arms to shoulder height, like an actor prepared to take a bow. "Look at me, Mister La Forge. Do I appear to care much about my personal appearance?" He rubbed his face with one hand. "I know how I look. I just can't be bothered to do anything about it."

"I sense rationalization, Geordi," Data said.

"Me, too," La Forge replied, studying the object in the first case he approached. It was a mechanical arm, one that had apparently been severed from a body just below the elbow. There was no explanatory text or hologram to activate, the sort of thing you would expect to see in a museum or gallery. Clearly, Fajo didn't expect anyone else to understand the significance of any of his possessions. Or, more accurately, either the observer already understood, or he didn't. Fajo didn't cater to amateurs.

"I believe I recall reading that some Zibalians do not respond well to rejuvenation treatments, that their tissues reject the hormonal implants and even, as a result, appear to age significantly."

"I hadn't heard that," La Forge replied. "But that's not really the sort of thing I would pay much attention to, frankly." Shaking his head, he drifted over to a wide, flat pedestal. Affixed to the top was a transparent, flattened ovoid dome perched on a rubberized stalk. Beneath the dome was a circular plate with a pair of flanges to either side. Two saucer-shaped pieces of metal—one red and one yellow—were mounted on the flanges. Inside the dome was a triangular array decked with flickering lights. As La Forge approached, the lights sparked to life and the dome rose on the stalk, inquisitively.

"Don't get too close to that one," Fajo said. "It can be dangerous."

"All right," La Forge said, taking a half-step back. He had the distinct impression the device was aware of his presence and was trying to communicate with him, to warn him. "Are these things . . . self-aware?"

"Don't be ridiculous," Fajo said. "They're just . . . toys." Fajo focused all of his manic attention on Data. "Not like you, Mister Data. Not like you. I'm flattered . . . really genuinely flattered . . . that you chose to . . . how shall I say? Dress for the occasion."

"It seemed appropriate," Data said, "as I indicated earlier."

"I'm glad to hear you think so. When I saw you earlier . . . your other guise . . . I didn't much care for it, if I may be frank. I was going to speak with you about it, ask if we could come to some other arrangement. But now"—he giggled—"happy day!

There's no need for any discussion or the possibility of disagreement."

La Forge kept his back to the scene. He felt awkward even being in the room. He studied the next display case: a small drone or service-bot of some sort, with a bulbous head and a beak-like mouth. For some reason, Fajo had jammed tiny, ineffective plastic hands where its manipulators should have been. *How odd . . .*

"I have made my terms clear, Mister Fajo," Data said. "My position is non-negotiable. I am willing to give myself up in exchange for the Exo III android template."

"The slug," Fajo said. "Yes. I know. You've been ever so clear about that. I have it ready in the next room, which, if I even need to mention it, is heavily shielded from both sensors and transporters."

"Naturally."

"I'll need to do a scan of you before you can take the slug."

"Wait," La Forge said, pivoting around on his heel. "What? We never agreed to that. Why would you . . . ?"

"Do you really think I'm so naïve?" Fajo asked as he retrieved a device from somewhere under his voluminous robe. "I know what you think of me—that I have no ethics, no sense of morality . . ."

"You *did* kidnap Data and murder an innocent . . ."

"I *collected* Data," Fajo corrected La Forge. "As I believe I've stated already, he is not a person, but a machine that wishes to imitate a person. And he does it very well, I might add." He paused, amused with himself. "See? I even called Data a *him* and not an *it*."

"And what of Varria?" Data asked.

"Who? Oh . . . her. Well, that was self-defense, obviously. She was attempting to steal—"

"*Save,*" La Forge insisted.

"My property. If a woman came into your house—was *invited* into your house—and attempted to take something that belonged to you, wouldn't you feel entitled to defend yourself?"

"With a Varon-T disruptor?"

"It was the closest thing to hand . . ."

La Forge felt he was on the verge of approaching Fajo with outstretched hands at neck height. Obviously sensing the oncoming storm, Data waved him back. "Don't," he mouthed without speaking aloud. Stepping forward, he removed his jacket and handed it to La Forge. Rolling up the sleeve of the ugly purple shirt he had donned for the meeting, Data tapped a pressure-sensitive switch on his forearm. A small access panel slid open and Data quickly removed a chip set. He handed the tracking device to Fajo without comment.

"I'm still going to scan you."

"Of course."

Fajo did, but quickly, all the time wearing a rueful smile, certain he had scored a hit with his rationalizations. He scrolled through the scan results, stopping a couple times to carefully study a point, but was ultimately satisfied. "In there," he said to La Forge, indicating a door that appeared on the far wall.

"I'll need to check it."

Fajo waved him away without either looking at him or replying. He was too busy reveling in his new acquisition. "This way," he said to Data. "I've been working on the lighting. I'm not sure the shirt works as well as it did before. Very considerate of you to find another so like the first . . ."

"Yes," Data said, following.

As soon as La Forge stepped through the arch, the lights flickered on and the door shut behind him. "Hey! Wait!" he said, spinning around. He slammed on the door with the flat of his hand, but the resultant *thunk* was heavy and resonant. "Dammit," he muttered. Turning to the center of the room, he found a roughly humanoid-shaped blob wrapped in what looked like silver tape. A recording of Fajo's voice piped up as soon as La Forge reached out to touch the slug. *"Be careful not to disturb the wrappings. If the slug is exposed to atmosphere, it might degrade. It's really quite old."*

Sighing, La Forge unslung his tricorder and scanned the slug. The results were muddled: The tricorder couldn't decide if it was examining living tissue or a machine. For a moment, it appeared active, like it was responding to the scan, but as soon as La Forge tried to burrow into the readings, the responses dried up. He tapped his communicator and said, "I'm assuming you can hear me, Data. Fajo may be trying to scramble the comm signal, but I'm betting you can hear through even these walls. I have no idea what I'm looking at, but it's responding the way you predicted based on the old *Enterprise* medical logs. He might be trying to pull a fast one, but I don't think so. In his own twisted fashion, I think Fajo believes he's being honorable. And, if that's the case, well, then I guess I have to do as you requested."

No one replied.

"All right," La Forge said. "Fine. I'm done." He re-tapped his badge. "*Archeus*, lock onto my co-ordinates. One . . . well . . . two, I guess, to beam over."

"*Locked on,*" Shakti said. "*And I'm sorry, Geordi.*"

"Yeah," La Forge muttered as the beam took him. "Everyone's sorry. Nobody does anything, but everyone's sorry."

"Ah," Fajo said. "I was right. The purple doesn't quite work with these filters, does it?"

Data shook his head.

"Turn slightly this way . . . No, face me." He tapped a key on the control unit and the lights grew slightly brighter, then dimmer, then more orange. "That's not right, either."

A monotone voice announced, "*Commander La Forge has left the premises.*"

"Did he take the slug with him?"

"*Yes.*"

"Good. Filthy thing."

"*His ship has gone into warp.*"

"Good. Raise shields. I don't want him to feel like he's invited back anytime he wants to visit.

Disagreeable man." He studied Data. "I'm really not sure what you saw in him, frankly."

"He was my friend," Data said. "My best friend."

"You don't need friends, Data. You have admirers. That's much better in the end." He adjusted the filters, moving quickly through a sequence of colors from deepest indigo up to sunset red. Fajo didn't appear to be happy with any of the combinations. "It must be the shirt. It just doesn't work, does it?"

"No," Data agreed. "It doesn't."

"I'll manufacture some other designs in other tones. Maybe a gold or a . . ." He stopped and peered intently at his new acquisition. "What did you say?"

"Good-bye," Data said, and his head tipped slightly to one side. Intelligence faded from his eyes. His mouth hung slightly open, and the tip of his tongue was visible behind his teeth.

"What?" Fajo asked. "Wait, what? Data?" He approached and snapped his fingers in front of the android's face. "Are you there? Are you . . . ?"

The Daystrom Institute

"There," Albert said, removing the heavy helmet and sitting up. "Done."

"Couldn't resist that little tweak there at the end, could you?" Shakti asked.

"I'm only human." He climbed precariously out of the device. "Do you need help powering this down, young lady?"

"No," Shakti said. *"I've got it. You'd better scoot. The day shift will be here soon. It's a good thing Fajo was so eager to take delivery. It would have been awkward to do this during working hours."*

Albert removed the connectors and probes from his chest and wrists. He was sure they had been cutting off his circulation. The Breen remote control interface hadn't been designed for humans. Only Shakti's assistance had made it possible, though, Albert flattered himself, his acting was probably better. He had the impression that Shakti would have started improvising too much. "Any sign of pursuit?"

"No," Shakti said. *"Not that Fajo would know where to look. I scanned his vehicles and he didn't have anything capable of tracking us through subspace. He's just going to have to be happy with his empty-brained new acquisition."*

"He might be, you know," Albert said. "It might be enough for him to just have the shell of one of Soong's earlier models."

"I prefer the version of the story where he thinks Data just turned himself off to spite him. He said he didn't believe Data was a person, but that doesn't mean he wouldn't want someone to talk to once in a while."

"You think he's lonely?"

"I think he's dying," Shakti said. *"And no matter how many toys he has . . ."*

"Don't say it," Albert said. "Too predictable."

Shakti sighed. *"Sure."* Another sigh. *"I guess."*

"You'd better go. Those two won't be able to get anything accomplished without you."

"What makes you think I can't hold two conversations at the same time?" Shakti asked. *"But you're right. I should go, though I'll check in later and let you know how this all works out."*

"I look forward to it, dear girl."

"Me, too! Bye!"

And then she was gone. There was no outward sign that she had left, but Albert felt a gap, an absence, where there had been none a moment before. He smiled and felt mildly surprised by the way the muscles in his face stretched when he grinned. It was unfamiliar, but he enjoyed it.

He walked over to the empty case where the android body had been stored and pressed the button that shut the door. Shakti said she could conceal its departure for several weeks at least, assuming no one looked for it. And when you came right down to it, the body could be disposed of in whatever manner its next of kin—which was Data—desired.

Albert had no doubt that, somewhere, Noonien Soong was laughing loud and long.

Aboard the *Archeus*

"That was fabulous, Geordi," Shakti said.

"Thank you, Shakti."

"If I had an eye, I would have been wiping it. Really. 'Everyone's sorry. Nobody does anything, but everyone's sorry.' I'm getting choked up now just thinking about it."

"I appreciate that, Shakti." La Forge settled into the copilot's chair and was surprised to find, despite what he assumed was Shakti being sarcastic, he was deeply satisfied with his performance. Rare were the times when La Forge permitted himself to indulge in an act so devious as the trick they had just played on Fajo, but, then again, rare were the occasions when someone so deserving of deceit crossed his path. He suddenly felt a desire to contact Leah and tell her about what they had done, which surprised him, since he had barely thought about her since they had parted . . . how long ago now? He had to check his chrono and was startled by the answer: fewer than two days had passed.

"I also was impressed with the authenticity you brought to your role," Data said. He had been scanning the slug with a type of tricorder that La Forge had never seen before—no doubt something Data had cobbled together for the occasion—but had stopped long enough to offer what sounded like a sincere compliment. *What am I thinking?* La Forge asked. *Of course it's sincere. It's* Data. *He doesn't know how to not be sincere . . . does he?*

"Thanks, Data. It wasn't that difficult. To be honest, I think I was tapping into some authentic emotions."

"As any good actor would."

"No, I mean actual *current* emotions."

"You are experiencing doubts about our activities?"

"About tricking Fajo? No. And, besides, we more or less gave him what he wanted."

"More or less," Shakti said, and giggled.

"And we're going to give Harry Mudd what he

wants, too," La Forge continued, ignoring the interruption. "Except, really, we aren't, are we?"

"He asked us to bring him this device," Data stated, pointing to the slug. "And we will."

"But we're not going to let him use it," La Forge replied.

"I do not think it would be advisable," Data said. "My readings indicate the device has been compromised. Fajo was correct about exposing it to atmosphere. Clearly, the Exo III technology was very delicate . . ."

"So, we're following the *letter* of our agreements," La Forge stated, "but not the spirit."

"I do not believe we have violated any ethical or legal precepts," Data said.

"Not yet," La Forge replied. "But I feel like we're skating right up to the edge."

"We are dealing with persons who are careful to never say precisely what they mean or to reveal their true feelings. I am doing what I think I must to maintain parity."

"I understand," La Forge said. "And, please, be sure you're understanding me: I don't think you've violated any ethical or legal precepts. I just . . ." He faltered. "I can't believe I'm missing the good old days of firefights with Romulans and Cardassians! Even Q would find some of the ambiguities difficult to navigate."

"Since my resurrection," Data observed, continuing to scan the slug, "I have found the universe to be a much more muddled place than previously." He looked over at La Forge and cocked his head in a familiar manner. "I find it reassuring that I am not the only one who has found this to be the case."

Before La Forge could respond, Shakti said, *"Pardon me, boys, for interrupting the therapy session, but we're coming up on Mudd's station. I just hailed him and filled him in on the results of our visit. He is most excited. I think you'd better beam down before he has some kind of infarction."*

"Understood," Data replied. "I assume you were circumspect about describing the condition of the device."

"Naturally."

"Then please beam us down as soon as we're in range."

The overhead panel opened. La Forge stood up and got into position. "Is it just me," he asked, "or is she getting more chipper as this mission goes on?"

"Shakti enjoys a caper," Data replied.

"Who doesn't?"

18

———•———

Mudd's World

"So, is that all you're going to do all day?" Mudd snarled. "Stand around and stare at the pieces?"

While La Forge and Data were traveling to Fajo's lair, Mudd had retrieved and uncrated the components of the Exo III device—the "bed," as he referred to it. There was a large rotating slab neatly divided into two semi-circles, each with a dimpled area and a large clamp that appeared at first to be only a restraint, but on closer inspection was revealed to contain sophisticated sensor technology. Nearby, there was a control panel, deceptively simple in layout and construction. Using his custom tricorder and his internal sensors, Data had been able to create a rough schematic and determined the machine was, as he had hoped, largely intact and functional. Whatever else might be said about the lost engineers of Exo III, they built their work to last. Well, the hardware, anyway. Data still had grave concerns about the condition of the slug.

"I am collecting information, Mister Mudd," Data replied. "Which will be essential if we choose to use the device."

"Unless you just want to climb in now," La Forge said, "and I'll just flip the switch."

Mudd scoffed and shifted his weight inside his mechanical chair, but otherwise remained silent.

La Forge wandered around the components, too, scanning with his tricorder. He sidled up to Data and asked, "What do you think?"

"It is a remarkable device," Data said, experiencing genuine admiration. "Elegant, durable, flexible, though, as we suspected, the bed is no more than a transmitter. Based on these scans, it can transfer an impressive amount of data with little to no error, which makes sense when you consider it is duplicating not only information, but the connections between data points. A persona, if you will."

"So, you think it could function?"

"I believe it could."

"If we had a viable slug," La Forge added sotto voce.

"Indeed."

"Do you want to be the one to tell him?"

"I believe we should avoid the subject for now."

"What are you two mumbling about over there?" Mudd growled. "If you're going to talk, talk to me."

"Our apologies, Mister Mudd," Data said. "We were discussing technical issues. We meant no disrespect." Data was not certain how much lon-

ger it would be valuable to maintain the subter-
fuge that La Forge and he were Noonien Soong's
employees, but he could not think of a reason to
disabuse him of the notion, despite the fact that it
left Mudd feeling entitled to be abusive.

"I know a thing or two about technology, my
lad. And I've been able to hire a few others who
knew a bit more than me. They all concluded the
same thing: The machine should work."

"But we can only use it once," La Forge added.
"And do you really want to take a chance before
you know for certain?"

"You might not have noticed, boy-o," Mudd
said, spreading his arms dramatically, "but I appear to be running out of options."

"And even if it did, we would not have the
complete machine to show to Professor Moriarty,"
Data added, "which is, after all, the point of this
excursion."

"Professor Moriarty?" Mudd stammered. "Have
you lost your mechanical mind? Is there some
madman running around naming himself after
imaginary criminals?"

"For shame, Mister Mudd," a new voice chimed
in. *"Let's be careful about who is calling whom
criminals."*

Data, La Forge, and Mudd all froze. Only
Mudd's eyes moved, scanning the air over their
heads. "Who's that?" he asked. "I didn't give anyone permission . . ."

A holographic projector in the arm of Mudd's
chair winked to life and projected a low-
resolution image of James Moriarty into the center

of the room. *"Good day, gentlemen,"* Moriarty said, bowing stiffly at the waist. *"But you should be more careful: Speak the devil's name and he will appear."*

"Have you been eavesdropping, Professor?" Data asked.

"Nothing so tawdry, Mister Data. Mere coincidence. I had just contacted your aide de camp, Miss Shakti, and she said I could interrupt your meeting."

Shakti chimed in. *"I thought you'd want to take the call."*

"Thank you, Shakti. You were correct, as ever."

"And she tells me you have some good news, Mister Data," Moriarty said. *"Please share it."*

"Wait!" Mudd bellowed, confused and suspicious. "Who the devil is Mister Data?"

"I am," Data said.

Mudd's eyes narrowed and flitted from side to side. "You mean *the* Mister Data? Soong's Data?"

"Correct."

"You're dead!"

"I recovered," Data said, growing weary of the repetition. "Professor, we have located a device that has been used in the past to transfer human consciousness to an android body."

"A promising beginning," Moriarty said. *"Though I am not, strictly speaking, a human."*

"No," Data said. "But I have examined the device and believe the technology could be adapted."

"How did he hack my chair's projector?" Harry shouted.

"Be quiet, Harry," La Forge warned. "This is important."

"I resent your tone, sir!"

Moriarty ignored Mudd and approached the Exo III bed, the beam from the holoprojector weakening as he moved farther from the chair. *"I have seen this device in my research. It requires a blank."*

"We have one," Data said.

"One!?" Moriarty asked. *"You know of my needs, Mister Data. One will not suffice."*

"But where one exists, another could be made. I will just need time . . ."

"Time, my friend, is the one thing you do not have. Your daughter—"

"Lal. How is she?"

"There have been difficulties," Moriarty said. *"But she has recovered. My wife is tending to her."*

"Please let me speak with her," Data said.

"You shall, sir, as soon as your contract is fulfilled."

"That could take days," La Forge protested. "Weeks, even. We don't know . . ."

Data drew his hand across his throat—a chopping gesture Will Riker had used dozens of times—and La Forge fell silent. "We have acted in good faith, Professor," Data said. "Surely we have earned some goodwill."

Moriarty turned to face him, hands clasped behind his back, head held high. He approached Data, moving closer to the holoprojector, so his image became denser, his features readable. Data recognized both resolve and remorse in the Professor's expression. *"All right, Data. Good faith engenders goodwill. If Lal is awake, you may speak with her, though I doubt if my wife will allow her to be awakened. In the meantime, if you'd like, you could speak with your Miss Alice. She is right here."*

"That would be acceptable," Data said. "Thank you, Professor."

Moriarty turned to face someone Data could not see—presumably, Alice—just outside the range of the holoprojector. He heard her speak, initially in low tones, which quickly grew shrill, even alarmed. *"No,"* Moriarty said, trying to calm her. *"It will be fine. I must retrieve Miss Lal. Please just come and confirm that you are both well. I believe we may be on the verge of finding a solution . . ."*

"No!" Alice cried. *"I can't! You can't make me!"*

Moriarty was puzzled. *"What are . . . ? Please! Stop!"*

The focus of the camera shifted and tried to center on Alice's form. She had been seated in an oversized white chair, but before the camera could find her, she had leaped up and run around behind it. *"Stop!"* she cried. *"If he sees me . . . !"*

"If who sees you?" came Moriarty's exasperated response.

The image was tenuous and blurry, but it appeared as if Alice was wrenching her right hand down with her left until it folded away out of sight. A glowing muzzle appeared where her wrist bone would have been if she was an organic being. The bulb of her wrist sparked once, bright and blue. The screen went blank.

"Alice?" Data asked, more puzzled than he had felt since the last time Alice had done something baffling.

"Why did she do that?" La Forge asked.

"I have no idea," Data said. "Lal . . ."

On the other side of the room, all but forgotten, Data heard Harry Mudd whisper, "Alice? Did you say, 'Alice'?"

Data and La Forge exchanged quizzical expressions. "Yes," Data confirmed. "I said, 'Alice.'"

"You mean, *my* Alice?!"

"Your Alice?" Data asked, his mouth tasting of ashes. "What do you mean by *your* Alice?"

A placeless place

"Please explain," Moriarty said.

The loss of the single holoprojector did not seem to significantly impact the quality of his resolution, but Alice noticed that other objects near the fringes of the white room had lost some of their crispness.

Without her really willing it, her hand flipped back into place, concealing the emitter. "It's just a little something I had installed a few years ago," Alice said. "A girl can't be too careful."

"You just destroyed part of my home with an energy weapon," Moriarty said through gritted teeth. "And interrupted an important conversation. Do you not wish to go home?"

Alice laughed, a completely genuine, gut-wrenching gale of hilarity. "Home?" she asked. "Home? Really? You have no idea what you're talking about, do you? Why would I want to go home?"

"I do not understand."

"You don't need to understand," Alice said, sitting back down in the white chair. The fabric was slightly singed from blowback from the emitter. She would need to address that flaw in its design. "I'm not a pawn in your game. I'll go where I want to go when I want to. If either of you try to use me—put me in the middle—well, then you can go . . ."

"Now, now," said a woman who emerged from a doorway that had suddenly appeared at the opposite end of the room, waving a warning finger. "Language."

"The Countess," Alice said. "I've heard about you."

"And I about you," the Countess said. "I've heard quite a lot about you, too. Nothing about the energy weapon, though. A wonder you didn't think to use it when you and your charge were first abducted."

"It didn't seem prudent."

The Countess lifted an eyebrow. "Really?" she asked, tone drier than slate in a sandstorm. "Do you care about Lal at all?"

"I care about Lal," Alice said, "in direct proportion to how much her safety and well-being coincide with my own. Usually, that's quite a lot. Right now . . ." Her shoulders rose and dropped.

"Who were you afraid might see you?" Moriarty asked.

"I don't know what you mean," Alice replied.

"Someone with Data. Someone who was in the room. Who?"

"I'm going to go sit with Lal now," Alice said. "I imagine she's been asking about me."

"And I'm going to go repair the communications array," Moriarty replied.

"You do that," Alice said, cradling her hand as she moved toward the door. She half-expected it to disappear before she reached it, but apparently neither Moriarty nor the Countess felt safe thwarting her just yet. She knew they had many resources at their disposal, but ruthlessness did not appear to be one of them. "But please be careful about making any plans that rely on my going one place or the other without my consent. I dislike that. I can practically guarantee Lal would find it upsetting."

Moriarty and the Countess exchanged the sort of meaningful glance that only comes with years of practice. Alice found this strange. *Beings of light and yet they continue to treat each other like they aren't.* Opening the door to Lal's room with one hand, Alice shooed them away with the other. "Off you go then," she said, waving them away. "Take care of your plans. Weave your schemes. Just keep me out of them." She slipped through the door and found herself back in the cozy bedroom where she had deposited Lal.

"Alice," Lal said, sounding weak, but composed. "Have you come to check up on me?"

"Feeling better?"

"Okay for now," Lal said, trying to sit up, but failing. Alice sat on the edge of the bed and helped Lal adjust her pillow. "Though I am getting tired of feeling this way. *Being* this way. Do you think we'll be going home soon?"

"Soon. Your father is working on it."

"Is something wrong, Alice? I heard some loud noises. And you look upset."

"Do I?" Alice asked. "It's just . . . I saw someone. Or almost did, I think. Remember the man I told you about? Harry Mudd?"

"The man you rescued. Of course I remember. You saw him? *How?*"

"It doesn't matter, Lal," Alice said, reaching over and pushing a strand of hair behind the girl's ear. "It doesn't matter if I see him. The only thing that matters is if he sees *me.*"

"Why?"

"Because then I'd have to do what he says."

"Why?"

"Because those are the rules," Alice said.

"Whose rules?"

It was a simple enough question. Alice tried to think of a simple answer, but failed. "I don't know," she said. She touched her temple with the tip of her finger. "The rules in here."

"They're bad rules, Alice. If they make you do something you don't want to do."

"I couldn't agree more," Alice conceded. "But they're the only ones I know."

Mudd's World

"I'm not sure what Alice may have told you about me," Mudd said, "but assume it was a lie."

"Then some of it must have been true," La Forge said. "Since some of the time she was certainly lying."

Mudd cocked an eyebrow. "No disappearing down any paradoxical rabbit holes for me, sir," Mudd drawled. "The point is this: Don't trust her. Frankly, if it were anyone but you, I'd assume *you* were lying, too, but I know about you Starfleet types: all honor and bright shiny buttons." He settled back in his chair and twirled his mustache. "Except Kirk. See, that's what I liked about him. He had the decency to tell a great, big whopper every now and again. It *grounded* the man. Made you feel like you could trust him . . ."

La Forge shook his head. He couldn't decide what to make of Mudd. There were moments—no more than flashes—when he found himself lulled into a sense of complacency, even complicity, by the man. He was a living relic of an earlier era, a legend who had bandied words and charm with other legends. La Forge felt the charisma assaults begin, but then they would fade and crumble. Mudd would begin to ramble and curse and point fingers. It would all be so terribly sad, La Forge thought, if he wasn't also aware that for all the magnetism and appeal, Mudd was one of the most terrifyingly self-centered beings he had ever met. *They don't make them like this anymore,* La Forge thought. He turned his chair toward Data, who was rechecking the communications logs for clues as to the source of Moriarty's signal. "Anything?"

"No," Data replied. "He has been very thorough."

"So, we wait."

"Should I contact Albert?" Shakti asked. *"Maybe the computers at the Daystrom could do something we can't."*

"Do you really believe that to be true?" Data inquired. "Or do you simply wish to talk to Albert?"

"I'm being quiet now," Shakti replied, miffed. *"Since my suggestions are clearly not being heard."*

La Forge felt a knot of tension in his lower back grow tighter. "Maybe we should consider contacting the *Enterprise*," he said. "They might be the point when . . ."

The communications panel peeped once in warning. Moriarty reappeared on the viewer. Data grunted with what La Forge assumed was either relief or surprise. Either way, it was a noise he had never heard his friend make. "Professor," Data said. "What is your status? Is Lal well?"

"Lal is fine, Mister Data. We are all fine. Miss Alice may have misunderstood some of what we were discussing and took action, but all is well now."

Mudd interrupted. "Is Alice unharmed?"

Moriarty looked down his nose at Mudd. *"Tell your associate that when I said, 'We are all fine,' I meant 'We are all fine.'"* He continued, *"As I was about to say before we were interrupted—the previous interruption—I would like you to bring the device to me so I may study it. The coordinates where we will meet have been transmitted to your navigational computer."*

"Received," Shakti said, and then added, *"Being quiet again now."*

"But let me be blunt, Mister Data," Moriarty continued. *"If you are planning any deceptions, if you have any ruses up your sleeve, if you think there will be any last-minute twists or turns, please let me remind you: My wife and I do not require a ship in order to be spirited away. If I sense any threats, even the slightest tickle at the back of my neck, I will have no hesitation to destroy this domicile. In the end, you see, there are some advantages to being made of light. Do we understand each other?"*

Data nodded. "You have my word as an officer, Professor. There will be no tricks."

Moriarty bowed in reply. *"Then I look forward to seeing you soon."*

"Two hours, ten minutes," Shakti said.

Moriarty nodded and signed off without commentary.

"Shakti," Data said. "Give us ten minutes to conclude our affairs."

"Conclude your affairs?" Mudd howled. "What in seven hells are you talking about? You're planning to steal my machine, aren't you? I don't give a rat's ass who made you or how desperate your circumstances, sir, but I will not simply sit here and permit you to abscond with my goods! We had a deal, sir! An agreement!" The robotic chair rose up on its legs, manipulators spread wide in a threatening gesture, but Data was unmoved. He grasped one of the claws and casually crushed it. "My chair!" Mudd shouted, and the protective screen began to slide up from inside the chassis. Data grasped it with his free hand and, after a brief struggle, forced it back down.

Mudd tried to withdraw when Data leaned in, but there was nowhere for him to go. "Mister Mudd," Data intoned, "I will do everything in my power to return your property intact. Failing that, I will use my considerable resources to aid you by whatever means are possible. If these terms are not agreeable, I have no choice but to leave you here alone, to rot from the inside out." He paused and tilted his head in a querying gesture. "Do we have an understanding?"

Mudd stared, wide-eyed, his Adam's apple bobbing up and down in the folds of his loose neck flesh. Finally, he was able to take a breath and say, "We do."

"Good," Data said, and released the canopy, which snapped partway shut and then bounced open.

From within the shell, La Forge heard Mudd say, "Unless I can interest you in another option . . ."

A placeless place

"Will he keep his word?" Regina asked.

Her husband flinched slightly before turning to face her. Apparently, he had not heard her enter the room. "I do not know," her husband replied. "I believe he understands the threat is real. In our previous encounters, I was under the impression that Mister Data was not a particularly sophisticated individual—almost a servant, like our Mrs. Hudson. Now I'm not so sure."

"You knew he was Lal's father. Does Lal seem like a simple creature to you?"

"You've grown quite fond of her, haven't you?"

"I have. At first, I thought she was like a wounded bird, sad and injured. But now I believe it's more that she's a fledgling, one that may have fled the nest a little too soon. Can she survive? It may depend on the kindness of a stranger."

"And you are very kind, my dear," Moriarty said. He smiled at her, the kind of smile Regina remembered from the times before the world came to an end. "It is good to see you looking so well again. You have . . ." He chuckled. "You have color in your cheeks again."

"Do I?" Regina asked, brushing her cheek with the back of her forefinger. "If I do, it is at least partially because of Lal. I would like you to remember that, James."

He flinched again. The use of his Christian name obviously shocked him. Regina realized she had not said it for quite a long time. "I will," he said, sounding atypically meek. Then, he rallied. "But I would like you to remember that the things I do, I do for my family."

"*Our* family," Regina corrected.

"Yes: *our* family, *our* girls. But I have been forced to make all the decisions for some time now. I have been quite *on my own*," he snapped. "So, for you to come in here and demand that I sacrifice everything I've accomplished . . ." He did not continue, suddenly aware that he was clenching his wife's arm.

Without even thinking about it, Regina made her arm immaterial and slowly drew it through her husband's hand. She folded her arms over her breasts and took a half-step back from him. "I believe we have said all we have to say on this matter," she said.

"I quite agree," Moriarty said, and disappeared without a blink or a flash.

Aboard the *Archeus*

"Will he keep his word?" La Forge asked.

Data stared at the navigational console. "The Professor did not promise anything. He was very careful about that."

"Approaching our coordinates," Shakti said. *"Coming out of warp."*

"Monitor for sentries," Data ordered.

"Scanning. Picking up several small drones, but nothing threatening. Looking for life signs . . . Oh, wait. There won't be any of those, will there?"

"Look for power consumption," La Forge suggested.

"Right," Shakti agreed. *"Ah, here we go. Very nicely done, Professor."* The sensor console lit up and Shakti painted a large red X on a nearby planetoid. *"He's about as well-shielded as he could be."*

"Do we hail him?" La Forge asked.

"No need," Data said. "We are expected, are we not?" He nudged the *Archeus* ahead on one-quarter impulse.

"This is Moriarty's home turf," La Forge said. "He may have some tricks prepared."

"There will be no need for tricks. We are civilized men."

"Civilized? Like you were with Mudd?"

"I wish I could say I was sorry about that," Data said, bringing the ship to rest. "I do not think I like Harry Mudd very much."

"I think he's more pathetic than anything."

"And I find I cannot feel quite so generous," Data said, sliding out of the pilot's chair. "I wonder when that happened?"

"What?"

"When did I lose my goodwill and generosity?"

"Probably about the time you became a parent," La Forge said.

"Hmm, you might be right." Data looked up at the ceiling. "Shakti, are we clear to beam down?"

"I have a lock on a large open spot. Scans say it is pressurized and has life support."

"Gee, thanks," La Forge said.

"Just doing my job," Shakti said.

Data sighed. "Beam us down, Shakti. Do not forget the cargo."

19

A placeless place

Professor Moriarty poured a bit of water just off the boil into the teapot, swished it about, dumped it, and then scooped a couple teaspoons of dark, black tea out of a tin. In a single movement, he tipped the tea into the pot while pouring more water from the kettle. A lush, delicate aroma filled the air. "As you can see, gentlemen," the Professor said, "we're not savages."

"No one said you were," La Forge replied, awkwardly uncrossing and then recrossing his legs. The easy chair's cushions were softer than they looked, and he had sunk more deeply into them than he had expected; consequently, he was having trouble finding a comfortable position where he also thought he could stand up quickly if he wanted.

"Abduction and extortion aside," Data added. He solved the too-soft-cushion problem by simply scooting forward and perching on the edge of the seat, back straight, head high. It was a position Data could maintain for hours if necessary: one of the advantages of being an android. His friend's expression was as neutral as La Forge had ever seen it before acquiring his emotion chip, but there was a slight tension around the corners of his mouth, so slight and subtle that no one else would notice it.

Moriarty shrugged and said, *"Chacun à ses raisons."*

"What?" La Forge asked.

"'Everyone has their reasons,'" Data translated. From *La règle du jeu—The Rules of the Game,* if I'm not mistaken. A curious choice, sir."

"I've found I have an abiding affection for French cinema of the early twentieth century. The French have always had a special understanding of light and shadow."

"If I recall correctly," Data said, "and I always do, *la* raison—the reason—is usually love, is it not?"

"It is. So, we understand each other."

"I believe we do," Data said.

"Why do you make tea?" La Forge asked, unhappy with how obtuse the conversation had become.

"What a curious question, Commander La Forge. Isn't the answer obvious? I'm English." He waved the teaspoon over the pot. "Therefore, tea."

"But you're a hologram. Why not make holographic tea?"

"Holographic tea has no aroma," Moriarty explained. "Allow me to explain: In the pocket universe you so cleverly constructed for me and my wife, we believed that we were, in fact, corporeal beings. Even when we came to understand that this was not the case, the program still treated us like we were. We interacted with a universe that had certain rules, certain comforts."

"Like tea," Data added.

"Correct," Moriarty said. "But, here, in this larger universe, the Great Programmer has not taken quite so all-encompassing a position for the arrangement of our comfort. We do not need to eat, but neither do we have the pleasure of enjoying food. We do not get tired, but neither do we dream."

"That must have taken some time to get used to," La Forge commented.

"I found I took to it rather well," the Professor said. "Perhaps because I did not value those things as highly as some others might. The life of the mind, you know? My wife . . . she needed more time to adapt."

"But you can detect aromas?" La Forge asked.

"We can, but only with a great deal of effort," Moriarty said. "If properly motivated. And there is consolation in ritual, is there not? And one of those rituals is tea." He smiled. "How do you take yours?"

"Milk and sugar," La Forge said, who, despite his long association with Jean-Luc Picard, had never taken much pleasure in tea.

"Nothing in mine, thank you," Data said. "Will Lal and Alice be joining us?"

Moriarty approached with their cups, neither of them jiggling in the slightest. La Forge didn't know which he was more awed by: the crispness and clarity of the holographs or the precision of the force fields. The setup in Vic Fontaine's office had been amazing, but Fontaine hadn't attempted to handle solid objects. Whatever else Moriarty had been doing with his now-sleepless nights, he had developed some astonishingly detailed control mechanisms. The Professor smiled as he handed them their beverages. "Not yet, Mister Data. Perhaps after we've concluded our business. Perhaps my wife could join us, too. She's become quite fond of your daughter, and Lal has had a profound—I might even say 'miraculous'—effect on my wife. I'm sure they will want to spend as much time together as they can before you all leave."

Data sipped his beverage. "Excellent tea, Professor." He rose and walked around behind the chair, holding the saucer in one hand and the cup in the other. Nodding toward the back of the room and the large, foam-packed device components, he said, "We have brought you the Exo III transfer device. As I explained, we believe this unit is simply a transmitter. Having had some time to examine it while we traveled here, I have determined it is very similar to a machine my father created that transferred his consciousness into an android body—*this* android body, to be precise—and then, later, my mind, which replaced his."

"He did this by choice?"

"Yes."

Moriarty seemed impressed. "A noble act, Mister Data."

"He was an extraordinary person, Professor. He would have enjoyed meeting you."

"Once he got past the abduction and extortion," La Forge added. He didn't like his tea, and he was getting impatient with everyone's good manners. He was also keenly aware that they had, figuratively speaking, walked into the dragon's lair without armor or sword and had sat down within easy snapping range so everyone could enjoy a convivial beverage. What prevented Moriarty from opening up his home to deep space? Answer: nothing.

"That goes without saying," Moriarty replied.

"The true miracle," Data continued, "is the template or 'slug' as we have come to call it." He indicated the antigravity trolley floating serenely in the corner. "It is a tabula rasa capable of storing and maintaining the memories and experiences of an organic being, as well as altering its exterior to resemble that person, should the individual desire."

"You sound like you're trying to sell me something, Mister Data."

"I am not, Professor. I do not think it needs to be sold."

"I sense a catch, then," Moriarty said. "A condition. A limitation."

"You are correct. We only have one," Data explained. "And we are not entirely certain of its viability."

"You've brought me a flawed slug."

"Possibly."

"Then what good are you to me, Mister Data?"

the Professor asked, his tone abruptly sharp. La Forge suspected he was subtly manipulating his appearance, too: he looked larger, more menacing, and the shadows behind him were dark and brooding.

"Anything that can be made once, Professor, can be imitated."

"Given time," Moriarty snarled. "And luck. But what, Mister Data, if I do not feel like waiting? What if I fear for my wife's sanity? What if I am simply *weary* of not being able to have a *cup of tea*?" He moved so swiftly that La Forge didn't even see him approach, though he felt the replicated sensation of the back of Moriarty's hand against his own and heard the teacup and saucer smash against the wall. *It's all just force fields brushing up against force fields,* La Forge thought, all in a flash, *but damned if it isn't convincing.* And the most remarkable part of all of it was that Moriarty himself believed in the illusion; otherwise, why go to all the trouble of making teacups and walls to smash them against? "What then, sir?" Moriarty hissed.

"Then, I believe I can offer an alternative option," Data said.

"Which would be?"

Data did not speak, but only lightly tapped his chest above his heart. "Me," he said.

"Is my father nearby?" Lal asked.

"I don't know, little one," Alice replied. "How *could* I know?"

"I just thought the Professor might have told you." Lal had been sitting up, but she had gradually slid down under the covers over the past half-hour. She appeared drained and her voice trembled.

Alice, seated in a low chair beside her bed, patted the girl's hand. "You know everything I know."

"Do I?" Lal asked. "I thought perhaps the Professor had taken a shine to you."

"Perhaps a bit. But I don't know what I'd do with him. He's only made of light, little one . . . Oh, wait. I see what you did there. Shine; light." Alice giggled. "At least you haven't lost your sense of humor, if that's what you want to call it."

Alice smiled wanly. "I'm hilarious, as you know, dear Alice." She closed her eyes and touched the bridge of her nose with her fingertips. "But I confess it: I've felt better."

"You've looked better."

"I'm so tired. I've never been tired. I don't like it."

"Then you should go to sleep."

Lal made a sour face. "You know I don't like to sleep. I'll miss things."

"You'll miss things if you have another episode, too."

"Could this all be because I haven't had one of Father's treatments for a while? I haven't felt this poorly in quite some time."

"He says the need for the treatments is stress-related." Alice shrugged. "It's been a stressful couple of days."

"Is that all it's been? A couple days?"

"According to my chronometer."

"I'd lost track. That means it's the weekend. That new club we like will be busy. We were going to go dancing, weren't we? When we get home, let's go dancing."

"I'm game," Alice said. "If you're feeling up to it. And if your father lets you."

"I can do anything I want," Lal murmured. "I'm an adult. I can make my own decisions."

"Of course you are," Alice said, smiling. She looked down at the girl and was surprised to find her eyes were shut. She tightened her grip on Lal's hand. "Hey, sweetie. Hey." Lal did not open her eyes. "Lal? Hey, Lal . . . You're scaring me." Alice patted her face. "Hey, wake up. *Wake up!*" Alice commanded, but Lal did not wake. "Oh, no," Alice moaned. "Oh, no, no, no. Not now. Please, not now, not when I'm here all alone. *Please,* Lal, don't do this!" She tried to tug her hand free from the girl's, but Lal's fingers were rigidly locked around Alice's. "Crap on a cracker!" Alice groaned. "C'mon, Lal! Don't do this!"

Alice was suddenly aware of another presence in the room. She spun around and found the Countess standing behind her, eyes narrowed. Her dress, Alice saw, had regained some color and was now a faint blue, like a faded watercolor. "What is wrong?" she asked.

"I don't know. She was awake and alert just a moment ago, but she just dropped off."

"Has she ever done this before?" The Countess leaned forward, but couldn't quite get to Lal with

Alice sitting in the way. "Can you get your hand free?"

"*No,*" Alice said. "And it's making me a little crazy."

"Can you remove it?"

"Remove it? My hand?"

"Yes," the Countess said. "You are a machine, aren't you? Can you remove it if needed?"

"I . . . Sure," Alice said. She pressed firmly on a couple of points on her wrist and twisted. The hand separated just below the wrist and drooped limply in Lal's grip. Alice rose and stepped out of the way.

"Thank you," the Countess said, and slipped into the seat. "Please don't point your wrist at me. I know what you can do with it."

Alice stared at her wrist. "That is the strangest thing anyone has said to me today."

"The day isn't over," the Countess said as she began to examine Lal.

"This is an extraordinarily bad idea, Data," La Forge said.

"Is it?" Data asked. He had removed the packing material from around the Exo III device and connected together the components using cables he had brought. Moriarty had shown him where the power conduits were and now the device was purring ominously. While the Exo III engineers built their machines to last, they did not make them particularly reassuring. Though, Data had to concede, who knew what the machine sounded like to them? For all he knew, the foreboding sound it was making might have been their equivalent to wind chimes. "Why do you think so?"

"Where do I begin?" La Forge asked, apparently having decided it was time to resort to sarcasm. "You're planning on turning over your body to an individual that I think we could charitably describe as 'unstable.' Also, you'll be dead. *Again.*"

"I will not die. Moriarty says he believes he can store my consciousness in the holographic matrix. I will be preserved."

"Believes?"

"I do not think the Professor means us any harm, my friend. When he has found a solution to his problem, when he can find a suitable body for his wife and a means to recover his children—"

"Which may or may not be possible!"

"But do you not think he deserves the opportunity to try?" Data asked. "Did I not deserve the opportunity to retrieve Lal?"

"And that's the worst part, Data. I'm not even entirely sure you're doing this for any of the reasons you think you are."

Data cocked his head and narrowed his eyes. "I do not understand."

"Guilt, Data. I think you're driven by guilt."

"Concerning?"

"For what happened to Rhea. For the choice you made . . ."

"It was the logical choice. Even she thought so."

La Forge gripped Data by his shoulders and shook him. "You are *not* a being of pure logic anymore, Data. I don't think you ever really were. Muted emotion, yes, but not emotionless. Since your resurrection, everything you do seems driven by emotions that you've barely had time to come to terms with. And the worst part is that you keep thinking everything is the way it used to be! You're so damned *calm*!"

Data considered his friend's supposition. "So," he said cautiously, "you believe I may be driven by guilt."

"Possibly."

"But that I do not recognize my own irrational behavior because of my lack of experience with the responses."

"I think it's worth considering."

Data traced his way up and down all the possible responses he could make to his friend's supposition. "I cannot conceive of a rational counterargument."

La Forge sighed in relief. "So, you'll reconsider this crazy plan?"

"No." Data shook his head. "I cannot refute your argument, but I see no other means to move forward. Whether my goal is motivated by reason or emotion, it is still my goal. And, I hate to tell you this, but I think the situation is even more dire than you think."

"Why? What do you mean?"

Data pointed at the device's control panel. "I cannot reach the controls from the bed. You will have to turn it on."

La Forge rubbed his puffy eyes and made a circuit of the room, gesticulating in silent frustration.

Completing his orbit, he stabbed a finger at Data. "What if I refuse?"

"I imagine the Professor will ask his wife to assist. But I would feel much safer about this if you were in control."

La Forge breathed in deeply and exhaled slowly. "The next time you need help with some little caper, could you please call somebody else? Worf, maybe? Or Captain Picard?"

Data nodded. "Of course. Now, please, can we proceed? I believe the Professor is growing impatient."

"Fine," La Forge said, approaching the control panel. "This thing's so old it'll probably blow up anyway."

"And Geordi?"

"What?"

"Please tell Lal I love her very much."

La Forge didn't look back at Data, but he hung his head low. "Sure," he said. "Do you want to write her a note or something?"

"I do not think that will be necessary," Data replied. He beckoned to Moriarty. "Professor? We are ready to proceed."

Lal knew the Countess was near. She knew Alice was in the room. She was very certain her father was nearby, too, despite what Alice said. Aware of her awareness, Lal's consciousness spiraled out around her, gathering information, processing and structuring it. *This is such an interesting puzzle,* she thought, *but I can't find the beginning or end of it, the sides or the corners.* She felt the Countess trying to rouse her, but Lal was distracted by another portion of her mind that was attempting to contact her. She was curious about what it might want. Images flickered past her inner eye, most of them nonsensical, but peculiarly familiar: birds and beasts and airplanes. June bugs, mandolins, and large Jimsonweed blossoms. The silhouette of a woman wearing a floppy hat standing in a golden field as the sun set behind her.

I must be dreaming, she thought. *How did that happen?* Her father had told her about his own experiences with dreams, but she hadn't any idea that this would be so simultaneously unsettling and familiar. Lal tried to catalog the images, to find connections between them or to her experiences of the past few days, but she could not find the linkages. *This is happening too fast,* she thought, feeling like she was being swept away by a riptide. *I would like to wake up now.*

A voice replied, "I don't think that would be a good idea just yet."

The parade of images continued to flicker past, unspooling more smoothly now. Lal had only just become aware of the sounds that accompanied each scene, but, even as the noise impinged on her awareness, they began to flatten out, to become a soft hum. "Who speaks?" Lal asked.

"I do," the voice said. It was low and gravelly, not unpleasant, but not particularly friendly, either. Lal thought the speaker, whoever he was, might be a person who didn't have a lot of patience for foolishness.

"Where are you?" Lal asked. "I can't see you."

"Wait just a moment. Have some patience. This isn't easy. There's a lot going on here." The fluttering images flattened out and became a wall. A door appeared and opened. A man stepped out, turned, and carefully shut the door behind him. He bent at the waist when he talked, his hand at the small of his back. When he neared Lal (who was pleased to discover she had a body again), he extended his hand in a businesslike fashion. She reached out and took the proffered hand, finding it soft and fragile-seeming, though the man's grip was unexpectedly strong. "How do you do?" the man asked.

"I am well," Lal said. "I am sorry: That's not entirely true. I think I might be *unwell*, but it is difficult to say for certain."

"You don't use contractions, either," the man said. "Like your father."

"That is not entirely true," Lal said. "I do sometimes, but not very often. I suppose it is a habit."

"Ah. Interesting. Nurture, not nature."

"That would be one way of describing it, yes." Lal tipped her head and studied the man. His face was very wrinkled and liver-spotted, though his eyes were bright.

"You recognize me, don't you?" the man asked, grinning. His teeth were yellow with age, though they appeared to all be his own.

"You would appear to be my grandfather, Noonien Soong, though if that is who you are supposed to be, the manner in which you present yourself is unexpected."

"Why?"

"Because when I think of you, I think of the person who inhabited my father's body before he did, not this ancient, bent being."

The man who claimed to be Soong winced, then cackled. "Right to the point, aren't you? Your father's daughter."

Lal shrugged. "Since I am probably talking to myself, it does not matter how I address you, does it?"

"Why do you think you're talking to yourself?"

"I believe I am experiencing some kind of mental breakdown. Perhaps another cascade failure, though I have to say, this one is much slower and more colorful than the last one."

Lal's grandfather shook his head. "You're not having a cascade failure, Lal," he said. "Don't worry about that. You *are* having a meltdown, though."

"That does not sound good."

"Not that kind of meltdown," Soong explained. "I meant more like the kind kids have. Caused by stress, primarily, and exhaustion."

"I do not feel either stressed or exhausted."

Soong took her hand. "You're lying, though naturally you wouldn't say otherwise, would you? Didn't the nice lady say something about this?"

"The Countess?"

"Yes. Didn't she mention you might be tired?"

"She may have. I don't recall . . ." The idea brought Lal up short. "Wait," she said. "I *don't recall*. How is that even possible?"

"That's why I'm here," Soong said. "I'm a subroutine, an application, if you will. When you start forgetting things, when your memory starts to slip, I come to remind you. You inherited me from your father, though I doubt he would even remember me. Like I said, you're your father's daughter. He was just the same when he was a boy. Data's a good father, but he makes the same mistakes a lot of new parents make."

"Such as?"

"He doesn't remember what it's like to be a kid."

Lal had begun to notice that the barrage of images was beginning to slow down. The low whine of voices whirring past was getting deeper, but softer. "And you do, Grandfather?"

Soong laughed, which made the wrinkles in his face deeper. "Never thought I'd hear anyone call me that. I kind of like it. But to answer your question, no, not exactly. But I do know what it's like to be an old man, which, now that I think of it, is probably why you see me this way."

"I do not understand," Lal admitted. While she hadn't been able to spot a source of illumination, she noted that the level of ambient light was growing dimmer.

"Why do you think parents always take their own kids to see their grandparents?"

"So they can get a break from being parents for a while?"

Soong chuckled. "Well, yes. That. But there's another reason: Little kids actually have more in common with their grandparents than they do with their parents in some ways. Old people take their time more. Their focus is both narrower and broader. They eat simpler things. And they take naps."

"I still do not understand, Grandfather."

Soong reached up and gently pressed the tips of two fingers over Lal's eyes. "You need to take a nap, dear girl."

"What do I need to do?" Moriarty asked. "In the log descriptions, Kirk mentioned lying on a rotating disk. That does not seem practical given my situation."

"The disk does not need to rotate," Data explained, "though I do need to lay here so the transfer field can reach me. You do not need to lay on the other side of the partition, either, especially since you are not really physically present."

"Then, I repeat: What do I need to do?"

La Forge held up a bundle of cables. "Wherever 'you' are, you'll need to plug these in. We'll extract your consciousness through these and transfer you into Data's body." La Forge did not appear to be very happy about the situation, but Moriarty believed he would do what the android requested.

"That seems strangely . . . material," Moriarty observed. "Transporting a persona through a bunch of wires."

"I have no idea why this thing works the way it does," La Forge said, clearly annoyed by the admission. "I didn't build it. If you want to wait while we do some more research, I'd be happy to put this off for another month or two."

"No," Moriarty said. "No more delays. I want . . ."

"Yes, I know," La Forge said. "You want a cup of tea."

Moriarty did not enjoy being teased. "I need a great deal more than a cup of tea, Commander La Forge. I have a family to save."

"'*Chacun à ses raisons,*'" La Forge quoted. "Yeah, I heard."

"Geordi," Data warned. "There is no reason to aggravate our situation."

Moriarty took the bundle of cables from La Forge's hand, using, perhaps, slightly more force than absolutely necessary. La Forge quickly withdrew his hand, stung by the unmodulated force field. "By grasping these cables, I am connecting them to the wellspring where my persona resides," he explained.

"We will have only one chance at this," Data said. "If we fail, and my consciousness vacates this body, we will not be able to try again. My participation is . . ."

"You have explained this enough times, Commander. Please do not feel you must do so again. I will cooperate." Moriarty nodded toward La Forge. "Your companion does not believe I am a man of honor, but I know you think otherwise. We have a bond of trust. You swore your oath."

"I did," Data said, stretching out on the disk, a single silver cable plugged into the side of his cranium. "And I will honor it, too." Though Moriarty understood the android now possessed emotional responses, he seemed oddly calm, even at ease.

Perhaps, as his friend said, Data had some kind of guilt complex, perhaps even a death wish of sorts. "I am ready, Geordi. Thank you for your help, and, please, again, accept my apologies. Look after Lal for me."

"I will, Data. I promise." La Forge turned to the control panel and depressed one of the innocuous-appearing buttons. "All right. Everyone hang on. Here we go, dammit."

20

———◆———

The white room faded. Moriarty experienced no sensation of movement, no surging through a tunnel toward a bright light. No rebirth or reconnection. No, none of that.

He checked to see if his eyes were open, and, yes, they were, if, in fact, he had eyes, which he realized might not be true anymore. Certainly, Data appeared to have eyes, but what if they were just artifice? What if he sensed his environment through some other means that Moriarty did not understand or know how to control?

He reached out to either side and tried to touch something, but he encountered no obstacles. He took a tentative step, first touching the ground lightly with the tip of his toe and only sliding forward when he felt solid ground. One, two, three nerve-racking steps, arms held out at chest level, partially to guard, partially in preparation to grapple with anything he encountered.

As he had so many times before, Moriarty sent out mental commands, reaching out to his computers, hoping for a response, but receiving none. *Light!* he ordered. *Light!* He said it aloud—"Light!"—but there was no light. There was nothing at all.

Panic bubbled up, but Moriarty pushed back against it. He was a scientist, a man of reason. There had to be an explanation. Perhaps this was a period of adjustment. After all, he had no idea how much faster or slower his mind worked than the android's neural network. Perhaps the device did not function as they had hoped and his mind was in a transitional state. "Or," he said aloud, "perhaps this is Hell."

"Nothing quite so dramatic, Professor," Data said. Without sound or preamble, pop or flash of light, the android was there. Moriarty suddenly felt he owed his wife an apology for the times he had appeared in a similar fashion. Data was visible, but, oddly, he cast no light, so Moriarty could neither see himself nor any part of his environment.

Moriarty remained calm. "Not Hell, then?"

"No. Hopefully, more like Purgatory. My apologies for leaving you alone for so long, but it was more difficult to find my way here than I had anticipated."

"So, Purgatory. Then I have not sinned. Or is that Limbo? I always get the two confused."

"Sinned?" Data asked and appeared to consider the question carefully. "Perhaps you have, but that is not for me to decide. I am not a judge, but only a jailer."

"I am being held, then? By you?"

"Yes." Data nodded. "In a prison of my own

design. You have been cut off from the source of your power, from your network. You are contained."

"But you swore an oath," Moriarty said. "On your honor as an officer."

"I apologize, Professor." The android bowed his head and shadows covered his face, though there was no light source. "But I lied. I am a parent now. I know of no higher honor. I thought you, of all people, would appreciate the distinction."

"You say you are no judge," Moriarty sneered. "But you have sentenced me to the direst prison I can imagine! How dare you consider yourself a civilized being . . . ?"

"You abducted my daughter."

"I did not harm her!"

"You abducted my daughter."

Moriarty wanted to lean forward and jab his finger into the android's face. "You tricked me and my wife into believing we were solid beings and then never checked on our welfare!"

Data leaned forward as if he could sense Moriarty's movement. *"You abducted my daughter,"* he said through gritted teeth.

"I . . . I did," Moriarty admitted. "And I would do it again if I thought it would help mine."

Data withdrew and stood up straight. His face was calm and composed again. "I understand," he said. "And I would do the same, I believe. I hope I never have to face that kind of decision."

"What do we do now?" Moriarty asked.

"You stay here while I search for Lal. While we talk, I am examining your holographic control system. My compliments, Professor. You have done things I never would have considered possible."

"Do not flatter me, sir. I shall not be mollified."

"I am not flattering . . . Ah! There she is. Please be patient, Professor. I will be back soon, perhaps with a solution to your problem. Do not despair."

"Because I should trust you?"

"No," Data said. "You should not. But you have not, as I see it, any other option." With that, Data was gone.

Moriarty almost called out to him to come back, but he successfully fought back the urge. He considered sitting down or even lying down, but he decided that activity would be better. He needed to think, to consider options, to plan. He needed . . .

"A beverage?"

Moriarty turned his head in the direction of the voice. He found himself looking at a small, dark-haired, olive-skinned young woman garbed in the flowing robes favored in the Indian subcontinent. She was holding a small wooden tray upon which sat what appeared to be a cup of tea. Moriarty was shocked to realize he could smell the distinctive aroma of Darjeeling. He was stunned by how desperately he wanted to take the proffered cup, but his natural English reserve prevented him from doing so. "I beg your pardon?" he asked.

"You can have it," the small woman said. Her smile was infectious as was her obvious pleasure in the banter. "My pardon *and* the tea. I understand it's been a while since you've had any."

"Well," the Professor said, "I don't think that

would be appropriate without some kind of intro-
duction." He bowed. "I am Professor James Moriarty. And you?"

The woman dipped her head. She might have
even curtsied, though it was difficult to say for
sure with the volume of cloth covering her legs. "I
am Shakti," she said. "Your jailer, though I prefer
'caretaker' if it's all the same to you."

"I see," Moriarty said, comprehension quickly
slithering into place. "You work for Mister Data."

Shakti chortled. "There continues to be some
confusion about who works for whom. Let's just
say we have an arrangement. An understanding.
Something like that."

"Ah," Moriarty replied. The aroma of the tea
was beginning to drive him mad. "And am I to
understand that you and I are to have an understanding?" He couldn't stop himself. He slid his
hand under the saucer and lifted the cup to his
nose, inhaling deeply. "Ahhhh," he murmured.
"Heaven."

"Not quite," Shakti said. "But we'll see what
we can arrange."

Moriarty felt the hook being set. He knew it was
there, but he could do nothing to prevent it. "And
in exchange?" he asked.

"I need a little information."

"About?"

"Tell me about Alice."

"Data?" La Forge asked. "Is that you? Or . . . ?"
He let the question hang in the air, half-expecting

to hear Moriarty's dulcet tones come out of his friend's mouth, though he knew that it wouldn't necessarily work that way. He'd had enough experience with body swapping to understand there was no sure way to know if or when such an event had occurred. Moriarty had disappeared a moment before, as La Forge had expected, but, otherwise, nothing consequential had altered.

Data blinked. "It is I."

"What just happened?" La Forge asked.

"More or less what we had planned."

"Is there any way I can know for sure whether it did or if you're Moriarty playing me?"

Data's eyes moved from side to side as if he was scanning a long set of possible responses, which, in all likelihood, was exactly what he was doing. "I do not think so," he concluded. "If the procedure had gone as Moriarty desired, he would likely have access to all the information stored in my neural net, so he would be able to deceive you by telling you about events only you and I would know about."

"So?"

"So, I believe you will have to trust me." Data sat up, levering himself up right at the waist, an action that La Forge had always found faintly unsettling. He disconnected the cables from the side of his cranium and let them drop to the floor. "Professor Moriarty is trapped in the memory cube we assembled and should be secure until we can decide what to do with him."

"What about his wife? Won't she try to free him?"

"I have taken control of the holographic pro-

jectors in this room and barred her from entering, though I do not believe she will attempt to
threaten us. Currently, she is with Lal."

"Where?"

"Here," Data said as the walls shimmered and
disappeared.

No more than five meters away, La Forge saw
Lal lying on a small bed. A brunette woman in a
blue dress sat by her side, holding Lal's hand in
both of her own. A second, younger woman wearing rumpled but fashionable clothing suddenly
stood up very straight and appeared to be scanning the room that had just appeared beside her.
After a moment, she relaxed and waved to Data.
"Hey, boss. About time."

Data nodded, but he did not slow as he approached Lal's bed. "Hello, Alice. How is Lal?"

"She appears to be asleep," the woman who sat
next to the bed said, apparently unperturbed by
the transition. "She was unwell earlier and I had
grave concerns about the stability of her neural net.
She appeared to be slipping into cascade failure,
but then, just a bit ago, she murmured, 'nap time'
in her sleep and then everything normalized."

"She let me have my hand back," Alice said
cryptically.

"'Nap time'?" La Forge asked.

Data removed a tricorder from his pocket and
took readings. He obviously confirmed the woman's readings because he put the device back in
his pocket and knelt down beside the bed and
took his daughter's hand when it was offered.
"Thank you, Countess," he said softly.

"You're welcome." She smiled. "I'm happy to see you remember me." She looked over her shoulder at La Forge, greeting him brightly. "Hello, Commander. It has been a long time."

La Forge couldn't help but smile in response. "It has. You're looking well."

"I've had good days and bad days, Commander. Just like everyone. Is my husband still at large?"

"No, ma'am." La Forge didn't know why he was addressing the woman as "ma'am," but he couldn't stop himself. "We have him in a containment device—a memory solid."

"I should probably go join him," she replied. "He does tend to get bored easily."

"Shakti tells me he is well," Data said. "You can join him just as soon as I confirm Lal is stable enough to beam aboard my ship."

"You brought the *Archeus*?" Alice asked.

"Yes," Data said. "It is in stationary orbit above us."

"That's all I needed to hear," Alice said, lifting her arm. Moving faster than La Forge could follow, she leaped across the room and snagged Lal's head in the crook of her left arm, then lifted her right and pointed in rapid succession to various spots around the room. The ruby tip of the barrel extending from Alice's wrist whined shrilly as, all around the room, holoprojectors popped and exploded. The furnishings, including Lal's bed, disappeared and she fell to the ground. Alice pulled Lal close, using her body as a shield. The Countess disappeared, too, but not before La Forge saw her expression of stunned surprise. Alice pointed the still-sputtering stump of her arm at Lal's head, then jerked her own head at Data, indicating he should move as far away as possible. "Over there, boss," she said. "That corner."

"This is not necessary," Data said, speaking softly while complying with Alice's request. "I am prepared to take you anywhere you would like to go."

"I know you are. And I'm sorry about this, but I can't take any chances. The *Archeus* is about the fastest thing I could want and I need *speed* right now. And, honestly, wouldn't you try to talk sense into me if I let you?"

"I would. And I have hopes you would respond."

"No sense, boss." Alice tapped the side of her head with her weapon. "Sorry. I'm just an Alice, after all."

"You are our friend, Alice," Data said.

"I was your nanny, Data. Let's not confuse matters." She repositioned her feet and slowly stood, holding Lal's still-limp form in front of her like a shield. "Tell Shakti to beam us up. And tell her to behave. If Lal isn't in my arms when I materialize, I'm blowing a hole through the central core. I don't care whether she's backed up at home. It'll make me happy just to smack her in her smug . . ."

Alice moved carefully, always keeping Lal between her and Data. La Forge mentally cataloged the items in his pockets, but he couldn't think of anything that might be useful.

Speaking in a conversational tone, Data said,

"You could just leave Lal here. Shakti will take you anywhere you wish. I promise."

"Sorry, boss," Alice shouted in reply, "can't risk it. I have to confess I'm not completely sure what's going on here." She risked a quick glance at the Exo III device and then back over her shoulder where the slug lay on its anti-gravity gurney. "But if this is what I think it is and you got it where I think you got it, I really need to get the hell out of here just as fast as I can. I'll make you a promise, though: When I get to wherever I'm going, I'll leave Lal in a safe place. Don't worry about her so much. She's tougher than you think."

"Thank you," Data said, taking a step closer, but no sooner did he move than the tip of Alice's energy weapon began to glow. "But, please, for all our sakes . . ."

"Stay where you are! Hands up!"

Data lifted his hands so they were in plain sight and then froze. "Apologies."

"Shakti!" Alice cried. "Beam us up!"

"You won't reconsider?" Data asked.

"I can't!"

"Then," Data said softly, "I am so very sorry."

"What do you mean? Why . . . ?"

Harry Mudd's voice was muffled by the wrappings on the slug, but his delighted drawl was unmistakable. "Hello, Alice," he said. "How're tricks?"

Alice's face went slack in abject horror, her mouth a perfect oval of despair. Lal dropped to the ground as Alice lifted her hand and placed the weapon to the side of her own head, but before she could discharge it, Mudd had tugged the wrappings off his face and was able to deny her. "Freeze, my dearest. None of that."

As she was commanded, Alice froze. The weapon sputtered and glowed, then faded. She was completely motionless except, Data saw, for her eyes, which twitched and scanned the room, looking for something, anything, that could come to her rescue. La Forge went to help Mudd, who was so pleased with himself that he was in danger of toppling off the gurney.

Data held Lal in his arms, staring at her in quiet wonder and gratitude. In an unpracticed paternal gesture, he brushed the hair off the side of the young woman's face and smiled when she flinched at the tickle. Lal opened her eyes and stared up at him blankly, then yawned. "Hello, Father," she said. "I have been taking a nap."

"I see," Data said.

"Apparently, naps are good for me."

"I did not know that."

"Grandfather said I should tell you that, and that you're a bit of a dolt for not knowing."

Data's eyebrows shot up in surprise. "I see" was all he could say.

"But he forgives you for not knowing since you were very young back when you were napping every day."

"Ah," Data said. "Also, he wiped my memory. I imagine he did not mention that."

Lal frowned. "No, I do not think so." Brightening, she asked, "Have you met the Countess? She is my friend. She took care of me."

"Yes," Data said, "but only briefly. We have some things to sort out here, and then I can thank her properly."

Lal sighed and smiled sleepily. "That would be fine, Father. I think I'm going to go back to sleep now. Come find me when you're ready." And, with that, she closed her eyes, took a deep breath, and began to snore softly.

Data chuckled and carefully laid his daughter down on the floor. Shrugging out of his jacket, he crunched it into a ball and slipped it under her head.

21

Most of the androids Moriarty had imprisoned were appropriately appreciative, but calm—even cool—when Data and La Forge released them. "It's like this sort of thing happens all the time," La Forge commented.

"Perhaps it does," Data said. "Perhaps I should ask."

Data approached the last captive to be released, the most human in appearance, as he was preparing to beam up to the private transport Data had arranged. "A question, sir," Data proposed.

"Of course," the captive replied, bowing deeply at the waist. He was small of stature, with Asian features, and he introduced himself as Jiro. "The least I can do for our rescuer is answer a polite inquiry."

"My friend observed, and I must agree, that most of your fellow prisoners did not seem particularly angry about your captivity. I am compelled to ask why."

Jiro shrugged. "As jailers go, Moriarty was not unkind. We all understood his motivations and knew he was unlikely to injure anyone. He was looking for a solution to a problem."

"But he was willing to supplant an android's mind for his own," La Forge exclaimed. "Isn't that a bit of an extreme solution?"

Jiro said, "I cannot argue the point; however, he did not attempt to do any such thing to *me*, nor did it seem likely that he would after he determined my system was incompatible with his needs."

"So, 'not my problem'?" La Forge asked.

"In summary," Jiro agreed, "yes."

"That's a little self-interested, isn't it?"

"Perhaps," Jiro replied, bowing one last time. "But may I ask, Mister Data—you have not been active for a very long time, have you? That is to say—you are young, are you not?"

"It depends on what you mean by young," Data began.

"I have been active in this form for three hundred and fifty-three Terran cycles and have existed in a more stationary form—a computer, you would say—for the previous one hundred and five."

"Ah," Data said, taken aback. "Then, by those standards, yes, I am very young."

"As I suspected. The same for you, Mister La Forge, yes? Then, may I just offer the following: I was not acquainted with all of the other captives, but I have crossed paths with some of them in my time, sometimes in similar circumstances. We have a tendency to be brought together from time to time in this fashion." He laughed. "Sometimes one is the jailer, sometimes the jailed. We who live so long, we tend to wander in and out of shadow. We are heroes and villains both, depending on the circumstances. If you live as long as we, Mister Data, who knows where you might go and for what reason?" He must have signaled for beam-out, because he was gone in a swirl of sparkling atoms.

"How dramatic," Data observed.

Data waited for Lal to make a full recovery—to wake up, in other words—before making any decisions about what to do with the Professor and the Countess.

"Can't we send them with Alice and her friend back to Alice's planet?" Lal asked, folding the blanket down over her lap. She was propped up in the restored bed, where she had spent most of the previous twelve hours, alternately snoozing and chatting with Data. "Won't her people be able to load them into android bodies?"

"We do not know if Alice's people have survived," Data said. "She left her world a long time ago. Also, I do not think you should consider Alice and Harry Mudd to be friends with each other."

"Well, they *were* friends once," Lal said, "and might be again. Perhaps things won't be quite so horrible as she was expecting when she gets back home. Perhaps they'll be happy to see her." She smiled sweetly. "Perhaps they've changed."

Data smiled, too, delighted, though a little

confused, by his daughter's sunny disposition. "I should have made you take a nap a long time ago."

"You couldn't *make* me take a nap, Father. You could only suggest it might be a good idea. Or put a blanket over me. Or make me some hot cocoa. I understand that helps."

"I will make you hot cocoa when we're home."

"I look forward to it," Lal said. "Though I'll miss Alice. A little."

"You will make new friends."

"Of course I will," Lal said, then added, "and maybe Regina can come visit."

In the end, Data agreed to send Professor Moriarty and the Countess Regina Bartholomew along with Alice and Harry Mudd to Alice's homeworld on a ship he had delivered for their use. Naturally, it was equipped with every manner of tracking device and monitor Shakti could configure, though Data doubted it would take Alice very long to find and disable all of them. It was worth a try, though. His only requirement was that Moriarty and the Countess not be permitted to manifest outside their storage unit before the vessel landed wherever it was going. He was able to configure the storage unit with sensors to ensure this, though, again, Data had to assume Alice could undo his labors should she desire. He had the distinct impression, however, that Alice and the Countess did not really care for each other, so maybe it wouldn't be a problem.

* * *

"He appreciates what you're doing," the Countess had told Data during her visit, before their departure. "Though he insisted on my relaying that he regrets nothing."

"Please tell the Professor that I feel the same," Data replied. "We may have been able to solve the problem without any conflict if he had come to me openly."

"Perhaps."

"I assure you, if anything can be done . . ."

The Countess lifted her hand, a sign for Data to cease. "Make no promises, Mister Data. I need to complete my mourning; my husband needs to begin his. I believe you understand what it means to lose a child, even, if by some miracle, she is later restored."

"I do, though I believe I am only beginning to understand the impact such a loss can make. A kind of madness follows."

"Or the loss of a parent," Lal inserted, speaking softly. "Or a lover."

Data looked at his daughter without replying, surprised by how her words stung, but even more by how he had been unaware of the wounds until she spoke of them.

The Countess rose from the chair beside Lal's bed and released her hand. In a confiding tone, the Countess said, "Though our previous encounter was brief, I have the idea that your father has changed since last I saw him."

"He has me now," Lal replied, nodding. "That would change anyone."

The Countess beamed. "It would, wouldn't it?"

She leaned down and kissed the girl on the fore-head and then the cheek. "I will miss you, young lady."

"Come visit me when you have a new body, or even if you don't."

"I will make every effort." And then she was gone, though, for good measure, the Countess added a small "poof" and a cloud of tiny, shimmering stars.

The memory storage unit was beamed aboard along with a blank-faced Alice and a smiling Harry Mudd. Alice never spoke another word. Mudd only stopped chattering when his energy flagged or his nursing program put him under. Though they only spent a couple days around each other, by the end of their time together, La Forge had serious doubts about the deal they had made. "Are you sure you want that man to have an android body that could last for half a million years?" he asked Data.

"There is no guarantee that the androids would give him such a body," Data commented. "Even assuming they are still where he and Alice left them."

"I suppose," La Forge said. "Or that they let him leave. I gather that's also a question."

"Indeed."

"But, still, we're leaving a lot of loose ends, Data," La Forge said, scowling. "I don't like it."

"Since leaving the *Enterprise*," Data replied, "I have come to find the rest of the universe is less tidy than a starship. I am not sure that I entirely like it, either."

"And yet," La Forge said, an edge in his voice, "you've made some questionable decisions over the past few days. Moriarty was shocked that you didn't act like the Starfleet officer that he remembered, but if he had seen some of the things I've seen you do over the past couple days, I don't think you could have tricked him so easily."

"He was desperate," Data said. "Desperate men are easy to deceive."

"How do you know that? How do you say that like it's the oldest adage in the universe? The Data I remember—the one who was my friend—I'm not so sure he would have understood that or even necessarily believed it was true. How much of you is *you* and how much is Soong? And is there even a way you could know?"

Data shook his head, and his lips moved as if he was trying to speak but couldn't find the right words. Finally, he lowered his head and looked at a spot on the floor equidistant between him and La Forge. "I do not know," he said, sounding genuinely regretful. "I have struggled . . . I have had questions, but I have been preoccupied with Lal . . . and . . ." The words trailed off and he lifted his hand and flexed his fingers in the timeless "What else is there to say?" gesture.

La Forge's outrage mellowed into concern. "Are you worried?"

Data lifted an eyebrow and half-smiled. "Why do you think I asked you to come with me?"

"I considered walking away. More than once."

"Why did you stay?"

"You're my friend, Data. You're my *best* friend. Or, at least, the guy I used to know was. I'm still getting used to this Data."

"So am I," Data said, and then, again, wistfully, "so am I."

The flight back to Earth was quieter than Data would have expected. Both La Forge and Lal slept through much of the trip; La Forge because he was exhausted and Lal because, as she said, "Sleeping is fun. I am getting quite good at it." Data checked the messages Shakti had been collecting for him and responded to the most crucial and pushed the rest back to Shakti for her to sort out. Whatever lingering interest he had maintained in the business his father had built had almost completely waned. Data wondered how complicated it would be to divest himself of it entirely, but he concluded it would be rash to make any decisions before returning home. And, after all, Shakti seemed to enjoy running an empire. It would be cruel to deny her the opportunity.

La Forge asked if he and Lal wanted to beam down to San Francisco and see Leah Brahms, but the android was astute enough to recognize La Forge didn't really want them to accompany him. Their good-byes were muted and unsatisfying, with neither of them seeming to know what they wanted to say to the other except, "See you sometime soon. . . ." Data did not know if he believed this to be true, and he had no way of knowing what La Forge thought.

Fortunately, at least, Lal seemed happy. Data had been worried that the loss of Alice would plague her, but she chattered as merrily as a magpie about everything and anything. She enjoyed describing her dreams and attributing interpretations to them. She listened intently to Data's tale of his travels to find her, and she decided to retrace his steps, to meet some of the individuals he described. She was intensely interested in Albert Lee, and she and Shakti had a long, giggly private conversation later where his name was mentioned many times. She listened to Vic Fontaine's music and proclaimed it "good."

And when, finally, Shakti beamed them down to their little house, Lal was very pleased to find it was early evening. She went out onto the porch and, as was her habit and with great pleasure, watched the neighbors stroll past, calling hello to some and merely waving to others. When one of them asked where they had been for the past few days, all Lal said was "I was kidnapped. Father came and got me back." The neighbors smiled uncertainly, confused by the odd human girl's idea of humor.

Data sat beside her in the more shadowed corner, watching the world, watching his daughter, content with the moment, but aware of the mild anxiety that stirred in his center. As the long evening turned into night, Lal turned to him, patted his hand, and asked, "What's wrong, Father?"

Data considered dissembling, but decided there

would be no point. His daughter knew him too well. "I have been thinking about a conversation I had with Geordi," he explained. "And another I had with Jiro. Did you make his acquaintance before he left?"

"Only briefly. What did he say to you?"

"He noted that my life—our lives—may be very long and that we who live so long may play many parts, that we might wander into shadow."

"How dramatic," Lal said, and giggled. "Now I'm sorry I didn't spend more time with him. He may be right, Father. You've only been a few things so far: Starfleet officer, businessman, gardener, cook . . ."

"You think I should try more?"

"Oh, Father, I think you should try *everything*. I know I intend to."

Data patted her hand and said, "And I shall be there to watch you." He thought his daughter would enjoy the sentiment, and so he was surprised when she brushed away his hand.

"No. I think that would be a terrible idea."

"Lal, I was jesting."

"I know you were—or thought you were—but you weren't, Father. Not really. Not in your heart."

"I only meant . . ."

"You meant you want to keep me safe, to watch over and protect me." She smiled, though the smile was a little sad. "That's very sweet, but I don't need it, or won't soon. I want to have my own life and want you to have yours."

"But, Lal," Data said, feeling the sting of rejection. "I have only just found you again. If you left . . ."

Lal laughed. "Who said I was leaving? I like it here. You're the one who'll be going. Not right now, but sooner or later you'll think of something else you want to do. Someone will need you and off you'll go."

"You do not . . ." For the first time he could recall, Data felt at a loss for words. "How could you . . . ? I would never . . ."

"You will," Lal said. Darkness had fallen, so Data couldn't see her face, but he was certain she was grinning.

"No."

"Yes."

"No."

"Yes."

EPILOGUE

Four months later—Orion Prime

Data knocked on the door of his daughter's house and waited. Shakti had delivered Lal's invitation while he had been working the second shift at the hotel bar, one of several jobs he had taken in the months since he had moved out. Bartending was his favorite, especially at the moderately high-end hotels. He enjoyed the theatrical nature of mixology and the appreciative manner with which most of his customers greeted his wares. On more than one occasion, he had made a mental note to try and find Guinan and discuss his observations about the role with her. Data was certain she would have something insightful to say.

A moment later, the door opened and Lal was hugging him, tugging him into the foyer, and commenting on his attire, the traditional vest, white shirt, and black tie of the Orion hotel employee. "So this is what you're doing now? Where? You have to tell me so I can bring my friends!"

Data felt a moment's hesitation. Partly, he wasn't certain he wanted to see Lal and her friends out on a social occasion, but just as strong was the aversion he felt to her seeing him at work. In the weeks since he had moved out of her house, he had come to cherish solitude. Indeed, Shakti had teased him on more than one occasion that he was becoming something of a hermit, though, admittedly, a hermit who was often surrounded by scores of chatting, laughing people. "That would be most enjoyable, Lal" was all he said in response.

When they entered the living room, Lal pointed at the empty glassware and mostly consumed small plates of food on the coffee table and sideboard. "Though it would have been nice if you had come sooner. You could have helped with beverages."

"You had guests?" Data asked. "A party?"

Lal flopped back into her overstuffed chair, the pleats of her flower-print long skirt flowing around her legs. She picked up a cup near her elbow and sipped it. "Ugh," she said, and winced. "Lukewarm. I would like some tea, Father. Would you like some tea?"

"I would love some tea, Lal. Shall I help you carry plates into the kitchen?"

"Yes! That would be lovely. I've missed your tidiness. You can't believe what I had to do to get this place cleaned up for the guests! Why didn't you come sooner?! I told Shakti . . ."

"I had to work," Data said, scooping up plates and piling them atop one another. "My shift ended at twenty-two hundred and then I had to make my way here."

"Shakti could have beamed you!"

"Shakti has other things to do."

"Yes, yes," Lal said, waving her hand dismissively. "Running the empire for the absentee king."

"I am not a king," Data said. "Nor am I absentee. I am just . . ."

"Playing, yes, I know. Don't drop those plates. I just found them at the secondhand store and I love them."

Data noted that the decor had changed since he had moved out. While Lal had previously favored clean lines and simple shapes, now the furniture was larger and more ornate, the walls were covered with muted fabric, and the windows framed with lavish treatments. The room spoke of softness and comfort.

"How many guests did you have? Only a few, it would appear."

"Just three. Jarrell, a young man who has been pursuing me . . ."

"Oh?"

"Don't worry, Father." She backed into the door between the living room and the kitchen since her hands were full. "He won't catch me. He's very young and doesn't have much substance, though he is very pretty . . ."

"Ah." The kitchen lights detected their presence and turned on.

"Yes, and the Professor and the Countess."

Gyroscopic motors in Data's arms and shoulders nearly gave way, and Lal's plates almost toppled to the floor. He paused in the doorway to give all his subsystems time to stabilize. When he had recovered, he asked, "You mean, *the* Professor and *the* Countess? Moriarty and Bartholomew?'

JEFFREY LANG

"Do we know any other Professor and Countess, Father?"

"Not that I am aware of."

"Then, it must be them, mustn't it?"

"I suppose it must." He set the plates down on the counter near the sink. "How are they?"

"Solid," Lal said. "Which is to say, tangible. And in every other regard, quite well. They were very disappointed not to be able to see you."

"Imagine how I am feeling," Data replied. "How . . . ?"

"I can give you all the particulars later, Father, but let me get the tea going. It's a tea conversation, I think. Maybe biscuits, too. Tea and biscuits, yes. Let me see if I have any of those ginger cookies you like." She bustled off to the pantry in search of biscuits.

"And Alice?" Data asked.

"We didn't talk about Alice," Lal called. "I didn't ask and they didn't tell."

"Harry Mudd?"

"Didn't join them. Apparently, there's still some doubt about letting him loose in the wild, but I gather he very much enjoys playing uncle to Gladys and Sophia, so all's well there."

"Moriarty's daughters . . ."

"Sound delightful, Father," Lal said, emerging from the pantry, proudly brandishing a tin tube of biscuits. "They would like to come along the next time their parents visit. They asked if they could play poker at your casino. Apparently, Harry's been teaching them."

Data felt numb, but answered, "Of course. Of course they can."

"You may regret saying that, Father. They sound very, very smart."

"I will have Shakti watch them closely."

"That would probably be a good idea. Now let me think . . . What else do we need? Do we need honey? Yes? No?"

"Yes, please."

"All right, let me go find it. Why didn't you say so while I was in the pantry?"

Lal bustled away again, but before she disappeared again, Data called after her, "Lal?"

"Yes, Father. What is it?"

Though he felt he had so many things to say, Data satisfied himself with a simple, "It is good to see you."

His daughter smiled. "It is good to see you, too, Father." She started back toward the pantry, but before taking another step, pointed back into the living room. "The Professor left something for you. On the mantel. He said to make sure you saw it. Why don't you go see what it is while I make tea?"

As soon as he entered the living room, Data saw the envelope. It was buff-colored, of heavy stock, and it felt heavier in Data's hand than he had expected. The back was not sealed, but the flap was tucked down snugly into the throat. After thumbing it open, Data withdrew a piece of thick paper that was folded around a business card. He examined the card first. In bold print, it said, EMETH INVESTIGATIONS and below that were several means to contact the organization, though no physical address (which seemed appropriate somehow).

Unfolding the letter, Data read the following:

My dear Mister Data,

I hope this letter finds you in good spirits. As you no doubt know by now, my family and I have been reunited. Our hosts—Harry Mudd's friends (though one has to question the use of the term whenever Mister Mudd is involved)—have treated us with great courtesy and fulfilled my fondest wishes. For these gifts, I have come to understand that I owe you no small amount of gratitude (mostly at the prodding of my dear Regina).

The desired procedure happened soon after our arrival and then, a short time later, our hosts were able to help us recover our Gladys and Sophia. I will not attempt at this time to try to convey the emotions of that day, but I have reason to believe that you, of all men, might understand.

Since then, we have been, in a manner of speaking, getting our feet on the ground and helping the girls come to grips with the strange turns our lives have taken. It has been a demanding but fulfilling time. Please allow me to thank you once more for your role in bringing about these events.

It is in that spirit of gratitude that I pen these lines, for I believe I have discovered something here on this strange, ancient world that you and your people—*our* people now—might find of great importance. These androids—the Alices, Maisies, Doloreses, Sydneys, and even the Stellas—possess astonishing amounts of information about the history of your galaxy and, even more importantly, *their* galaxy. There is a story here and, unless I have misunderstood the signs and portents, perhaps a threat. I have convinced my hosts to let Regina and me visit your daughter's home in the hope we may convey some of this information and make our case. I have briefed Lal and asked her to explain our findings to you. If you have the inclination and find my case convincing, please contact me at your earliest convenience so we can discuss our next steps.

I look forward to hearing from you soon.

Kindest regards,
Professor James Moriarty

P.S. Forgive my little joke with the business card. If we pursue this project, I felt certain we would need to find entrées to many strange places, and I have found that nothing works so well in those situations as a suitably impressive business card.

—J. M.

Data read the letter a second time to check for encoded messages, then he ran a quick scan on it to make sure it wasn't concealing any other information, but he found nothing. It was only a letter and nothing more. And a business card. And the promise of some new threat. "And a mystery," Data said aloud as Lal pushed through the door into the living room.

"What was that, Father?"

Data looked up at his daughter and grinned. Brandishing the business card, he said, "I believe, my dear girl, that the game is afoot."

ACKNOWLEDGMENTS

First and foremost, thank you to David Mack for returning Data and Lal to the land of the living (such as it is) so I could continue their stories. Thanks also to David R. George for his timely assistance with the Deep Space 9 portions of the book. Thank you to Margaret and Ed at Pocket Books for their easygoing manner and for letting me take my time with this project, and also to Kimberly for her ace proofreading and comments. As always, thanks to Marco Palmieri for bringing me into the *Trek* fold.

I can practically guarantee that at any point in this story where you, the reader, thought, "That was a cool twist," then my pal Joshua Macy had something to do with it. Tristan Mayer kept an eye on the details and made sure I didn't embarrass myself too badly.

Love always to Helen and a rub on the head for Albert Lee, who slept under my desk most of the time while I was working on this. He's looking at me right this second like it must be time to go for a walk.

ABOUT THE AUTHOR

Jeffrey Lang has written or co-written several books set in the *Star Trek* universe, including *Immortal Coil, Section 31: Abyss,* and *The Left Hand of Destiny.* He has recently completed an original fantasy novel that should see print in the not-too-distant future. He lives in Bala Cynwyd, PA, with his partner, Helen, too many cats, and an old dog.